THE
SADDEST
GIRL
ON THE
BEACH

THE SADDEST GIRL ON THE BEACH

Heather Frese

—BLAIR—

Printed in the United States of America
Cover design by Laura Williams
Interior design by April Leidig

Blair is an imprint of Carolina Wren Press.

The mission of Blair/Carolina Wren Press is to seek out, nurture, and promote literary work by new and underrepresented writers.

We gratefully acknowledge the ongoing support of general operations by the Durham Arts Council's United Arts Fund and the North Carolina Arts Council.

This novel is a work of fiction. As in all fiction, the literary perceptions and insights are based on experience; however, all names, characters, places, and incidents are either products of the author's imagination or are used fictitiously. No reference to any real person is intended or should be inferred.

Quotes from *How to Read a North Carolina Beach: Bubble Holes, Barking Sands, and Rippled Runnels* appear throughout the text of this book. Copyright © 2004 by Orrin Pilkey, Tracy Rice, and William Neal. Published by the University of North Carolina Press. Used by permission of the publisher. www.uncpress.unc.edu

Library of Congress Cataloging-in-Publication Data
Names: Frese, Heather, 1974– author.
Title: The saddest girl on the beach / Heather Frese.
Description: [Durham] : Blair, 2024.
Identifiers: LCCN 2023048655 (print) | LCCN 2023048656 (ebook) |
ISBN 9781958888186 (hardcover) | ISBN 9781958888261 (ebook)
Subjects: LCSH: Grief—Fiction. | Self-realization in women—Fiction. |
North Carolina—Fiction. | LCGFT: Novels.
Classification: LCC PS3606.R47 S23 2024 (print) | LCC PS3606.R47 (ebook) |
DDC 813/.6—dc23/eng/20231018
LC record available at https://lccn.loc.gov/2023048655
LC ebook record available at https://lccn.loc.gov/2023048656

For my dad. This is me, standing by the ocean, telling them everything.

PART ONE

January

One

My hand was bleeding when I touched Nate for the first time since I'd arrived at the inn, when he glided his kayak across the Pamlico Sound and pushed up beside me on the dock. I'd reached out to grab the paddle as Nate pulled the kayak in, scraping myself on the rough post of the dock as I stretched out over the water. Tiny red rivulets ran down my wrists and dripped on the pier, the bright crimson out of place on this dimly bruised January day. A sharp wind kicked up whitecaps, ruffling the muted reeds until they bent their heads low.

Nate grabbed my right hand, cold beads of water dripping off his arm and landing on my own. He brushed at the red, saw that it came from a thin scratch. "Stigmata?" he asked lightly, wiping the blood away.

The old me, the one standing in front of the dividing line of my father's death, would've laughed and made devil horns. This new me only vaguely recognized that Nate's question was intended to be lighthearted. The water lapped against the dock, and I closed my eyes.

"Charlotte?" Nate asked, his voice soft. "Are you okay?" He pulled my hand closer to his chest. The scratch started to throb, and it felt like something I could anchor myself to, an echo of the way pain used to feel.

I opened my eyes and turned away. Back at the inn a light flicked on, illuminating a second-story window. I nodded. "Fine," I said through the tightness in my throat. I pulled back from him and ran my other hand across the rough post, pressing down to see if I could bleed again, to see if I could feel something. I stopped when I saw Nate watching me. "How was kayaking?" I asked.

Nate shrugged. "Chilly, but I needed some water time after being stuck on the mainland." I'd been here for three days, but Nate had been visiting friends in Raleigh the whole time.

The breeze kicked up, damp and fish-smelling. I knew I should ask about his trip, force a smile and listen with interest, but the prospect exhausted me. "I'm going to go back and help with dinner," I said. The wind lashed my cheeks as I walked down the boardwalk, heading toward the light.

The Pamlico Inn was the only thing keeping me steady. The inn and the water. I was otherwise loose, untethered and distant from my brother, James, and my mother. I couldn't stand to be with them now that our family was only three. At home, I'd been constantly aware of the friction caused by my father's absence, the space where he should have been—my father, stable and strong and reassuring. A beacon. He'd been gone for four months now.

Gone.

Nine years ago, when I was ten years old, the National Park Service moved the Cape Hatteras lighthouse. I thought it would crumble and fall, afraid its solid, striped body, the steady golden sweep of its beam across the night, would be lost. The Park Service was moving the lighthouse away from the pounding waves and eroding ocean. But I imagined the black-and-white spirals, all 208 feet of them, swaying, rocking, left, right, catching momentum, crashing to the sand. Piles of black-and-white bricks. Everywhere dust, rising and billowing and choking me with grit. Days later I would still be spitting out rogue grains when I brushed my teeth.

But the lighthouse didn't fall. It just moved, the glimpse of black-and-white spirals no longer visible from Lighthouse View Road, the rotating beam now illuminating maritime forest instead of dunes and beach and frothy waves. Still, what once was can haunt a person, can make them run away from home, and this is where I ran, where I landed, this great gray seashell of an inn tumbled onto the shore. I was still running.

I ran away from Nate, up the boardwalk and toward the inn, the cuts on my palm stinging against the salty breeze. The inn had three stories, with ramps along the outside connecting the new addition to the original, with lace curtains fringing the windows of rooms named after North Carolina wildflowers. My best friend Evie Austin's parents owned it. The inn closed every year for the month of January, so the Austins let me choose whichever room I wanted. I picked a small, yellow room overlooking the sound, the Primrose Room, in the old part of the inn. I liked it because of its coziness, and I liked being close to the family quarters. Mr. and Mrs. Austin had a bedroom tucked behind the office in the original part of the inn, along with a living space, and Evie and Nate had rooms overlooking the garden since tourists wanted a water view.

Once I was inside the inn, I went upstairs, hid in the Primrose Room, and let myself cry about my dad. I felt so stupid getting upset in front of other people, hated the way the grief still rose in my throat unexpectedly. It'd been four months now. Four months and eighteen days.

Someone knocked on my door, and I wiped my face with my bleeding hand. "Charlotte," Evie said. "I'm coming in."

"Don't," I said.

"You better have pants on," she said, pushing the door open. Evie stood with a hand on her hip, her eyes shadowed. Then she rushed forward, touched my face, and pulled back, her fingers damp, red. "Why's your face all bloody?" Evie asked. She pulled a tissue from the side table and rubbed my cheeks.

I showed her my hand. "There's something sharp on the dock post," I said.

Evie walked out of the room and came back in with a box of Band-Aids, unwrapped two, and put them on my palm. I swallowed hard, swallowed again, stared at Evie as her dark hair fell forward, shiny, and straight and long. She threw away the Band-Aid wrappers, and I sat down on my bed.

"When are you going to unpack?" Evie asked, pulling a pair of pink socks out of my bag and tossing them at me. "You're home."

I shrugged, let the socks fall. I didn't bother telling her that nothing was permanent, not even home, especially not home. That I'd watched my father die, packed my bags, and left late for my first semester of college, because he'd wanted me to go. Because everyone said it would take my mind off it. Him. September, October, November, I did everything but think about him. I unpacked my luggage and hung posters on the walls of my dorm room, and then, in December, Evie called to tell me she was pregnant, mingled notes of apology and terror in her voice. Two weeks before finals, I took a leave of absence from school. The form I filled out asked the reason for my departure. *Life and death*, I wrote. Melodramatic, yes, but that's how I was feeling at the time. And I left the solid Midwest and came down here to the Outer Banks, to this improbable strip of islands, this narrow, shifting place, more water than land, to be with my friend. To stare at the water and make everything go away.

Evie sat down on the edge of the bed beside me, tossing the pink socks up and down in one hand. "Did I ever tell you about the time my parents tried to make me wear a pink dress?" she asked.

I shook my head no and tried to smile, but really, I just wanted to be alone. *Please leave.*

Evie went on. "It was some awful Easter dress or something," she said. "I think I was seven. I was in my Sherpa phase. No way was that dress going on my body."

"Your Sherpa phase?" I blew my nose. *Please leave. Please leave. Please leave.*

"I was obsessed with climbing Mount Everest," Evie said. "You know, like a Sherpa." She got up and placed the socks in a dresser drawer. "I still think Sherpas are kind of sexy," she said.

"What's not to love?" I said.

A phone rang downstairs in the office. "I'll get it," Evie said. She walked to the door and paused with her hand on the frame. "I'll see you at dinner."

I went to the bathroom and washed my face, soaking my Band-Aids, then wandered over to the Sea Oats room to look out the window, relieved to be alone. Pampas grass shook and swayed in the wind around the curved gravel driveway. Winters on Cape Hatteras were more desolate and more compelling than I'd imagined. There was a quietness, a muted rhythm that made summer seem like a carnival of color and life. Ice cream stands, Putt-Putt courses, bright T-shirts flying from shop windows, all these furled in on themselves in winter. The island, extended and curved like a ballerina's arm, elegantly jutted people away in these windy, chilly months. I loved it both ways, winter and summer. My parents had only seen the summer months, had planned to see winter when they retired. My dad

would never see a Hatteras winter. Before the grief behind my eyes
could transition from a prickle to a tidal rush, I got up and walked
downstairs, hoping the motion would distract me. I picked at the
Band-Aids on my palm. Outside a tall sliding-glass door an egret
swooped down, landing in the marsh grass. The sun peeked above
the rim of a streaky, gray cloud, reflecting on the stillness of the
shallow bowl of water that was the Pamlico Sound.

I stepped outside, the breeze fresh on my face, and breathed. Then
I got out my phone and sent my mom a text message about the egret.
I hadn't been able to talk to her since I'd left, too tired and grief-
worn to withstand her asking me to come home. I put my phone
back in my pocket and walked downstairs to the kitchen, running
my fingers over the carved sign that said GALLEY, breathing in the
onion and potato smell of clam chowder preparations. Inside, Evie
and Nate bickered back and forth, and then Evie said something
about dying and I didn't want to hear them talk about my dad, so I
went in. Nate blushed and bent down to the sink, tall and lanky with
his wet suit peeled half-off. Before I could say anything, Evie grabbed
a handful of silverware in one hand and me by the other and spun
me out the kitchen door. We went to the inn's dining room, which
the family used as their own space in the offseason, and started setting out plates and cups and napkins for dinner.

"He's okay with it," Evie said. Her fingers flitted down forks, hummingbird quick.

"What?"

"Stephen," she said. "He's okay with the baby."

"I didn't know you told him." I passed Evie saucers. A gust of wind
shook the inn, rattling the window-lined dining room. I was still

getting used to the wind in winter, to the chill and the damp. "Did you tell your parents, too?"

Evie walked around the table. "Not them yet. Nate knows. I told Stephen last night. He freaked out, but then he rallied." She jostled the table with her leg and reached forward to steady a pitcher.

I stopped straightening the linen and looked at her, trying to peer past her veneer to see if she was actually upset. "He freaked out?"

"You know, whatever. 'How could you,' blah blah blah." Evie fluttered her hands in the air and rolled her eyes at the ceiling. A ray of sun shot through the window and danced across the table. "I mean, we haven't exactly talked about what we're going to do. But the point is, he's not mad anymore, and he's coming to dinner tonight. That was him on the phone."

Stephen Oden. I walked over to the other side of the table to a window overlooking the dock. At Thanksgiving, he'd taken Evie on the ferry to Ocracoke, got drunk, and left without her. It was his way of ending their relationship. She called me from the terminal as the last boat was pulling out. They'd been broken up for a few weeks then gotten back together, then Evie realized she was pregnant.

I turned and Evie was staring at me with round, dark eyes. "Okay," I tried to sound cheery. "Hey, I'll give him a chance." I smiled, and my face felt like it was cracking.

Stephen was late. Evie hadn't told her parents he was coming. Once he was inside the inn, she explained, Stephen had the safety of guest status. Even if the inn was closed for the season, her family was bound by politeness. Mr. and Mrs. Austin, Nate, Evie, and I sat around the long rectangular table and pulled cloth napkins onto our laps. Mr. Austin had always served breakfast to his guests but was planning to open the restaurant for dinner in the coming season. He'd been a chef before buying the inn, and so far, he was preparing the food himself, playing with dishes he thought might appeal to guests.

"This chowder sure is making me feel quamish," Evie said to her mother, throwing around the island word for queasy. Evie knew I collected words like people collect seashells, lining them along my windowsill, turning them over to discover their origins, grouping them by color and shape and size.

Mrs. Austin furrowed her brow at Evie's forced vernacular. She was short, like Evie, and looked like she ought to be at the kid's table, if there were one. There wasn't, because Evie's mom was the innkeeper and she said that everybody would be welcome on the same level at the inn, even children. Somehow, I didn't think she'd extend that policy to one of Evie's. Evie's dad's title was *innkeeper's husband*.

"*Quamish* is found in Shakespeare," I said. "I took a Brit Lit class this semester." The pliability of language amazed me, the way a word from Elizabethan England could migrate, twist, wash up on shore, and burrow into an island's dialect when it died elsewhere. It was a great word. *Quamish*.

"She knows," Mrs. Austin said. "Besides, nobody says those old words anymore."

Mr. Austin crumbled crackers into his chowder. "That's mostly so, but if you want to hear the brogue in full swing you ought to head down to Ocracoke and sit in on a poker night," he said. "It gets to be a regular pissing contest to see who can sound the most Elizabethan."

"Because Charlotte wouldn't be conspicuous at all during an Ocracoke poker night," Nate said. "Not like that would be awkward or anything."

Evie kicked me under the table. "Pass me the salt, Meehonkey."

Meehonkey was an old island word for hide-and-go-seek, and when I'd first heard it, I couldn't stop laughing. I said it so much it became a nickname. Nate reached for the lighthouse-shaped saltshaker at the same time I did and our hands met, then skirted away.

"Is your hand okay, Charlotte?" Nate asked. He passed the salt to Evie.

I looked down. "I'm fine. Just thin-skinned."

"Yoo-hoo!" A voice echoed around the dining room windows, and Evie and Nate's Aunt Fay poked her bedraggled head around the corner. "Look who I found," she said, ushering Stephen into the room like he was a lost puppy. People called Aunt Fay eccentric, or unconventional, or original. She drove a rattly old four-wheel-drive truck up and down the beach every day. Her other vehicle of choice was a school bus she'd painted green and emblazoned with her name. Part of Aunt Fay's lower jaw had been cut out because she'd chewed so much tobacco over the years, she got cancer. She liked to walk around naked in her house, and sometimes she forgot to put on clothes before she answered the door. Today she wore green corduroy overalls—that matched her bus—and a pink plaid shirt.

"Hey, Aunt Fay," Evie said and leapt up, hustling over to Stephen before he could say anything. She gave Aunt Fay and Stephen hugs and pulled them to the table, where Mrs. Austin set places and spooned chowder into big blue bowls. Mr. Austin creaked his tall frame out of the chair and got up to kiss Aunt Fay on the cheek and shake Stephen's hand.

"How are you, sir," Stephen said. He had a sharp chin and a wiry frame and was growing a mustache.

"Older, fatter, slower," Mr. Austin said, thwacking Stephen on the back and steering him to a seat. Evie's parents knew how much of a shit Stephen had been, but under guest status they treated him like they usually did, as a nice kid from a good Hatteras family.

"Hey, Char," Stephen said to me. "How was your trip down?"

Don't call me that. My mother got away with calling me Charly, and I let my brother tease me by calling me Charles, but nobody else. "It was fine," I said. "Long."

"Catch anything lately?" Stephen asked Mr. Austin. He sat between Evie and Nate, and his sandy hair glowed in the evening sun.

They started talking about fishing and the weather, and Mrs. Austin went to the kitchen and brought up a platter of fish and sautéed squash for the main course.

Nate took a filet and passed the plate to me. "If you want, I could take you down to Ocracoke. You can hear the brogue when the fishermen unload their boats at the docks."

"Hell, just teach her poker and take her to a game," Aunt Fay answered. She pointed at me with her fork. "Old tars won't know what hit them."

Evie took a piece of fish, and I thought suddenly about fish, mercury, and pregnancy. I cleared my throat and asked, "Evie, could you help me in the kitchen?"

"What do you need help with?" Evie finished her clam chowder and took a piece of fish.

"Is this grouper?" I asked Mr. Austin.

"Mackerel," he said.

Evie cut a bite. "Is it holy mackerel? Were you praying when you caught it?"

"Evie," I said. "Isn't some fish bad for—some people? At some point?"

"Shit, she's right," Stephen said. "Don't eat that."

The room quieted, a silver rim of tension stretching across the air. Evie looked at the floor, and Stephen tugged his hair.

"The trick to poker," Aunt Fay said, "is to play dumb." She poured herself some wine. "If you tip your hand, it's all over, so what you've got to do is just pretend like you don't know a thing." Outside, the wind gusted, and the sky smeared with fat, dark clouds.

Mrs. Austin was staring at Evie. "Is there a particular reason why you shouldn't eat the fish, Evie?"

"I don't want it," Evie said. She pushed her plate away with a flourish, like a petulant child. "I'm tired of fish. I want chicken."

I turned to Aunt Fay. "When I play, I'll call spades 'shovels' and clubs 'clovers.'"

Mrs. Austin pushed out her chair and gathered up soup bowls. They clanked together like thunderclaps in the silence.

Mr. Austin stood up, too. "Easy there, Mal," he said, taking a stack of bowls from her. "New dishes aren't in the budget."

I stood and moved toward Mrs. Austin. "I can get that," I said. I was trying to be as helpful as possible since they were letting me stay.

Mrs. Austin slammed a handful of spoons onto the table and turned to Mr. Austin. "You want to talk about dishes? Why don't we talk about your daughter?"

"So, she's not in the mood for mackerel. She can get something else." Mr. Austin set the soup bowls down on the sideboard and looked from Mrs. Austin to Evie.

"She's already got something," Mrs. Austin said, walking to the door. She stopped with her hand on the doorjamb and looked over her shoulder at Evie. "Don't you?" she asked, turning, taking a step forward.

Evie looked at Stephen then back to Mrs. Austin and raised her hands into the air, stiff and spread apart like starfish. "All right. Yeah. I'm pregnant. That's what's going on." She slammed her right hand down. "I was a bad girl. Is that what you want to hear? Do you want me to apologize?" Her left hand curled into a fist. "Do you?" She stood up and touched Stephen's shoulder. "Let's get out of here."

"Now, hold on here," Mr. Austin said, his voice calm. Outside, night was closing in early, tingeing the dining room bluish-gray. Shadows coated the corners like cobwebs.

"Sir, I can explain," Stephen said.

I thought Mr. Austin's eyebrows were going to fly off his forehead. "That's an explanation I don't think I need to hear," he said, his finger pointed at Stephen.

Mrs. Austin glared at Evie, then Stephen. "How could you be so careless? Didn't you even *think*?"

Stephen Oden's mouth pinched into a thin line. "It takes two, you know."

"Just get out," Evie said to Stephen. "Go home." She ran out the door. Nate stared at Stephen until he left, too, the outside door slamming.

Aunt Fay got up and flipped on a lamp. She stood with her arms crossed and glanced around the room, then walked over and sat back down. "I always did say those Oden men were dicks," she said. "Just didn't reckon on them knowing how to use them."

Mrs. Austin picked up the handful of spoons again and slammed them on the sideboard, the clang echoing around the room. Mr. Austin rubbed his forehead. I shifted in my chair, an outsider, an interloper with no Evie to act as a buffer between me and her family. The oak table shone softly in the lamplight; on my plate, a half moon of liquid marked where my chowder bowl had been. Nate stared at the floor, eyebrows drawn together. Mrs. Austin walked across the room and yanked curtains across the windows, shutting out the darkening sky.

"Not the end of the world," Aunt Fay said. She picked up a dinner roll and a butter knife.

"It's the end of hers," Mrs. Austin said. "She'll never finish school and get off the island now."

"Shouldn't you go see to Evie?" Mr. Austin asked his wife.

Mrs. Austin pulled the last curtain shut and walked out of the room.

———

Hi Charly,

I hope you're getting all settled in there and everyone is doing well. Give my best to Jacob and Mallory and, of course, Evie. What a rough time this must be for her. James brought home a D on his algebra test, then apologized for allowing his grief response to show in such a typical manner. I told him his dad would say that he needed to study. I don't know what to do with him.

I know you just got there, but think about this—if you came back in a couple of weeks you wouldn't miss any school, or if you missed a couple classes and exams, I'm sure you could catch up.

Can you show me how to change the email to take off your dad's name? I can't stand to look at it. Hope everything is well, honey, and that you're getting a little beach time, even in the winter. The Weather Channel says it's supposed to be in the seventies there this weekend.

Love,
Mom

Two

I could feel the storm that day before I opened my eyes. The sound of waves pounding away on the other side of the island jostled me in my bed. I woke up completely when I realized I couldn't possibly be hearing them this far away and it must be the wind instead.

"Charlotte."

I sat straight up at the sound of my name. Evie was curled in a yellow chair in the corner.

"Sorry," Evie said. "I didn't want to scare you." Her eyes were swollen, and she rested her chin on her knees.

"It's okay," I said. I rubbed my eyes and reached for my robe. "I had a dream about waves."

"Nor'easter's coming through," Evie said. "It's fixing to blow a gale all day." She sighed, opened her mouth to speak, closed it again. When she looked up at me her eyes were hollow and dark. "Charlotte, what am I going to do?" she asked.

I pulled her over to the bed and wrapped her in my blanket still warm from sleep, brushed the hair off her face. I told her it would be okay. I didn't know how, but it would be okay.

Evie flopped back onto the bed with a groan and threw her arm across her face. Sometimes I don't understand life. Most of the time I don't understand life. From the time I was little I'd wanted a family of my own. And Evie'd wanted adventures, mountains, Sherpas.

I nudged her with my foot. "Hey, Eves," I said, "last night kind of sucked. I blew it. I know you weren't ready to tell them."

She shrugged. "Ready is overrated," she said.

"But I'm glad the baby didn't get mackerel-poisoned," I said.

"It's not a baby," Evie said. "Technically. Technically it's just a mass of cells. A growth." She grimaced and glanced down at her flat stomach. "It's a bunch of cells, half of which were put there by Stephen Oden."

I walked over to the window and peeked out the lace curtain. The scrub trees shook their branches in a frenzied dance. I leaned my forehead against the cool glass. I remembered how I was supposed to act around other people, shook myself out of myself. "You could say it's cell-fish," I said.

Evie threw a pillow at me. "Seriously," she said, "it started out microscopic, and it's already the size of a blueberry. It's burrowing into my uterus like a stupid tumor. Would you want a partial Stephen Oden tumor growing inside of you?"

I sat on the edge of the bed. Some cells really were tumors. Some cells were death.

It was September seventeenth, James's birthday, when my father told us he had cancer. He wouldn't talk at first—*this is neither the time nor the place*—but we kept asking. The biopsy results were back, and the only thing worse than knowing bad news was not knowing anything at all.

Cancer. An astrological sign. A water sign, Cancer, the crab. In the stars. Cancers are supposed to be nurturing, protective, tenacious, and sensitive. If you were born with your moon in Cancer, as I was, you feel most comforted when you're caring for somebody else. If you have cancer in your lymph nodes, you have a 20 percent chance of living for five more years.

We were all sitting around our polished cherry dining room table. My brother had already blown out his eleven candles.

Miles away from that dining room table in Ohio, out on the Outer Banks, pellets of rain spatted the beach. The dunes and sea grasses blew sideways, and the next morning Hurricane Isabel gashed across the island, separating the village of Hatteras from its neighbors to the north with a watery swath. The destruction was awesome. My family and I glued ourselves to the Weather Channel and gaped at the new inlet, the Sea Gull motel spewed sideways into the center of Highway 12, the beachfront houses crumbled into the sea like brittle skeletons.

The force of the waves and the wind was just too strong for the island to stand. At its widest point, Hatteras is only three miles across. During our summers on Hatteras, my dad, the geologist, showed us fossils of sea creatures found in the Pamlico Sound, a record of how far the island had already eroded westward. In the early days when Native Americans lived there, Hatteras was lush with trees and vegetation that kept it anchored against the sea.

Now, it's just fragile, waving sea oats that hold the dunes in place, their horizontal root system a knotted web trying desperately to hold off the inevitable tide.

"Charlotte?" Evie said, nudging me with her knee, once again bringing me out of my own head when her own problems were so fresh. My best friend. She got up and walked over to my closet. "It's going to be cold today," she said. "Did you bring any sweaters?" She riffled through my suitcase and pulled out a cream-colored cable-knit sweater.

"Are you thinking of not having the baby?" I felt my ears reddening. It wasn't like me to just say something like that without mulling the phrasing over in my head a million times first.

Evie was quiet. Finally, she said, "I don't know. I just don't know."

"I'll go with you if that's what you want." I stood up and walked over to her. "If it's not what you want, we could move in together. Like the Golden Girls, only with a baby. And fewer shoulder pads."

Evie shook her head. "If I have the baby, I'll have to marry Stephen," she said. She tapped the door of the closet and kicked at my shoes, grazing the side of a cardboard box on the floor next to them. "Did you bring clothes you haven't shown me yet?" She tossed herself to the floor and flipped open the box's lid.

"No." The word popped out of my mouth like an ice cube. I shook my head. "Don't open that, please."

"Why?" Evie asked. "Do you have racy lingerie in there?" She raised the other flap. And I was frozen in place. I couldn't move, couldn't speak. Evie squinted into the box. "What is that?" she asked, poking at it with her forefinger.

"That's my dad." The words sounded clearly articulated in my head, but I don't think they came out that way,

Evie stepped over to me, her mouth rounded into a small *o*. "Your father's ashes?"

I nodded. "Your parents said I could leave it—him—here. He wanted to be scattered in the ocean. The family's coming in July. For the scattering. We're going to get one of those big houses on the end of the island, you know, down by the ferry, and hire a captain to take us out. We don't know if everyone is going out or just me and Mom and James, so I told Mom I'd look into that, look into boats, you know, and how many people can fit on one and how much it costs and if they can even do something like that. I mean, it's not like a religious service or anything but it is kind of weird. You know?" It felt like a torrent of words, a rushing release of the most language I'd uttered in days. But it wasn't cleansing or calming; it was a whitewater tumble over jagged rocks and coursing stones and scratching grains of sand. My throat tightened again.

Evie nodded. "We'll ask Nate, okay? He knows about boats." She touched my arm, rubbed up and down. "Let's go to breakfast. Nate'll be down there."

Nate was in the dining room balancing a platter of blueberry muffins in his hand. Evie grabbed one and sat down. "Nate," she said, "tell us about boats." She picked the blueberries out of her muffin and popped them into her mouth one at a time. The wind lashed around the corner of the inn, and outside, the water of the sound sloshed high over the curve of the dock. It wasn't underwater yet, but soon would be.

"Boats," Nate said. "What do you want to know?"

"How about the Miss Hatteras?" Evie said. "How many people can fit on her?"

"You all planning a blowout party or something?" Nate's eyelashes were thick and dark as he blinked at me.

Evie kicked him. "It's for Charlotte's dad's scattering."

Nate placed a muffin on a bone china plate with gold piping. He set it down softly in front of me. "The Miss Hatteras holds at least a hundred people. It's either that or a dinghy. Limit there's six." He passed me butter and juice. "But I have my license. I could take you out."

I ran my finger around the edge of the plate. The muffin was crimpled with French pastry topping. "Mr. Austin must've gotten up extra early to do that," I said.

"He's always up early," Nate said.

"It's just I should've gotten up to help him," I said, pushing my muffin at Evie. My stomach twisted, clenched with the thought of setting my dad to sea, and I couldn't sit calmly in the dining room, popping crimpled blueberry muffin bites into my mouth while talking about the pulverized remains of my father's body. I couldn't do it. So, I did what I do—I ran away, to the kitchen. "Hi, Mrs. Austin," I said, "can I help?" When the inn was open, Mr. Austin did breakfast and Mrs. Austin took care of afternoon refreshments. They'd been running practice sessions of breakfast and snack options along with dinners.

"I'm making carrot cake for today." She passed me a silver potato peeler. "And call me Mallory, hon."

I set myself up in front of the stainless-steel sink and palmed a carrot, slicked the skin off it with the peeler, and kept on whisking and skimming with escalating intensity until I scored across the side of my thumb. I sucked my teeth and threw the carrot into the sink. Not again. Two thin lines of red stung all the way down to my wrist. Two thin lines redly pointing out that I was still made of nerve and corpuscle, not ash and incineration. My blood pulsed, alive in my body. I stared at my torn skin and stood poised, ready to bring the grater down on my thumb for the second time.

The swinging door swished open, and Nate walked in bearing an empty platter. "Evie and Dad give the blueberries a thumbs-up," he said to his mother. His voice, deep and tar-thick, mingled with the new, percolating aliveness that cutting myself had created. He turned to me. "You okay?"

I ran my thumb under a stream of cool water, red swirling down the sink and into the carrot shavings. "I'm just helping peel."

Nate turned off my water and pressed a white washcloth onto my hand, his fingers long and brown and callused. "Not having much luck lately, are you?" he asked. Then to Mrs. Austin. "Mom, got any Band-Aids?"

"In the cupboard," she said, barely turning her head.

I let Nate bandage me up.

"You need some breakfast," he said.

"She knows to help herself to anything we have," Mrs. Austin said. I'd tried to think of her as Mallory, but I couldn't. Evie's mom's matter-of-fact prickliness made me uncomfortable.

"I wasn't implying you were a bad hostess," Nate said.

Mrs. Austin thwacked her spatula down on the counter. Little bits of batter splattered the counter. I looked out the window. Across the walkway the old part of the inn stood like a dowager, stocky and strong against the wind that tugged at her gray shingles. I wanted to be outside in that wind, wanted it to grasp my hair and pull until my roots tingled. I pushed past Nate and past the pool to the dock, toward the water, little spits of rain needling my face. I stopped at the curve in the pier where the water splashed up, occasionally covering the boards, and sat down, huddled with my arms around my knees so that I could feel my thumb throb when I clutched my hands together. Slowly, I pressed in. Pain coursed like waves and the wind rocked, and despite the clouds, I could see clearly for the first time in months.

Behind me, the dock rattled and swayed, and Evie came and sat beside me. "Nate said you cut yourself," she said.

"I was peeling carrots."

The sputter and huff of a boat churned out in the sound. "That looks like the *Celtic*," Evie said. The *Celtic* was Aunt Fay's fishing trawler, put together from a kit and souped up with a fast engine. She loved taking it across the inlet into the ocean, sidling up to fancy boats, and challenging them to drag races. She never lost.

Even though the day was overcast, Evie put her hand over her eyes to scan the horizon. Habit, I guess. She brought it down to her stomach and flinched. "Dad must've gotten some bad blueberries," she said. Another twitch. "Ouch."

Aunt Fay cut the engine but still pulled up to the pier in a foam of churning water. Evie and I got up and walked to the end of the dock, leaping over the boards that were covered in water. Aunt Fay stopped the boat and tossed a coil of rope to the dock. Evie hopped up to tie it off but doubled over before she could execute her slipknot.

"What's wrong?" I knelt and brushed her hair away so that I could see her face.

"You girls chat later," Fay yelled. "This boat can't wait."

"I don't think Evie can wait," I said, but I straightened up and tied off the rope, hoping I'd done it right and that the boat wouldn't float away.

"I'm okay." Evie moved over and held out a hand to Fay, who brushed it away and leapt onto the dock, her knees creaking as much as the boards.

"Got the morning sickness?" Fay asked, her eyes honing on Evie.

"I don't think so," Evie said. She winced again and sat down. "What are you doing out in the weather?"

"Needed a little adventure," Aunt Fay said, thudding Evie's shoulder. She looked like the Gorton's fisherman's sister in her yellow rain hat and overcoat. "Kid," she said. "What are we going to do about this?" We all walked back to the dry part of the pier, waiting for the waves to abate before we crossed the wet curve.

Evie and I sat back down, and I draped my arm over her shoulders. Even though it was windy and damp, I wasn't ready to be back inside, and Evie and Aunt Fay didn't seem to want to, either.

"I don't know, Aunt Fay," Evie said.

"You love him?" Aunt Fay crossed her arms.

"I don't know. I think so." Evie and Stephen had only started dating when they both went away to the same college and were homesick. But she'd been crazy over him in the beginning, elation in her voice when she called to tell me about their first dates.

Aunt Fay creaked down to sit beside us and popped two sticks of Doublemint into her puckered jaw. "I haven't lived all these years to not know a few things," she said.

"Enlighten me," Evie muttered. She hunched her chin over her knees.

Fay cleared her throat, moved the Doublemint around her cheek. "That boy is not right for you."

"I agree." My words rushed out, caught on the cold wind.

Evie lifted her chin. "Y'all don't know. Neither of you know what this is like. You saw how Mom looked at me last night. I don't even want to think about Daddy. If I have this baby and don't marry Stephen—" she paused. "They're old-fashioned." Evie's hair blew across her face. "I'm already the black sheep."

"She's right." Fay looked at me. Her accent slanted the word into *roight*.

"Golly gee, thanks, Aunt Fay," Evie said.

Fay continued, "Your folks are old-fashioned, but they got sense." She gave a quick nod of her yellow-capped head. "You'd be surprised what your daddy can forgive."

Evie turned her head, I thought to look over at Fay, but her whole body followed, crumpling into a ball as she cried out in pain. I turned and saw Nate walking down the boardwalk; his gait quickened to a run. Fay hoisted herself off the dock to meet him. "Get this girl to the doctor," she said.

Evie moaned. "No," she said. "Can't you help, Aunt Fay?"

"Something is wrong. You get to the doctor."

"There's the clinic in Avon," I said. I felt detached, calm.

"They know me there," Evie said through her teeth. "I won't go there. I won't do it."

"No lady parts doctors on Hatteras Island," Aunt Fay said. "Looks like that's what she needs. She's going to have to go to Avon to the regular one. Best we can do."

Nate bent down to his sister. "I'll go get the car. We'll take her up to Nags Head."

"Road's likely washed out at S-turns," Aunt Fay said. *Loikely.*

Evie looked up, her face white. "If you try to drive me to Avon, I'll jump out of the car."

"They know you in Nags Head, too, dude," Nate said.

Evie squinted. "Still. I'm not going to Avon."

"You could try to get past S-turns," Fay said. "Tide's rising. It'd be a gamble."

At least the doctor in Nags Head wasn't Evie's dad's best friend like she'd get in Avon. And maybe the road would be passable. "Let's go," I said. Evie nodded and took my hand.

———

Nate drove north, Evie lying down in the back seat, knees pulled to her chin. As we passed the local shops and restaurants along the sound in Buxton, the waves rushed in whitecaps, choppy two-foot riots in the normally placid water. A ray of sun wobbled briefly through the clouds and disappeared.

"How much time do you think we have to make it?" I asked Nate, keeping my voice quiet.

Nate squinted. "We'll see what the overwash is like up at the motels."

"It feels like someone is ripping the lining of my uterus from itself like Velcro," Evie said from the back.

"I'm going as fast I can," Nate said.

Ahead, as the road curved left, at the small row of beachfront motels, a sheen of water cascaded across the road, white-foamed and frothing. "It's flooded," I said.

But Nate drove on, slowing the car as he drove through the water. "That's salt water, so we have to go slow," he said. "It'll rust out the car. But it's not so bad yet."

I peered out the window, rolling it down to poke my hand out in the spits of rain. The tires made swooshes of wake, but Nate was right, I could still see the road beneath the spray. A tiny edge of red poked around my bandaged thumb, and I pulled my hand back and rolled up the window.

Nate crept out of the last splashing trail of overwash and gunned the engine, speeding up Highway 12, fast, past Canadian Hole, with Evie quiet in the back.

"Last chance to go see Doc Quidley," Nate said as he stopped at a red light near the Food Lion.

I turned to look back at Evie. Her dark hair spread across the car seat, hanging to the floor in a curtain that obscured her face. A jolt of real fear took hold in my stomach. "Maybe you should, Evie."

Evie turned her head toward me, her face still behind her hair. "No."

Nate sighed. I watched his long fingers on the steering wheel, the way the muscles in his leg flexed when he pressed the gas. "If we can't make it through, you're not going to have a choice," Nate said.

We kept driving north, fast, not stopping until we came to a line of cars at the north end of Rodanthe, right by the tall house they used in the movie from that Nicholas Sparks book. The rain had increased, gone from spits to an unrelenting gray film. Nate stuck his head out the window to flag down the police officer walking along the row of cars. Apparently, Nate knew him and, in a rapid exchange, got the officer to let us through. "Thanks, man," he said, pulling his head inside and rolling up the window. He shook his hair out of his eyes like a wet Labradoodle. "It's breached. They're shutting down the road after us," he said. The cars ahead inched forward. "Hang tight."

The road looked fine, looked like it always did, and then, as we followed the slow parade of people trying to get off the island, we came to the breach. The stormy ocean alarmingly, terrifyingly near, thrashing and dark, one small dune separating the rush and crash from my window. That one small dune was all that stood between me and the undertow, and then that dune was gone. Water flowed across the road and under our car in a torrent, pulling at the tires. All it would take was one rogue wave, one unseen extra boost of current to pull us out, for it to all be over. Nate drove, waves crashed, and my shoulders tensed and tightened. Evie raised up on her elbow in the back seat to see, and she caught my eye. I was partway out to sea in my mind, smothering in the wet darkness, when Evie stretched out her hand, whether to comfort or be comforted I didn't know, maybe both. I grasped on, and then we were through. The dunes rose again, the road wet but visible, and Nate passed the other cars in a spew of grit and foam. He slowed the car through patches of wet, but there was nothing else like that breach. Wind buffeted the car as we crested the Bonner Bridge, and I felt the urge to take Evie's hand again because that bridge always scared me. I planned my escape in case the bridge fell. It wasn't entirely an anxiety fantasy—that bridge was old and worn out. I'd seen an umbrella under my seat; I'd use that to break the window after we crashed into the water, and I'd pull Evie out of the back seat.

"Don't forget to breathe," Nate said, nudging me with his elbow. I blinked, back in the world, my arm warm from where he'd touched me. Driving down the last of the bridge off Hatteras Island, we skimmed through the gray and wind until there were stoplights, fast-food restaurants, the turn to the hospital. Nate parked.

"Can you walk?" I asked Evie. She sat up, but her hand still grasped her side, a jumble of silver rings bright against her teal jacket.

Before she could answer, Nate was outside; he picked her up and trudged toward the brightness of the hospital's front door. I followed, squishing through the mud and sand that covered the parking lot, whooshing through the sliding doors into the hospital smell, tracking dirt all over the antiseptically white floors. Feeling calm to the point of vacancy. Feeling nothing, really, at all.

———

I'm glad my father didn't die in a hospital. I'm sorry he didn't get to die at the ocean as he wanted. I wish that he didn't have to die at all. Hospitals, even when they're different, are all the same. Their scent crept into my skin and turned my stomach against itself. I declined the cup of coffee Nate offered, and the vending machine wares. We'd been at the hospital for a while—lunchtime had long passed, but I wasn't hungry. Or maybe I was and just didn't care. I poked at my sore thumb and excused myself to the restroom. Nate kept pacing and pushing cardboard food items at me; it was so much work to keep myself present and behaving the way I knew I needed to, to talk and interact even though being able to do all that effortlessly felt like a distant memory.

I turned on the hot water in the bathroom sink and waited for the steam to envelop my face and breathed in. Instead of masking the sterile ammonia smell, it seemed to amplify it, so I shut off the tap and walked back to the waiting room. Nate had stopped pacing. He sat on a pea-green plastic chair with his long legs splayed out, elbows on his knees and head in his hands. "Any news?" I asked.

Nate shook his head. He looked so sad and lost. My cut thumb pulsed, and for some reason this made me want to connect my body to Nate's, to reach out and put my fingers in his tousled hair. He looked up at me, the planes of his face angled and sharp.

"Do you believe in prayer?" he asked.

I sat down. It was an intimate question; one I couldn't answer because I never really knew in the first place. But I thought Nate needed me to say yes, so I nodded, looked down, and started counting the number of linoleum squares beneath my chair. Fifteen if I included the ones on the outskirts of my vision. I hoped Nate wasn't an out loud pray-er. His shoulders moved up and down, and I thought he was crying but then realized he was only stretching, shaking himself out.

Nate put his hand on my knee. "Thanks for that."

"Don't thank me," I said. I hoped he thought I was being modest. "But I think she'll be okay," I said, shifting my knee beneath his hand, enjoying the friction. I had no idea if she'd be okay.

Nate looked up at the ceiling. I wondered how many tiles were above my chair and if they corresponded with the ones below it. "It's in God's hands," Nate said.

I pushed my thumb into the chair's metal leg and then pressed even harder to relieve the idea that some fictitious higher power had a benevolent and all-knowing reason for all the awfulness in the world. That was no higher power. That was nothing I could bow my head before. We were alone in a cold universe; that much I knew.

A white-coated doctor stepped into the waiting room, doors swinging behind her. She peered over rimless glasses at a plastic chart. "Austin?" she asked, surveying the room. Nate stood up and walked over to her. "Are you family?" she asked.

"Yes," I answered quickly for both of us. Doctors never talk unless you're family.

"Have a seat," she said, motioning with the clipboard to the chairs. She tucked a strand of hair behind her ear. "We've examined Evie, and she's going to be fine. She's had what's called a subchorionic hematoma, which is a blood clot that forms behind the placenta. She had some bleeding, but the ultrasound shows that both she and the baby are healthy."

I smiled. Evie was okay. I pictured her blood pooling and rounding out and pushing her baby's placenta away.

"What caused this?" Nate asked. He hooked his thumbs around a belt loop on his jeans and creased his forehead in a frown.

"Sometimes these things just happen," she said. "Have Evie take it easy for a few days—no heavy lifting or intercourse. It was a fairly substantial clot, so have her follow up with her doctor for an ultrasound in a month." The doctor showed us to the receptionist. Nate made an appointment, and I tagged behind the doctor, asking if I could see Evie.

She looked fragile and pale when I pulled back the curtain, sitting on the bed wearing her teal patched jacket over a pink hospital gown that covered her legs. I remembered that I needed to say something and not just stand there lost in my own thoughts. "That's a nice look you're going for there," I said.

Evie lifted the corner of the gown with two fingers. "I always did say that puke pink was my color."

I brought her jeans over and set them beside her. "I hear it's the new black," I said, forcing cheerfulness, trying to connect my words and tone with the way I was supposed to feel when I said them.

"Charlotte, I don't have any underwear," Evie said. "I bled through them."

In the pseudoroom next to Evie, I could hear a man protesting that he didn't need a catheter, that he could take a piss by himself. The nurse answered back that he'd had twenty minutes to take a piss, and if he didn't do it soon, she was going to do it for him. I jerked my head toward the curtain. "Maybe you could borrow his. Doesn't sound like he's going to need them."

Evie laughed, a low and melodic ripple of sound. I went in the hall, explained the situation to a nurse, and returned with the prize.

"You have to be joking," Evie said, holding the adult diaper out in front of her like it might already be full. She shook her head while she put it on and asked for my help with her jeans. "Do you think this is a sign?" Evie asked, pausing with one leg in and one out.

"The diaper?" It took energy to remember how to be playful, to wrap my old self around me like an aura.

"This whole episode," Evie said.

I hiked the denim up her left leg. The center of her pants was stained dark. "If I believed in signs, I'd think it's a sign that you're pretty tough and so is your baby," I said.

Evie stood up and buttoned her jeans around the puffy elastic and plastic. "Maybe it's a sign the baby doesn't want to stay there," she said.

"Maybe," I said. "It's your body. You get to decide. I'm here either way."

Evie slid on her shoes in silence. She took my elbow, and we shuffled out to meet Nate.

"We've got to move," Nate said.

"I'm fine, thanks for asking," Evie said.

Nate stopped walking. "Sorry," he said, "but we've got to get back before S-turns blows out again."

"Maybe we should wait," I said. "Evie doesn't feel very good, and we could find somewhere to stay."

"No," Evie said. "I want to go home."

Evening was lowering when we stepped outside. Gray sky collided with gray water as we started over the Bonner bridge, a uniform blankness punctuated by rushing peaks of whitecaps.

"Wind is kicking," Nate said.

I grabbed Nate's leg when the car jerked, buffeted in a gust.

"Should've shown your hand to the doctor while we were there," Nate said, looking down at my thumb.

"No, it's nothing." The car swerved again in the wind.

Nate corrected the steering, lightly and gingerly. Rain started again, fat drops blowing sideways. I moved closer to the comfort of his solid body but took my hand off his thigh. We drove over the peak of the bridge, the car swaying.

I looked back at Evie. "You okay?" I asked.

Evie scrunched up her nose. "Nauseated, but fine."

"Good thing she doesn't get carsick," I said to Nate. Without thinking I reached back to his leg. Nate caught my hand, his fingers grazing the cut on my thumb. I pulled away, and he let go.

The wind and rain filled the silence, and the road unfolded in front of us. Something—pain or fear or excitement—fizzed in my veins, and when Nate glanced at me the bubbling feeling coursed up a notch. This time we caught S-turns before the tide had approached the road so closely. Still, though, the ocean roared right at the dune line, spewing froths of white spume.

When we pulled up to the inn, I couldn't open my car door because of the wind. Nate got out and pulled it open for me, and then we both helped Evie inside. We were soaked by the time we got to the door.

"Would we flood here?" I asked, aiming the question at no one in particular.

Evie flopped down on the sofa in the lobby. "I forgot all my stuff in the car," she said.

"My dad bought this property because of its elevation," Nate said to me. "The pool might flood in a hurricane or nor'easter, but we'll stay dry up here."

I nodded. "I'll go get your bag," I said to Evie. Nate said he'd help and, remembering the wind pressing against the car door, I agreed.

Nate held the back door open while I grabbed Evie's things. We stepped away from the car, and the door slammed in a gust.

I looked at Nate. "Kind of wet," I said. Cold rain spattered my face, but my stomach warmed. Touching him in the car had rocketed me back into my body, bridging the long hollow of grief separating me from myself. I wanted to feel that again. I stepped closer to him.

Nate shifted his weight from foot to foot. "Kind of."

Then I did what I'd been wanting to. I skimmed his cheekbone with my pinky finger. Nate leaned forward, bent his head down, and caught my bottom lip between his. I opened my mouth to him. He tasted like salt. My head buzzed. Then a shock of wind gusted frigid air across my fingers and face.

We parted and walked back to the inn. Evie came to the door with Mr. Austin behind her. Evie took her bag as I passed it to her, then looked at her father and went with him wordlessly, tucked under his arm. Watching Evie and her dad walk away together, the gulf of grief came back, and I drifted back into it like a boat coming loose from its moorings, like an astronaut drifting soundlessly into space.

Once we were alone together, Nate put his arms around my waist, but the sudden heat twisted my stomach and I shook away. He was too close, and somehow it was different when Nate initiated contact, when it wasn't me trying to trick myself into feeling alive. I didn't know what I was doing, and I didn't want to lead him on.

Nate looked confused. I started to speak, but what could I say? *I'm sorry, Nate. I don't know why I kissed you when I've only ever known you as Evie's big brother, but I suspect it's because I'm so lost right now and it made me feel alive, which is unfair since you probably think I'm really into you which may or may not be the case because you're also really cute and are probably a lovely human being in general, but I'm just so lost right now.* So, instead of saying anything, I kissed him again, feeling like I was back outside in that wind, so strong I could almost let myself fall against it. Could almost trust myself to let it hold me up.

I stopped inside the old part of the inn when I heard voices. Mrs. Austin—Mallory—her voice bright, welcoming someone in. All I could see of the other person was a long shadow cast by the chandelier in the dim evening. I heard laughter, deep and resonant, and I shivered in my wet clothes. I walked in the door.

"Michael." He was tall and blond, lean, and muscled. He was my favorite cousin Troia's boyfriend, and I hadn't seen him in years.

Michael looked at me, blinked, looked harder. "Charlotte?"

"What are you doing here?" We spoke the words together and laughed. Michael stepped across the room and gave me a hug.

"Sorry about the attire," I said, motioning to my soaked sweater and jeans.

Michael smiled. "Hey, no problem," he said. "Wet is the new black."

It took me a second to realize that the laughter I heard was my own, which was enough to make me stop. "What are you doing here?" I asked again.

"I'm researching currents and global warming for a grad class. Nate's parents are letting me bunk here for a few days."

"And here I thought you'd come all this way to see me," Nate said, appearing around the corner. He and Michael performed some kind of handshake slap combo before clapping each other on the back.

"Good to see you, man," Michael said. He turned back to me.

"I'm surprised you made it in through this storm," Mrs. Austin said. I'd forgotten she was in the room. "With the road washed out and all."

"Swan Quarter and Ocracoke ferries were still running," Michael said.

"Well, it's good to see you, Michael," Mrs. Austin said. She turned to Nate. "Where's your sister?"

"Haven't seen her since she came inside."

Mrs. Austin walked out of the room toward the family quarters. The storm lashed around the office windows, clawing and howling.

"That's some nor'easter," Michael said.

Nate walked to the bathroom off the office and returned with two towels and handed me one. I suddenly felt dizzy and sat down, then realized that I hadn't eaten all day. Michael sat on the sofa beside me.

"Okay?" he asked. "You look pale."

The room seemed muted despite the glowing lamps and chandelier. Michael shrugged out of his coat, shook it off, and placed it around my shoulders. I curled in. "I need to go get some food," I said. The residual body heat from Michael's coat warmed me. I leaned back.

"I'll get you something," Nate said. "Orange juice, too?" He left for the kitchen.

Michael looked around the room. "They've made some nice changes to the inn," he said. He got up and paced around the room, looking at the local artwork and a map with pushpins representing the guests' hometowns. "Sorry, kid. I don't know what to say. Is your mom doing okay? How about James?"

James. How was my brother? How could my little, thirteen-year-old brother possibly withstand any of this when I couldn't with six years on him? "Thirteen," I said.

Michael leaned his head in toward me. "James is thirteen now?"

I nodded. "The man. He thinks."

"Because of your dad."

I nodded again, my head heavy.

"I'm sorry," he said.

"Me too."

"I missed the service. I was out of state on research," Michael said. He moved over to the couch and sat down, patted my knee. And I didn't feel the need to speak, to explain myself, to figure out how to pretend to be happy for someone else's sake.

The door banged open and shut, rain blowing in. "Here, drink some of this," Nate said, handing me a glass of juice. The citrus burned and I coughed but drank some more, and the room grew brighter and the sounds less dim. Nate gave me a piece of toast, and I ate it. I sat up and took off Michael's coat.

"Do you want some tea or anything?" Nate asked.

"Beef jerky and a Budweiser," Michael said. "Let's do this Charlotte style."

Again, I was laughing before I knew it, the sound unfamiliar in my ears. "What has my cousin been saying about me?"

"Yeah man, how is Helen-of-Troia?" Nate asked, slapping Michael on the shoulder. Michael and Nate first met when they were teenagers, surfing and working and fighting over my cousin. In the end Michael won, and he and Troia dated through college.

"She's good," Michael said. "Started up a drama club at her elementary school."

"Sounds like her," Nate said. He leaned back in a chair. "You didn't know Charlotte was here?"

Michael grimaced. "Troia didn't mention it. But she's been busy, grade cards and all. Me too with classes and research." He drummed his fingers on the arm of the sofa. "By summer we should be able to move in together."

"We're having a service down here for my dad this summer if you'd like to come. Troia will be there," I said.

"I'd like that," Michael said. "He was a good man, your dad."

"The best."

Michael stretched and stood up. "Hey, I'm going to head up to my room. Long drive today." He gathered his bags, and I handed him his coat. "I'll see you guys tomorrow."

I sat still after Michael left, trying to will myself to look at Nate, but I couldn't. I studied the floor. Brushed toast crumbs off my pants.

Nate cleared his throat. "So," he said. "Be good to have Michael around for a while."

"Yeah." I nodded. I ran my finger up and down the seam of my jeans.

"Some storm," Nate said. "We'll have to go see what's blown up on the beach tomorrow."

"Sounds good," I said. "Maybe Evie will feel like going out by then."

"You want any more to eat?"

I shook my head. "No, thanks."

"You were looking a little faint there for a while," Nate said.

I sighed. "Yeah, it was just a lot. For one day, you know?"

Nate moved my plate and glass around on the coffee table, stacked them up and wiped a tiny spot of orange juice with the napkin. "I didn't mean to freak you out," he said. "Earlier."

"I don't know what happened," I told him. "I mean, I do. I remember. I just don't know why I weirded out." I massaged my temples.

"We don't have to talk about it," Nate said.

"Good." I said it a little too quickly, with a little too much force. I dropped my hand to my lap. "Maybe later."

Nate got up, set the plate and glass on the desk. "I'll get those in the morning. You should go to bed."

"I will," I said. I stood up, found my legs, managed a smile. "Night, Nate." He gave a small half wave as I walked out into the hall. When I was out of sight I stopped and leaned against the wall, let my head fall back and stared up for a moment. I turned away from my room, walked toward Evie's, and knocked on her door.

"I gave at the office," she said.

"Hey," I said, sitting beside her on the bed.

"Hey yourself, storm chaser."

"Doing okay?"

Evie sat up, stacked the pillows behind her back, and scooted over so I could climb in beside her. "I've had better days," she said. "You?"

"Same." We sat together and Evie leaned her head on my shoulder, and I leaned against her head.

"You're damp," she said.

"Sorry." I moved away from her, and Evie reached into a drawer and threw me some dry pajamas. I got up to put them on. "Did you know Michael's here?"

"Michael-Troia's-boyfriend, Michael?"

"Yeah." I got back in bed, snuggled farther into the covers, and yawned.

Evie pulled the sheet over our shoulders. "He's been down here a few times lately. Something with the Labrador Current and the Gulf Stream."

"Remember that summer we met him? That was the same time we met," I said. My words felt warm and hazy.

"He cut his foot surfing at night," Evie said.

"And almost drowned James," I finished.

"Charlotte?" Evie said.

"Mm-hmm."

"Let's go to sleep." Evie switched off the lamp and the soft darkness washed over us.

Three

The first time I caught sight of Evie I'd been spinning around on a sand dune. I was nine years old, and she looked about my age, all dark hair and little-girl bones, and specks of light. "Why are you naked?" she'd asked.

I'd stopped spinning and stared, arms over my chest. "Because I'm going to have a bath after my brother gets done with the bucket." I'd picked up a striped towel and wrapped it around myself. "Why are you in our campsite?"

"I was climbing," she said. Her legs sparkled with a fine coating of sand. "Why are you taking a bath in a bucket?"

I kicked a cloud of sand into the air. "The showers are too cold. Don't you freeze in them?"

Evie picked up a coquina shell and held it out to me. "I hate showers. I avoid them at all costs."

"Doesn't your mom make you?" The shell curved in Evie's brown hand.

"She moved away for the summer for an important job moving the lighthouse," she said. "We live in the campground with our aunt for now. Our family is making a sacrifice for the good of the island."

I told her my name and she told me hers and we picked up shells for a while. "Does this one have a name?" I asked. A creamy white whorl nestled in my palm.

"That's a Scotch Bonnet," she said. "They eat sand dollars." She sucked in her cheeks and made a slurping noise. "They suck out all the sand dollar juice."

I threw it back into the sand. "Gross. I love sand dollars. I've never found one."

"You can buy them at the Pirate's Cove."

"It's not the same," I said. "If I found it, then it would really be mine."

"You won't find one here." The breeze flipped up the pink ruffles on her swimsuit.

"I might," I said. I knelt and swished my fingers through the sugary sand, back and forth. "Do you know the sand dollar story?"

Evie sighed. She said that everyone knew the sand dollar story from Sunday school. The top was a poinsettia, the bottom a lily, five piercings where Christ was nailed to the cross, five doves of peace when you crack it open. I'd always thought they were angels, and I told her so.

My brother, James, blond and skinny and three years old, trotted up the sand dune. "Mommy says your turn," he said to me.

"James, that's Evie," I said, and hiked down the dune for my bath.

That evening after dinner James and I walked down the hill. We were swinging hands, and James grasped the drippy remains of a sno-cone. "Ask your mom if you can take a walk," I called when I spotted Evie at a campsite in the bend of the road, forgetting that she lived with her aunt.

She jumped up from the picnic table and ran toward us. "I can," she said. Her long hair swung jauntily in braids, and crickets whirred in the dusk. The lighthouse should have been sweeping its beams across the island, but that was the summer it was dismantled, ready to be moved inland, away from the eroding ocean. Evie took James's sno-cone wrapper, and I tensed, afraid she would litter. But instead, she tossed it in a trash can, clanging the lid. James put one hand in mine and one in Evie's.

"My mom's moving the lighthouse," Evie said. Her voice was almost defiant. "Well, she's helping the lighthouse movers. They're from Buffalo, New York."

"Swing me," James said. He stepped forward and lifted his feet, hanging between me and Evie.

"Won't it fall?" I asked.

Evie gave James an extra heave, and he kicked off a flip-flop. "It could," she said, swinging James back. "Nobody's ever done this before. We're the first."

I released James's hand and ran my fingers over the sea oats lining the road. "I don't like it," I said. "I think it should stay where it belongs."

"Lots of people think it should stay where it belongs," Evie said. She picked a sea oat.

"Daddy says you're not allowed to pick sea oats," James said, crossing his arms over his *Star Wars* T-shirt.

"It's okay," Evie said. "This one was dead anyway, see?" She showed us the frayed stalk.

"You must love living here," I said. We crossed over to the bathhouse and sat on the wooden steps. A tiny green frog leapt around the water fountain, and James chased after it.

"It's okay," Evie said. But something about her eyes, the casual shrug of her left shoulder, made me think that she really did love it.

For the next two weeks Evie and I were inseparable. Our families intertwined because of us. When Evie's dad came to visit after work he'd stay for dinner on the grill, flipping steaks and keeping the gulls away from the hot dogs, swapping fishing stories with my dad. Evie's Aunt Fay told us tales about pirates and shipwrecks, and my mom draped jackets around our shoulders when the wind chilled around the campfire. I didn't figure it out until later, when I was older, but Evie's mother had taken up with one of the contractors from Buffalo who was here to move the lighthouse. This was why Evie and Nate were staying with Aunt Fay for the summer, who liked to squat in empty campsites, moving in her RV with the big tan-and-brown-striped awning until the park rangers threatened to have it towed. Evie's mom rarely visited. Evie loved my family, my gentle mother and boisterous dad, my freckled little brother who followed us around, my older cousin Troia who Evie said looked like pictures she'd seen of mermaids combing their long, golden hair. That was the summer Troia met Michael, and he joined our circle, too. It was the first and only year my aunt Gwen, Troia's mother, had accompanied us on vacation. She spent most of her time complaining about the humidity, cold showers, and general lack of civilization. We spent our days on the shore, digging holes, playing Frisbee, poking at jellyfish with our sand shovels, learning to bodyboard.

In the ocean, my body floated buoyant, free, limbs supported by the soft, salty water. I splashed around with my dad one day, hanging on to the orange bodyboard as he positioned it into an oncoming wave. "Don't let go of me!" I yelled back to him. The wave rose in a crescendo above my head, and I clung to the board, trying to propel myself backward. It was a big wave, or at least it seemed that way when I was small, and I didn't want to ride it, but my dad pushed me into the curl anyway. And then I was rushed forward, lifted up, splashed down, and spit out in the shallow water, looking down at the little bubbly holes the coquinas and mole crabs made. I pushed the hair out of my eyes and ran back through the breakers, dragging the board behind me. "That was an elevator," I said.

Dad took the board's leash off my wrist and strapped it to his own.

"You go up and then down really fast," I said. I snorted gracelessly as a wave splashed up into my nose.

"Snort," my dad said, pulling his nose up into a snout at me then swirling me around in the water. I let loose of the bodyboard, and he grabbed it back, catching a wave before I could tackle him. I body-surfed into shore behind him. James and my mother were spread out on the sand building a mermaid, and Dad and I sat down beside them. It was what James and I called a plop-whopper day—waves that could do a number on you if you turned your back, but good for bodyboarding. I slapped at a biting fly that hovered around my ankle.

"We need seashells for her bathing suit." James motioned at the mermaid-in-progress.

"Oh, my God," Dad said, covering James's eyes with his hand. "Don't look, son. She's naked."

James took Dad's hand away. "There's sand on my face," he said, brushing it away. He turned and poked his finger into the mermaid's stomach, making a belly button.

I started scalloping the mermaid's tail, wondering when Troia would get back with Evie.

"It's about a million degrees out here," Mom said, wiping her forehead with the back of her arm. "I'm going in for a dip." The metallic gold thread in her bathing suit sparkled as she walked down to the water.

"Dad?" I asked. "Are augers bivalves?" I offered up a small pointy shell spiraled with brown stripes.

"Do you see two valves on it?"

I stuck the auger in the mermaid's mouth like a fang. "I don't see any valves," I said.

Dad picked it up. "Augers are univalve," he said, tracing it with his finger. "One-part shells. They're carnivorous gastropods. First showed up in the late Cambrian period. Remember when that was?"

"No," James and I said.

"About five hundred million years ago," Dad said, sculpting a small fish in the sand beside the mermaid. "Way before people. We can go get some bivalves tomorrow if you want."

"Let's get them now," I said. Bivalve scavenging meant rigging up an inner tube with a cooler in the middle, putting on rubber water shoes, and clamming in the sound. "After Evie gets back."

Mom walked up from the water, shaking her head and spattering water over Dad's back. He grabbed her and pulled her into the sand. "Cal," she said, laughing and slapping at Dad, then running her hand up his arm. She paused below his shoulder, pressing a finger into his reddened skin. "You need sunscreen," she said.

Dad shrugged, pulled her farther into the sand.

I stuck out my lower lip and blew my bangs out of my face, a technique I'd been practicing all summer, and shook my head. They were so embarrassing. "There's Evie," Mom said, pointing up to where the boardwalk opened onto the beach. She blew a kiss at Evie and waved.

Evie walked down to our umbrella, carrying a small plastic bag. She brandished it in the air. Evie had been shopping for stationery in Avon. We were planning to find a pen pal in Ireland because Aunt Fay had told us stories about Irish pirate queens.

"I got it," she yelled. "We can write it tonight at my camper," Evie said. "But I wanted to show you now."

"Where's Troia?" Mom asked.

"She stayed at the camper to read," Evie said. "I think her mom was mad." Mom shook her head and said she'd better go see if there was anything she could do. She headed off toward the sand dunes, twisting up her hair as she went.

Evie and I sat in striped beach chairs under the umbrella and looked at the stationary, pink paper with veins of fiber running through it. It bent backward in the breeze, and I tried to smooth it out, put it back in the bag.

"Shit," Evie said, "it's getting ruined." I looked up to see my dad raise an eyebrow at Evie's swearing.

"Hey, Big E," Dad said to her. "Come help us build this mermaid." He walked up to us and put his sandy arm over Evie's shoulder, giving her a hug as they walked down the sand.

"Only if you tell us the Story of Absolutely Everything," Evie said, kneeling beside James.

I put the stationary in the beach bag and joined them, sculpting curlicues for the mermaid's hair. I listened to my dad recount the Story of Absolutely Everything—he told about the universe before there was a universe, infinite density, cosmic inflation, quarks and leptons, matter and antimatter. I loved the part about dark energy and pictured a mysterious bearded warlock benevolently calling forth the stars and galaxies. Dad always ended the story the same way, with the formation of the earth, fiery and awful and pounded with comets, then the cooling and the water and the slow oozing forth of life. "So, when you think about it?" he said. "Everything in the universe was there in that first bang. All the building blocks of life. And those same forces—gravity and density and everything—are in you and me right now, and what's in you and me right now is also stretched way out to the very edges of the universe. Pretty cool if you ask me."

"So much better than Genesis," Evie said.

My dad sat back on his heels. "That doesn't mean Genesis isn't true, or that they can't both be right."

"My dad says the same thing," Evie said. "But my mom says, 'Don't encourage her.'" She patted sand into waves around the mermaid.

James jumped up. "Let's build a trench," he said. He bent over and started digging with his hands like a small blond dog. "So the water won't ruin her."

Evie put her hands on her hips. "When that tide comes, it's going to demolish this mermaid."

"It'll be okay, James," I said. "We can build a new one tomorrow." I smoothed my hand across her fin, the sand cool and moist under my fingers.

"All the particles will still be there," Dad said. "Now how about we get some seaweed for her hair?"

So we built mermaids out of particles from the farthest reaches of outer space and got sunburned from ultraviolet rays emitting from a molten ball of plasma and magnetic fields, and that evening I was allowed to leave my family's camper and stay overnight at Evie's, where we ate hot dogs and played cards and wrote to a boy in Ireland, asking if he'd ever seen a real pirate queen.

That night, Evie shook me awake. Moonlight sifted through the screen of Aunt Fay's camper window, coating the rumpled bedcovers silver. "Come on," Evie whispered. She threw back the blanket and shimmied out of bed, slipping silently over Nate's empty bunk to the floor. She motioned to me with her hand. I was curious, so I slid out of bed, too, and we tiptoed out the door, the camper creaking under our feet.

Once we were several campsites away from Aunt Fay, I stopped walking and tipped back my head. "Look at the moon," I said. It shined high and silver-white, diamond specks of stars peeking through its glow.

"I don't care about the moon," Evie said. "We have to go work a spell." She began walking toward the boardwalk to the beach.

"A spell for what?" I asked, stung that she wasn't sharing the enchantedness of the moonlight with me, wary about the idea of magic. I was old enough to know how the world worked but young enough to believe in possibility.

Evie stopped walking and put her hands on her hips, then came over to stand beside me. "A spell so the lighthouse won't fall when they move it tomorrow," she said.

My stomach dropped, and my heart pounded in my throat. I knew it. It was going to fall. "Did your mom tell you that?"

"It's like a séance," Evie said. "Only part prayer, too, so God will fix things." She took my hand and started walking toward the boardwalk.

"I'm not allowed to go down to the beach alone at night," I said. When I was at home, I didn't like sleepovers, because even when I was having fun, there would come a piercing moment of homesickness, a wild longing for the familiar that rose in me and canceled out everything else. At the beach, sleeping over at Evie's, I was braver and stronger and freer, and I hadn't felt alone or scared. But at that moment, I just wanted to go home.

Evie stopped walking and dropped my hand. "Do you want it to fall?" She went on ahead, without me.

I followed, afraid to be left alone, still curious about what would happen next. We walked down the moonlit boardwalk, then plodded over the sand dunes to the beach. The sticky, sweet, salt air brushed my bare arms as we stood watching the silvery ocean in the moonlight. At the high-tide line, a campfire flickered and crackled, and as we walked closer, I realized one of the shapes sitting around it was Troia.

I called to her. Evie grabbed my arm in protest, but it was too late. Troia came over to us. "What are you two doing out here so late?" she asked.

And with her anchoring familial presence, I felt safe again, like we could fix anything that might be wrong. "We're going to work a spell," I said. "Otherwise, the lighthouse will fall."

Troia's eyes widened. "What do you mean, it's going to fall?"

"Evie's mom works with the lighthouse movers," I said. "She knows."

"It's just a spell me and Charlotte have to do," Evie said. "That's all."

"No, Evie," Troia said. She leaned down and looked into Evie's eyes. "If your mom knows something is wrong but the government is moving it tomorrow anyway, then we can't let that happen. We have to talk to somebody." Troia straightened up, her white dress and blond hair luminous in the moonlight.

Evie shuffled her feet in the sand. "We could call my mom," she said. "We could get her to come to the lighthouse and show her what's wrong."

"And convince her not to move it tomorrow," I said.

Troia nodded. She waved Nate and Michael over and told them our plan.

Nate snorted. "Why are any of you listening to her? Trust me, the lighthouse is fine."

Troia turned to him. "But if your mom told Evie that it's going to fall, then we need to do something. What harm can possibly come from calling your mother?"

I remember the silence that followed, a moment when even the ocean held its breath, and then the crash of action as Nate put out the fire and we all ran up the boardwalk.

We walked up to the campground phone booth, and everyone looked at Nate. "Tell her we have to meet at the lighthouse," Evie said. Nate threw his arms in the air and went into the phone booth, silhouetted in the moonlight as he dialed and slapped away mosquitoes.

Evie stood near him and listened as Nate talked to their mom. "Now you have to call Dad, too," she said when he hung up.

"Why would I call Dad?"

"Dad knows things, Nate. You have to call him. You have to get him to meet us up there." Evie took hold of Troia's arm. "Right, Troia? Tell him."

"We should get Aunt Fay," I said. I dodged away from Evie before she could stop me, my bare feet pounding the blacktop.

"Charlotte, wait for me." Evie's voice trailed behind me, but I kept running.

When I reached Aunt Fay's RV, she was sitting up in bed smoking and doing a crossword puzzle by lantern light. "Seen the devil, child?" she asked, stubbing out her cigarette while I leaned over to breathe, and Evie slammed in the door behind me.

"The lighthouse is going to fall," I said. I bit my lower lip then let it go.

"I called Mom already," Evie said. "Dad's coming, too. We have to meet them up there."

Aunt Fay shrugged a purple chenille bathrobe over her pajamas and scooted out of bed. She held Evie's chin in one hand and mine in another, her eyes darting between our faces. "So how are we going to stop this?" she asked.

"When Mom and Dad get together, everything will be okay," Evie said. And then, softly, "Please."

Aunt Fay stared at her. She sighed, a short breath in her nose and then out. "Get in the truck," she said.

We drove north, Troia, Nate, and Michael in the back. The lighthouse relocation site looked like a ghost town. Machinery sat abandoned, and the track for moving the lighthouse snaked across the ground. Even though we parked near the new location, deeper in the trees, I could still hear the ocean pounding.

Aunt Fay opened the door, and Evie and I filed outside, meeting the others as they climbed down from the truck. The night was thick and damp and enclosed with pine trees. Their scent prickled my nose. Aunt Fay stopped at a picnic table. "Thing is," she said, climbing on top of the table, "everything's got its own energy. These trees. That lighthouse. Us people." She mulled her mouth around a chaw of tobacco and spat. "So, what we need to do here is send out some good energy to that lighthouse."

"We'll help keep it strong," Troia said. She hopped onto the table and stood beside Fay. I looked at Evie. She leapt up too and thrust out her hand to me. I held on even after I climbed up. Nate and Michael stayed on the ground, shaking their heads at us.

"What do we do now?" I asked.

"We chant the spell," Troia said. She threw back her head, hair silvering down to her waist, then looked down again. "Anyone know any chants?"

Aunt Fay cleared her throat. "Cats and dogs, pigs and hogs," she intoned, "sturdy up the lighthouse logs."

"That doesn't make any sense," Evie said.

"Cats and dogs, pigs and hogs," I said. We held hands and started circling on the table, the pine trees spinning overhead. We turned a little faster until Aunt Fay pulled us down and we sat in a circle. Blood pounded in my face, and Evie's hair tickled my arm.

Headlights swept over us as a car rumbled up the road and then parked. A man sat at the wheel, and Evie's mom hunkered in the passenger seat, her lips a thin line. Before we could go over to them, Evie's dad's rusted red Ford truck pulled to a stop and his long legs swung out.

Evie rustled beside me. "We've got to go get them to talk to each other."

"That's why you pulled this shit?" Nate asked.

Voices rose in the darkness, caught on the wind. They were talking, but not about the lighthouse. They were arguing about who called whom first, and why.

"Look here," Aunt Fay said. "We got to let them sort out their business." She patted Evie on the shoulder.

Nate leaned back and rested on the table. "Don't worry about the lighthouse, Charlotte. The pile of bricks is fine," he said, kicking at the sand. A sliver of white peeped out where Nate had struck, and I jumped off the table and rushed toward it. The moon had come to the ground, a round, white sand dollar. I picked it up, dusted it off.

"Look." I placed the sand dollar carefully in the center of the table, and we circled around—me, Evie, Troia, Nate, and Michael. Aunt Fay headed back to her truck, tapping out a cigarette as she walked.

"You have to break it," Evie said, smacking the table. "Nate's wrong. Everything's not fine." She started to cry. "It's not fine, and you have to break it."

The sand dollar was perfect and pure, and it was mine. I wanted to hold it in my palm, wear it as a talisman around my neck, sleep with it under my pillow. "You have to let the angels out," Evie said. "We have to fix things."

I traced the leaves of the poinsettia, smooth and coarse at the same time. My homesick feeling rose, a longing for things to be whole and how they should be. "I can't do it," I said.

"I'll help you." Evie picked up the sand dollar and held it out to me, an offering. "We have to let the angels out," she whispered.

I ran my fingers under the sand dollar, placed my thumb on top beside Evie's, rubbed it back and forth one last time.

"Ready?" she asked, her face tear-streaked and expectant, her dark braids shining in the moonlight.

I took a deep breath, all salt and pine. "Ready."

The sand dollar broke crisply, and five white angels scattered into the sand.

Four

My sleep that night, in Evie's room at the inn, was tangled like seaweed. I woke up gasping. The storm had settled, and an edging of daylight poked in, tracing Evie's face in profile. Asleep, she looked the same as she did when we were kids. There's an old story here on the Outer Banks about a witch named Cora. When she was burned at the stake, she vanished into smoke, the letters of her name seared into the tree she was tied to. As I laid there in bed after the storm, alone on the edge of the world with my family fractured and irretrievable, I looked at the thin red line on my hand under my bandage and I felt like that tree. Marked. Hollow. I rolled out of bed without waking Evie and slipped outside where a gray morning shimmered. The deck railing splintered under my elbows as I leaned against it, watching the lapping water and waving seagrasses and breathing in their scent.

"You're up early, little one." It was Mr. Austin. He was fond of telling me that my name meant "little and womanly," an interpretation I disliked but tolerated because he meant it kindly.

I nodded and we stared at the sound. He clapped his hands down on the railing. "Coffee?" he asked.

"No, thanks," I said. "I'm just going to shower and then try to call my mom before she leaves for work."

"Good deal," he said, squeezing my shoulder with his solid hand. "If your mom and James want to come down, they're always welcome," he said.

"I'll let her know." I scuffled my foot along the deck slats, thinking about families spiraling away from one another, wondering how they ever came back together, wondering if DNA bound us like gluons in an atom or if humans sparked randomly across the universe, alone. Evie's family had somehow come back together months after her mother's infidelity.

"It's an awful thing," he said. "Losing your dad." His form shrouded in the mist, and he disappeared toward the kitchen.

Evie perched on the counter as I surveyed the Frigidaire for omelet ingredients. I'd showered and dried my hair, and by the time I called my mom, she'd already left for work. Evie moved a little more slowly than usual but said she was feeling better. I found spinach, bell peppers, and cheddar cheese crumbles and set them on the counter.

"Maybe you should let me chop," Evie said, sliding off the counter and opening the knife drawer.

I tossed her a pepper. "I've been thinking about when we met," I said. I reached up for the green glass bowl I used to whip eggs. "The summer of the lighthouse move."

Evie whacked a pepper and seeds flew. "Summer of Buffalo Bob, you mean?" she asked. "I thought for sure they'd get divorced."

"What happened to make them stay together?" I asked. I fired up the oven and lined muffin tins with ruffled pastel papers.

Evie had moved on to the spinach, which she chopped with great gusto, wiggling her green fingers at my face until I swatted her. "I don't know," she said. "Family." She shook her hair back out of her eyes. "Or maybe Mom just changed her mind."

Mr. Austin ambled in and kissed Evie on the cheek, and then me. "How are my favorite girls this morning?" he asked, appraising our breakfast efforts.

"Good," Evie said. She bent down to wipe up the pepper seeds and rose in slow motion, carefully straightening her stomach. She tossed the dishrag in the sink.

"Talked to Stephen yet?" Mr. Austin asked. He broke eggs into a mixing bowl and added cream.

"Dad, it's the crack of dawn. I haven't exactly had a chance." Evie passed me a bowl of vegetables and washed her hands.

"I figured spinach omelets with potato pancakes for breakfast," I said. "If that's okay."

"Sounds fine," said Mr. Austin. "I'll finish up," he said, whisking the eggs into a froth. "Why don't you girls go rest or play or do whatever it is you girls do." He waved us out of the kitchen, and we crossed outside to a hammock swing, sat down, and pushed back and forth with our toes until breakfast was ready. We ate, then returned to the swing.

"Morning." Michael's voice reverberated around the corner, and he jogged over to our swing. "Who's up for seeing what that nor'easter blew in on the beach?"

"Sure," I said. The beach after a storm was always a surprise.

Nate came outside, yawning and stretching his arms over his head, his hair rumpled from sleep. "What's up, kids?"

Michael told him about the beach, and Evie scooted inside to get us thermoses of coffee. We grabbed coats and crunched down the gravel driveway to Michael's green 4Runner.

"Sorry about the mess," Michael said, picking up McDonald's wrappers and Coke cans and throwing them to the wayback. Nate got in the front seat, and Evie and I took the back.

"This feels like the old days," I said. "I like it." It was in the midst of moments like this, my body in motion, surrounded by people, heading toward a destination, that I could forget my dad. And then I'd remember I'd forgotten and be awash again in grief and guilt.

"Only we're less young and stupid," Nate said, drumming his fingers on the console.

"Less young, anyway," Evie said.

Outside my window the town of Frisco rolled by, little churches and a fire station with a yellow truck outside. The Pamlico glimpsed through in places, wide and calm. Duck blinds perched on the water, and every house had a pier. The trees grew closer together as we neared the old Trent woods, and I cracked my window to smell the pine.

"We had fun back in the day," Michael said, catching my eyes in the rearview mirror. "Looks like I might be spending a lot more time here if I get the internship I applied for."

"The Park Service one?" Evie asked. She bounced her knee up and down.

"Yeah, I'd be part of the geoscientists-in-the-parks program," Michael said. He turned left onto the campground road, and we passed the Billy Mitchell airport, a tiny patch of concrete and parked planes covered with tarps. "I'd get to do research on the currents and erosion."

"How long's it last?" Nate scratched the stubble along his jaw.

"Nine months." Michael stopped the car near the beach-access road. "Want to walk up or drive?" he asked.

I turned to Evie. "Can you walk that far?"

She waved her hand at me. "I'm fine. I could walk for miles." She cracked the door and pushed it open. The ocean pounded. "Probably good for the kid," she said.

"Kid?" Michael's brow furrowed as we started walking. We climbed over the rope blocking off the campground and made our way to the boardwalk.

Evie wrinkled her nose at him. "Nate didn't tell you?"

Nate lifted a shoulder. "Too early in the morning for family secrets," he said.

Evie nodded. "I'm kind of pregnant," she said.

"Just kind of?" Michael asked.

Evie held her finger and thumb together and then parted them minutely. "Very kind of."

We walked as Michael contemplated this. "Okay," he said finally.

"You're not going to question me? Ask me whose it is? What I'm going to do?" Evie grabbed Michael's arm and swooned sideways, looking up at him. "Why, oh, why can't you be part of my family?"

Michael laughed and put his arm around Evie's shoulders, hugging her to him as we trudged up the dune to the beach. "I pretty much am, right?" he asked.

Nate pretended to swoon and shook Michael's other arm. "Oh, Michael, you're the brother I never had."

I picked up a broken sea oat and tickled Evie. "Remember James yelling at you about picking these?"

"I was pretty impressed," Evie said. "That's how I knew you weren't just dumb tourists."

The dune ascended, and we plowed our way up, the surf getting louder with each step. I looked down for sandspurs, and when

I raised my eyes at the top of the ridge, I grabbed Nate's arm. The ocean had eaten the beach, and waves tumbled in a roaring green frenzy right up to the dune line.

I stopped and stared at the tumult, water droplets misting my face.

"Wow." I don't know who said it; maybe we all did. The wide, gentle slope of sand where we used to build castles and bonfires was gone, covered by an ocean gnawing at the sand dunes.

Michael shook his head. "I have got to document this," he said. Excitement prickled in his voice, and he turned. "Camera's in the car," he said, sprinting off down the boardwalk.

I felt pressure on my hand and realized that Nate was squeezing it.

"Haven't seen it this bad in a long time," he said. "Not since the triple strike in ninety-nine."

Right after the lighthouse was moved in the summer of 1999, Hurricanes Dennis, Floyd, and Irene slammed into the Outer Banks. They chunked away the beach where the lighthouse had stood. Later that autumn, Evie and Nate's parents reunited for their own season of repair.

"Nor'easters are sneaky," Evie said. She advanced toward the water and threw a shell out into the waves. It vanished in white froth. "They don't get names and news coverage, but they're as bad as hurricanes."

I pulled on Nate's hand, and we stood beside her. I didn't hear Michael approach until he tapped me on the shoulder, his camera in hand. He showed me the digital images of the waves but turned the camera off at a picture of Nate and me holding hands, the steaming ocean surrounding us, Evie off to one side.

I slackened my grip on Nate's hand, and he released it and crossed his arms over his chest. The sun was bright, and I moved away from the water to sit in the damp sand.

"You're going to need my diaper from yesterday if you keep it parked there," Evie said, casting a shadow over me. I pulled her down beside me, and we stared at the waves. "I need to go talk to Stephen," she said. "Tell him about yesterday."

"Want me to go with you?" I asked.

Evie rubbed her head and squinted into the sun. "No," she said. "I've got to do this myself."

Nate and Michael moved down the sand to shoot different angles, their feet planted sideways against the dune's edge.

Evie's gaze locked on the water. "I don't know what to do," she said.

"You'll figure it out." I wrapped her in a hug, and she felt bony and fragile against my shoulder. "And I'll be there no matter what you decide. I promise."

"I just need to get this over with," she said. The breeze kicked up, and Evie shivered. She collared her hands around her mouth and called Nate's name. "I'll have Nate drop me off and come back with the truck," she said.

Nate trotted forward, and Evie stood stiffly. Michael passed Nate his car keys, and Evie and Nate headed down the boardwalk, dark heads disappearing over the horizon. Michael eased himself into the sand beside me, and we looked at more pictures. He put the camera back in its case and kicked off his shoes. "You cold?" he asked.

I stretched my arms forward. "The sun's keeping me warm enough," I said. "But the sand is kind of wet." We spoke louder than usual over the crashing surf.

Michael furrowed his fingers around in the sand, picking up a smooth purple shell. "What's the story with you and Nate?" he asked.

The sun felt suddenly hotter on my face. "Nothing," I said. "There is no story." I picked up the purple shell and smoothed it like I was making a wish. "Did he say there was?"

"Nah," he said. Michael leaned on one elbow, then sat back up. "Sand is cold," he said.

The sunlight shimmered a rainbow mist over the sea spray. "I kissed him yesterday," I said. "I shouldn't have, but I did. And now I don't know what to think." My shoulders felt heavy, and I leaned forward over my knees. "I'm not thinking too clearly these days." I flipped at the edge of my bandaged thumb and sand stuck to it. It didn't hurt anymore.

Michael touched my back, briefly. "You've got a lot on your mind lately," he said. "Is there a reason you shouldn't have kissed him?"

"It's just that I shouldn't even be down here," I said. My hair blew over my mouth, and I wiped it away, sand sticking to my lips. "I should be home with my mom and James. Or back in school like my dad wanted." My dad had been insistent that I start college after he died.

"Hey, there's nothing wrong with taking a break," Michael said. "When my mom was sick, I took a year off school."

"But you were there with her," I said, straightening my spine. "You didn't run away." A wave crashed closer to the dunes than the rest, and foam washed up inches from our feet. We leapt up and staggered back. My foot caught in the sand, and I tripped backwards. Michael tried to catch me, but we both fell in a heap, a reed poking me in the back. I yelped and rolled to my knees, damp sand all over my jacket and jeans.

"See what happens when you start beating yourself up?" Michael said, holding my elbow and brushing himself off.

I shook the sand off his camera case and handed it to him. We stood up and moved closer to the boardwalk, sitting down on the crest of the hill. "My dad believed in science," I said. I pushed my hair behind my ears and took a breath. "But science doesn't believe there's anything after death." Lately, my grief had focused on this, the cold, empty probability that after our molecules dispersed into ether, there was nothing. That the feeling I'd always gotten in church, the tingle in my spine when the congregation's voice rose, *to save a wretch like me*, the flow of connection when I wrote without thinking, my hand moving across the page channeling *something*, all that was the make-believe of a child.

Michael placed his palm on the top of my head, squeezed, and ran his hand down to my neck. And that was the moment something turned. It was the touch of his hand on my neck, my hair shielding us from skin-to-skin contact, but still, in my body something changed, turned, awakened. It was like the times I had reached out for Nate to try and capture some feeling of being alive were just precursors, just placeholders for *this* touch that ricocheted me back into my body, that pulled me from my contemplation of the cold depths to this simple leap and spark of atoms.

It didn't make sense. I didn't care.

"If you want to talk about it, I'm here," he said.

"Especially if you get the job," I said. I moved away from him slightly, trying to shake off the feeling I'd just had.

"Yep." He opened the camera case and looked at the images again. "The water is crazy today, Charlotte. Wild. All over the place." He shut the lens, stood up, and pointed at the waves to the north. "See that?" he said. "Up there around the point you could usually see the Gulf Stream. It's like a giant river inside the ocean." He held his hands out to his sides. "It comes sweeping up from the equator, bringing all kinds of life with it. Just teeming with life."

"But then it meets the Labrador from the north," I said, colliding my hands together. "Pow. Graveyard of the Atlantic."

"Exactly." He walked closer to the water, and I followed. "Here and Newfoundland are the only places in the world where those two currents meet like that. Add the shoals off the cape and you've got a recipe for shipwrecks and crazy weather." The wind blew Michael's hair back from his face.

I wanted to run into the water and let the currents wash me anywhere they wanted—north, south, up, down. I took off my shoes and edged down the dune toward the surf. "Let's get our feet wet," I yelled to Michael, bending down and rolling up my pants legs.

"You're a glutton for punishment, my friend," he said, but he pushed his jeans up too.

We picked down to the shoreline and the spuming water iced over our feet and ankles. I shrieked and ran backwards, jumped over a wave and chased it forward. Seaweed tickled my toes, and I splashed a handful of the frigid water in Michael's direction.

"You're going down, McConnell." Michael chased me, and I dodged him. A wave slapped foam up to my thigh, and I sprinted back to the dryness of the sand dunes. I leaned over with my hands on my knees, breathing hard. My thumb stung from the salt like it was newly cut. I shook it out, and Michael asked if I was okay. I kicked some wet sand over his feet.

"I'm good," I said. "But you're going to have to rinse off your feet now."

"Oh, really?" Michael balanced a heap of sand on his right foot and hovered it at me, but I pushed him off-balance and the sand flew to the side as he stepped down. I turned to run and just missed crashing into Nate.

"You two been swimming?" he asked, his gaze skating over my wet jeans.

"Sure," I said. "The water's fine." The ocean rumbled and thrashed under the bright sky. Three seagulls flapped by, looking confused that the beach was gone.

"Yeah, you should take a dip," Michael said. "Like bathwater."

"Like bathwater on crack," Nate said. I walked over to my shoes, sat down, and unrolled my pants.

"Did Evie get to Stephen's?" I asked Nate.

He nodded. "She's there now." The clear morning sun dimmed a bit, and the day seemed cooler.

"Let's head back to the inn," I said. "I want to be there when Evie gets back."

"I want to upload these photos." Michael brandished his camera and stuffed his feet back in his shoes. We trudged through the sand to the boardwalk. I turned back to the ocean before the rise of sand dune obscured it from view. In its wildness, in its crashing green-gray glory, it was an entity unto itself, a tumultuous crowd that made me feel small and insignificant.

Charlotta Divine—
Just a quick note while I'm on my lunch break. It's Salisbury steak
day. Which made me think of you.

Love and squishes,
Troia

PS—I forgot to tell you that Michael is coming down there. Have much more to discuss on that subject.

———

I walked down to the pier in the afternoon sun, the stillness of the Pamlico seeping into my bones, soft and calm after the jumble of ocean that morning. Alone, quiet, I stared into the water, which was the clear, comforting color of hot tea. Funny little crabs with one large claw and one small claw sat in the shallows, waving their large-clawed arms in the air like they were holding lighters at a Lynyrd Skynyrd concert. *Freebird.* Then they levitated sideways through the water. I sat on the dock and watched them, this proliferation of *life* all around, biology and motion, nothing stagnant, always moving. Until it stops. Until it's over.

It was just a matter of time before Evie would come bounding back from Stephen's and dinner preparations began, but just then it was me and the tide flowing in and back out. Me and some rock concert crabs. I took off the Band-Aid on my thumb and pressed on the cut. It stung, but it didn't make me feel alive like it had yesterday. Michael's hand on the back of my neck. Nate's mouth in the inn's parking lot in a storm. That made me feel alive. I poked at the cut again, stared at my fingers—long and tapered with oval nails that squared off at the tips. The hand that looked like my father's hand. The hand that looked more like his the sicker my father got. He used to palm igneous rocks in front of a classroom, lift slabs of malachite and granite as if they were made of chalk, haul bits of the earth out of their resting places to teach about where they had once been. As the cancer crept into his bones, his hands lost strength. The clay coffee mug James made in art class shook when my dad lifted it to his mouth. He still had hair then, but when it started to fall out from the radiation, he asked me to shave his head. We sat outside in the spring sun, and I pretended that I was a famous hairstylist flown in from Paris for the occasion. I clipped his hair short, then buzzed it with a razor. The fine strands tickled across my fingers and when I was done, he ran his hands over the smooth baldness, the bones of his fingers lacing over his skull.

I heard my name and turned to see Evie traipsing down the walkway to the pier. She lifted her arm and waved, and I ran down to meet her.

"Did Stephen drive you home?" I asked. We walked back out to the end of the pier.

"We want to have the baby," she said.

"You do?" An egret lifted into flight, its white wings pushing into the sky. "Both of you?" We reached the dock and sat on the edge.

"He says he'll take care of me," Evie said. She gazed out over the water and twirled a strand of hair around her index finger. "Maybe I'll be like a 1950s housewife. That wouldn't be so bad, right?"

I bit my lip. "Not if you got to wear vintage kitten heels." I paused. "Do you want to have the baby?"

Evie threw a twist of hair over her shoulder and turned to me. "I want to go see Aunt Fay," she said.

"Nate took your mom's car up to Food Lion," I said.

Evie drummed her fingers on the pier. "You and Nate seem to be having a lot of communication lately."

The wind cooled across my burning cheeks. "What. He's your brother. I can't just not talk to him."

She looked at me and tilted her head sideways. "You'd make a cute couple. You could stay on Hatteras and get knocked up, too, and then our babies would be cousins." Evie pulled her knees up to her chest and chipped at a scab on her ankle. "Let's go see Aunt Fay. We can take Dad's truck."

Aunt Fay lived down the island in the village of Hatteras. It was the place she loved best, and she wouldn't leave her stilted shack even when a storm threatened. Evie pulled the car around a gravel driveway that snaked through wind-stunted trees. Everything leaned to the left, including Aunt Fay's house. It bobbled on top of its stilts like an unsteady pelican, thrusting its gawky head as high as it could, slanting forward over a narrow but deep canal where the *Celtic* anchored. Aunt Fay's house was surrounded by large vacation homes—three-story beach mansions that lined the canal like haughty flamingos dressed in pastels. When this part of the island began to develop, Aunt Fay refused to sell her land and remained ensconced in her own quarter acre of tangled island growth. We climbed out of the car, and I stopped to inspect the orderly row of seven plaques, each bearing a picture of a black-and-tan Yorkshire Terrier and the name *Walter*.

"How old is this Walter installment?" I asked Evie. Whenever one of Aunt Fay's dogs died, she replaced it with another and gave it the same name. She claimed she couldn't keep any other name straight and would just end up calling it Walter anyway.

Evie stepped around the Yorkshire Memorial Gardens and made her way to Aunt Fay's rickety steps. "A few months," Evie said. She turned and motioned for me to follow her. "He's kind of a shit."

We clacked up the steps, and Evie pounded on the door. It was painted red and gleamed against the weathered boards of the house. Evie pounded again and turned the knob, poking her head through the door. "Aunt Fay?" she called into the house. Strains of a Mozart concerto drifted out, mingled with the yap of a small dog, and we walked inside. Aunt Fay stood in front of a tall easel wearing an apron, humming, and sweeping blue paint on a canvas in wide strokes, keeping time with the music. As we got closer, I realized that she was wearing only an apron. She looked up and smiled her caved-in grin. "Hello, girls," she said, splattering paint on the carpet as she turned to us.

"Aunt Fay," Evie said. "Clothing?" The Yorkie bark ratcheted up in volume and intensity.

Aunt Fay put down her paintbrush and shook her head. "You know I can't paint like that." Her accent rhymed *can't* with *paint*. "Sit," Aunt Fay said, pointing at the green chenille sofa. I sat and picked at the raised balls of fabric while Aunt Fay pulled on a bathrobe. She walked to another room and came out carrying a wriggling mass of black-and-tan dog with sharp, pointed ears.

"Tea?" Aunt Fay steered Evie toward the sofa, handing her the dog, then went into the kitchen and ran water into a black teakettle and lit the gas stove. She came back into the living room, sat down, and put a gnarled hand on Evie's knee. "How you feeling?"

Evie shrugged. "Fine. Making important life decisions." She tussled Walter around on her lap, sticking her hand in his mouth.

"Important life decisions." Aunt Fay hoisted herself up. "You need me to fix up that tea." She clattered mugs down from the kitchen cabinets and put them on a bamboo tray.

"Fix up the rest of my life while you're at it," Evie said. She placed Walter on the floor, leaned back against the sofa, sat up, and pulled a quilt off the back to wrap around herself. "This looks like Nate's baby quilt," she said. It was blue with squares of smiling yellow ducks. I touched its soft, frayed, satin edge and watched Walter stalk a housefly.

"It is," Aunt Fay said from the kitchen. "He found it the other day and wanted me to fix up the bald patches. He loved that thing raw." Aunt Fay carried the tray to the living room and placed it on a coffee table made of gas cans and mirrors. I picked up a mug with a logo of the Frisco Rod and Gun—two fishing poles crossed like clashing swords.

Evie lifted the mug of tea to her lips, drank, and made a face. "What is that?"

"Ginger," Aunt Fay said. "Settles your stomach." The Mozart concerto wound to a close, and Aunt Fay started to stand to change the music. Walter abandoned his housefly and attacked Fay's slippered feet. She shook him off.

"I'll get it," I said. The symphony emanated from an antique record cabinet that hid a CD player. I selected some Beethoven and stopped at a framed picture of a man in uniform on the wall. "Was his name Walter?" I asked. The mystery of the Walters had long haunted me.

"Of course not," said Aunt Fay. "Walter's a dog's name." She settled back into the sofa, smoothing her bathrobe around her knees, and pulled Walter onto her lap. He yawned. "His name was Charlie Anderson. Mainlander. Been dead for years now."

"I'm sorry," I said. I sat back down. Aunt Fay's house smelled vaguely damp, and the paint fumes were making my head hurt.

"He was the great love of your life, right?" Evie asked Aunt Fay. "But then he was killed?"

"Something like that," Aunt Fay said. She patted Evie's knee again, then petted Walter's fur in solid strokes. He fell asleep. "Now look here. I'll tell you this like I told your mama a long time ago. All men are pricks. You got your good pricks, and you got your bad pricks, but all men are pricks. You need to know that, and you need to know your family is going to be right here for you whatever you decide to do. You just need to know that." Aunt Fay hugged Evie to her.

I picked up the tea tray, carried it into the kitchen, and rinsed out the teakettle. The water and Beethoven's Fifth Symphony drowned out Evie's and Aunt Fay's voices. A surge of homesickness rose in my stomach; I wanted my mom and dad to tell me they'd be right there for me no matter what. The sun began to lower over the canal, pink brushing the sky. When I went back in the living room, Evie was still nestled under Aunt Fay's chin like a child.

Charls,
Mom said I should write to you.

James

I texted Michael: *I found this book in the common area and adopted/ stole it to my room.* How to Read a North Carolina Beach. *This is the shit you study, yeah?*

Michael texted me. *That's my shit, girl. What's your favorite part so far?*

I wrote: *"Once the waves have broken, they form a sheet of water called the* swash. *The swash zone is the area on the beach where this thin, relatively smooth, shallow layer of water constantly moves back and forth. As the tides rise and fall, the swash zone moves up and down the beach." Page 14.*

Michael wrote: *Good stuff.*

I'm the swash zone, I wrote. *A shallow layer of grief constantly moving back and forth.*

Michael texted back. *Page 11: "All beaches have swash marks. The way each wave breaks depends on the slope and shape of the ocean bottom." The slope and shape of your ocean bottom is solid, C.*

I blushed and texted him back. *You said "bottom."*

Through the glass of the inn's office window I saw Nate standing on the pier, his frame dark against the pink-and-violet sky. I put down my phone, told Evie I was taking a walk, and made my way down to the water. I had to get rid of the homesick feeling in the pit of my stomach that wouldn't go away. I needed my body to remember that I was tied to the earth. The wind gusted, and Nate's flannel shirt billowed out. I crept up behind him, stood on my toes, and brushed my lips across the nape of his neck. He started and turned his head, his dark hair tickling my nose, and I slipped my hands underneath his flannel, pressed my breasts to his back. He smelled like woodsmoke and pine and salt. Nate turned, and I pushed my hands up the front of his blue thermal undershirt, the nubbins grazing across my knuckles. He touched my face, skimmed a long finger over my cheek, and I raised on my toes again to match my mouth to his, to run my hands around his back, to knead his shoulders, to pull him down to me.

At dinner that night I stole glances at Nate as he chewed his food, raked his fork across his plate, lifted his glass of iced tea to his lips. We all sprawled around the table like lazy cats after the meal. Michael reclined, golden and bronze in his chair, telling Evie stories about Lake Michigan while Mr. and Mrs. Austin conferred over some bit of business, their heads bent together.

"Coming to church with us tomorrow?" Nate asked me. His shirt collar turned under, and I wanted to straighten it.

"Sure," I said. "I guess."

Stephen Oden poked his head into the room, and the easy camaraderie of the evening halted.

"Mr. Austin," Stephen said, taking long strides to shake hands. "Mrs. Austin. You're looking lovely tonight." Mrs. Austin smiled and motioned for him to sit down.

Evie tensed forward and laced her fingers together. "Hi," she said. Stephen nodded to her and smiled, his teeth whiter than the China cups. He still had that ridiculous mustache, and I wanted to pin him down and pluck it out hair by hair.

Michael raised an eyebrow at me, and I cleared my throat to introduce them, but Nate beat me to it. "This is Michael Holden," he said. "He's here doing research."

"What field?" Stephen asked, and everyone relaxed as Michael talked about the Gulf Stream.

Stephen picked up the iced tea pitcher and filled Evie's glass, then his own. I filled my lungs and exhaled, trying to navigate the new swirl of dynamics in the room. Evie and Stephen. Nate and me. Michael.

Five

The next morning before church, I went to an empty room overlooking the water, sat on the deck, and called my mother. The morning had dawned crisply, full of salt and promise, the Pamlico a deep, waving, navy blue.

I told my mom I couldn't talk long, that I had to eat and get ready for church. "I was thinking we'd go to breakfast after, but there aren't any restaurants open," I said. I sat in a rocking chair and pulled my feet up.

"That must feel isolating," Mom said. "To have nowhere to go."

I stared out at the horizon, the gentle, lapping water. "Not really. Not yet anyway."

Mom filled me in on all the gossip from home, how she suspected our next-door neighbor was having an affair with the contractor; that my second cousin went to the hospital for a heart attack, but it turned out to be indigestion; the pot roast she'd gotten at the Golden Dawn grocery meat sale two for one. That the light switch in the kitchen had started smoking and smelling hot. That Aunt Darcy and Uncle Emmett were remodeling their kitchen, picking out stainless steel appliances together. That she really, really missed my dad. "Your brother refuses to talk about him. It's like he never existed at all."

In my chest, a string of guilt tightened and pulled outward, a taut line of shivering remorse binding me to the family I'd run away from. If I hadn't left, I'd still be home over Christmas break, and when school started again, I'd only be an hour away. "He probably can't yet," I said. I couldn't. I told my mom I had to go, that I needed to find Evie and Nate and I didn't want to be late for church. I pressed my phone's end button and stared at the water until the pull lessened.

I went to the kitchen to look for Evie and found her staring glumly at the coffee maker. "You'd better drink an extra cup for me," she said. "It turns out that zygotes hate caffeine. It makes them have little bitty zygote attacks."

"I went off caffeine a while ago," I said. I grabbed an English muffin and spread it with peanut butter and jam. It stuck in my throat. I thought that if guilt could taste like anything, it'd be peanut butter.

"I don't know why anyone would voluntarily go off caffeine," she said. Evie had arrayed herself for church in a silver skirt with a sequined belt that highlighted the flat line of midriff between it and her purple shirt, but she was still barefoot.

"You're going to freeze in that," I said. Rays of sunlight filtered through the kitchen windows, catching dust motes. The only dress clothes I had were the ones I wore to my father's service, and I couldn't take the black silk of the funeral clothes touching my skin, so we went to Evie's room so I could plunder. I started to tell Evie I'd talked to my mom, but being around her had lifted my mood and I didn't want to go back to the sticky sorrow of our conversation.

"Fifty-one," Evie said. "That's the maximum temperature for Hatteras in January." She went over to her closet and slid on silver heels, fastening the ankle strap. "It's supposed to be in the seventies today." Still, she slung a furry white jacket over her ensemble.

"Fluffy," I said. Sometimes, around Evie, I forgot to be sad, just for a moment.

Playing in Evie's closet promised to be a challenging adventure as Evie was at least six inches shorter than I. Evie pointed out the divisions of her wardrobe—comfortable, trampy, and good girl. "You should probably stay away from my pants," Evie said.

"But I've always wanted to get in your pants," I said, thumbing through her clothes.

"Get in line," Evie said.

I pulled out a hot pink fringed tank top. "Wasn't this the swimsuit you wore when you were nine?"

Evie pushed the shirt back into her closet and twisted my shoulders toward the good girl section of clothing. "You stick to these," she said. "I need to glory in the trampiness while I still can." She smoothed a hand over her stomach and did a little spin, stopping with her hand on her hip.

I selected the most churchy-looking dress I could find, a black and teal polka-dot number that barely skimmed my knees, and Evie undid the black leather cord she wore around her neck.

"Here," she said. "This'll go with your outfit better." A chunky gold cross dangled from the worn leather strip, and Evie tied it around my neck.

Nate stood on the steps and whistled as we came down. He was dressed in pants and an Oxford cloth shirt, his only nod to the beachy day a pair of sandals instead of loafers. "You look nice," he said to me.

My cheeks warmed.

Nate turned to Evie. "Okay," he said. "Charlotte and I are going to church. We'll pick you up on your street corner afterward. Is 12:30 good?"

"Shut up," Evie said, prancing down the stairs in her heels. She flung open the windows and leaned outside, looking out at the sound.

"Is Michael coming?" I asked.

"Michael doesn't do the church thing," Nate said. "He's a scientist." He made air quotes around "scientist."

Michael walked into the room in his bare feet, a bagel in hand. "I don't know what you're talking about," he said. "I've got services scheduled at the lighthouse beach in half an hour." He flopped on the sofa and crossed his legs, jiggling his right foot up and down.

"There's no church at the lighthouse beach," Evie said.

Michael grinned and shrugged.

"Church of the Atlantic?" I asked.

Michael nodded.

"He's going surfing," I said to Evie.

"Water temp isn't even fifty yet," Nate said.

Michael popped the last bite of bagel in his mouth. "I got a wetsuit." He stretched his arms above his head. The breeze from Evie's open window wove through his hair, and I felt like singing. I squashed the feeling down, and when that didn't work, I tried redirecting it at Nate.

The church was small, and the congregation showed up in everything from suits and ties to camouflage and fishing waders. Many of the pews remained empty, though Evie told me there was standing room only during the summer. I tugged the hem of my dress to my knees and crossed my legs at the ankles. The wooden pew was scratchy and hard but the rose-colored light streaming through the stained-glass windows made up for it. The church buzzed with voices, and Evie put her hand on my arm and groaned.

"Oh, God," she said. "Hide me." Evie unfolded a hymnal in front of her face.

"You're a little hard to miss in that outfit," I told her. The sequins on her belt caught the light, and a little rainbow danced around her.

"There's Misty Garber," Evie said. A petite blond with Chiclet teeth wound her way through the aisle toward us, waving a program up and down. Misty Garber had been Evie's sworn enemy since kindergarten when they had both brought in seahorses for show-and-tell and Misty stomped Evie's into the ground.

"Evie Austin," Misty cried in a singsong voice, advancing on us, and stopping with her hand on Nate's shoulder. "And hello, Nate," she said, her square white teeth shining as she smiled.

"Good morning," I said. Evie didn't introduce me.

"So, when are you heading back to school?" Misty asked Evie, cocking her head.

"I don't know yet," Evie said. The church hummed a little louder as the choir filed in, Mrs. Austin leading the line. Their red robes swished as they walked.

Misty leaned in toward Evie. "I'm glad I decided to stay here and work at the store," she said. "I can't imagine being so far away from home. But at least you have Stephen," she said.

Evie stopped pretending to shuffle through her hymnal and closed it. "Can't seem to get rid of him," she said.

Misty walked away, and the singing started. Then the praying and the preaching and the praying again. It wasn't that I'd never gone to church or that I didn't realize I'd be surrounded by people. It was that the candles flanking the altar reminded me of the power outage at home last summer. The way the candlelight played across my father's bald head. How it was his last rainstorm. How we opened the windows and let the droplets mist in and the wind chimes we'd bought at the beach swung madly, singing and clanging and echoing. They pealed round full notes that rolled around the emptiness inside of me. It was that the emptiness that was still there did not match up to the glorious heaven the preacher described.

And something in me cracked. I wanted to believe. I couldn't. And yet I couldn't not believe, couldn't go on thinking that nothing of my father remained. I pulled Evie's jacket over my hands, ran my finger across the Baptist program until the thin line of a paper cut stung through me. The church felt stuffy, and the pew pressed the backs of my legs. Nate and Evie sat on either side of me, and I turned my shoulders to try to create space, to try to breathe, but it wasn't working. Nothing was working, and I was trapped until the last hymn, the last prayer, the last handshakes, and then Evie and I got in the car and waited for Nate and I begged him to take me to the beach.

"Please," I said.

"What's wrong?" Nate asked.

I balled my hands together to keep from pounding the dashboard. I wanted to run behind the car and push it to the beach.

Evie patted my bare knee. "Let's go see if Michael's still surfing," she said.

The lighthouse beach was a few miles up the island, the spot just above the jutting cape of Hatteras. The curve of the island created some of the best surf on the East Coast, and I wondered how this beach had fared after the nor'easter, whether it was eaten like the one in Frisco. Nate parked the car in a paved lot, and I scrambled out into the wind and sun. I looked up into the blue space where the black and white of the lighthouse had spiraled for so much of my life. A ring of stones commemorated the spot, the home of the lighthouse from 1869 until its move inland in 1999. A ghost lighthouse. The ocean thundered, and I threw my shoes into the car and ran toward the sound of the waves.

The wind was alive, steadily blowing my hair behind me like a kite. My calf muscles strained as I plowed through the sand, sharp bits of dried seagrass and pebbles poking my toes. The lighthouse beach had fared better than Frisco, and I ran down the strip of sand until I was out of breath.

Salt stuck Evie's dress to my body and coated my skin, and I opened to it, stretching my arms to the sun and the sea. The waves crashed in hollowed curls that then receded in a mesmerizing rhythm. Two fishermen stood to my right with their feet planted in the sand. Michael rose out of the water, carving his surfboard into a wave, skimming, sailing, flying. He made the board look like a part of him, an extension of his feet, and when the wave lost strength, I was surprised to see the surfboard shoot out in front as Michael fell back into the water.

I sat in the sand for a long time, watching the breakers, the swoop of gulls, the scurry of sandpipers. Evie and Nate walked up the beach in the other direction, and I breathed in the thick air. Evie's jacket didn't have any tissues in the pocket, just a movie ticket stub.

I dug my hands into the sand, and the grains pricked my paper cut. I gathered damp handfuls, throwing them as hard as I could. It satisfied me to see the sand splattering apart, and I moved down to the water, bending as if I were making snowballs, heaving them into the ocean, disrupting the white foam. I threw until I couldn't distinguish the wetness on my face from the sea spray. My dad had known the earth and the sky. I missed him with an ache so sharp I thought it would pierce my skin. A sandpiper flitted, leaving delicate footprints in its wake, and I moved up to the middle of the beach to write a message in the sand.

The sun was hot on my back, the breeze sharp and cool and salty, and I drug deep furrows with the sharp curve of a broken shell, spelling out tall block letters. *Dad*, I wrote. *Let's pretend you're out there watching.* I stood beside it, breathing the clean air and letting the waves crash all thoughts out of my mind. I turned to walk back to the car, glancing over my shoulder for a last glimpse of—what? The ocean? Michael? Then a glint of gray, a shine of silver sluiced out of the water. More than I'd ever seen in my life—twenty, thirty, fifty dolphins leaping and arcing and surfing in the waves and coming close to the shore and to Michael. I ran up the beach, shouting, waving at Evie and Nate, at Michael bobbing on his board. Evie and Nate dashed to meet me, and we ran closer to the shoreline for a better view. Sleek noses rising and falling, tail flukes slapping the water, light glinting on curves of dorsal fins. They broke free of the deep, soared and splashed.

Michael surfed in and dropped his board on the beach, then ran up and stood beside me. "I almost touched one," he said.

We clustered together until the dolphins moved south down the beach. I couldn't bear for them to go. "Let's follow them," I said.

The four of us raced together down the shoreline, kicking sand on each other's legs, splashing water up in the air, laughing into the wind.

PART TWO
March

Six

The air was sticky with humidity the week of Evie's wedding to Stephen Oden, March pretending to be July. We crossed the Herbert C. Bonner Bridge over Oregon Inlet, and I rolled down my window. Wind rushed over my face and lifted my hair, and down below the currents of the Atlantic Ocean met with the Pamlico Sound in swirling, green-bottomed eddies, shoals of sand rising out of the shallows. From the top of the bridge the distinction between sand and sea, sea and sound, blurred into blue.

"Maybe I'll name it Herbert," Evie said. She sat in the front seat beside Michael and peered over the bridge at the ocean. Something had changed in Evie. Her laugh was sparse and sharp nowadays, her lips a tight line. We were taking a day trip to Nags Head to arrange the wedding details and find Evie a dress.

"Herbert Oden?" Michael asked. He hung his left arm out the window and pushed it through the air, undulating it up and down like a porpoise, steering loosely with his right hand. "You can do better than that."

You can do better than Stephen. But Evie had decided. She would have the baby, and the only way she would have the baby was if she and Stephen got married.

The bridge crossed over swampy reeds, and we coasted onto Bodie

Island, past its black-and-white-banded lighthouse and the Oregon Inlet campground.

"How about Bodie?" I asked. I pronounced it the way it looked, not the way it was spoken here, *body*.

Evie's color drained until the contrast between her dark hair and pale skin grew sharp and she asked Michael to stop the car. I stood with her on the sandy shoulder of the road, passing her a tissue and reaching inside for my water bottle. Evie drank and handed it back to me. "You keep it," I said. Evie nodded, got in the car, and crossed her legs beneath her.

"All right?" Michael asked, starting the car and pulling back onto the road. The beach houses of South Nags Head rose, brown and weathered and capping the shore.

Evie crumpled the tissue and threw it on the floor. "Great," she said. We passed out of the National Seashore limits and into Nags Head, the red-and-white-striped awning of a Kentucky Fried Chicken marking the difference. "Just great."

———

The bridal shop was housed in a corner of the Beach Barn, a yellow building filled with new-age trinkets, beach souvenirs, and clothes. Evie pulled a fuchsia blouse off the rack and splayed it over her chest. I put it back and handed her the first white dress I saw. "I think Stephen likes hot pink," Evie said.

"I think your mother might prefer a more traditional look," I said. "Try this on."

"I will if you will," Evie said, grabbing another dress and dashing to the changing room. "There's no rule that says the bride and maid-of-honor can't match."

I crossed my arms. "We don't have time for this," I said. "Michael will be back in a few minutes."

"All you ever talk about is Michael," Evie said, pulling the curtains around her with a flourish. The shopkeeper looked up over her half-moon spectacles, and I shrugged a shoulder in Evie's direction. She smiled and went back to pricing stained-glass wind chimes. I hoped that Evie wasn't right, that all I talked about was Michael. I'd tried to stop feeling keyed up and alert when I was around him, tried to stop the flutter of my heart against the back of my ribs. He was my favorite cousin's longtime boyfriend, for crying out loud. And I had Nate paying attention to me, complimenting me, asking me out on dates. I'd gone out with him and genuinely enjoyed it. Him. Myself when I was with him. Nate was a steadying presence, one I'd outrightly pursued, a solid foothold in a slippery world tilted askew. But I couldn't make the chemical response to Michael go away.

"How does anyone ever get into these things?" Evie made struggling noises from inside the curtain then stepped out in a pouf of white.

"Pretty," I said.

"I look like a cupcake," Evie said, moving in front of the mirror. She squinted at her reflection and bobbed her arms up and down against billows of fabric like a penguin flapping its ineffectual wings.

"Is there something I can help you with?" The voice and the man were thin and reedy.

"Wedding gowns," I said.

"Bridesmaids," said Evie.

"Mother-of-the-bride, flower girl, tuxedos." I ticked them off on my fingers. "We've got a lot to do."

"I take it you're the bride-to-be?" The reedy man looked at Evie and smoothed his purple tie.

A smile twitched across Evie's lips, but all she said was, "Yes."

"And when is the wedding?"

Evie grimaced. "Three days from now?" She asked it like a question.

The man was visibly horrified, eyebrows raised and mouth gaping. "That will severely limit you to floor pieces in your size, you know."

"That's fine," I said. "We're trying to save money, anyway." I raised my chin. He didn't get to be rude to Evie.

"I'll start a room for you," he said, and walked smoothly off to the white aisles lining one end of the shop.

Evie went back into the dressing room to retrieve her jeans and sneakers. Before Stephen left for school, that day after the nor'easter, he and Evie had taken a walk on the beach. Evie saw a set of little footprints, like from a child running in the sand. She took it as a sign, and they decided to get married. All that was left were the details. All that was left was for Evie to be married—*married*—to Stephen Oden.

Evie started off to the white section, and I followed. "Hey, Eves." I paused and placed my finger in the center of an iridescent sequin adorning a white gown that trailed the carpet. Evie turned to face me. "Are you sure?"

"Sure of what?" Evie's right leg jiggled up and down, vibrating a taffeta dress.

"Stephen. The wedding. All of it." The words clawed into an ache at the back of my throat. "Are you sure he's right for you?"

Evie exhaled through her nose. "I've made my decision. This is it." She outstretched her arms at the dresses surrounding us, fingers flicking open.

I stepped toward her, lowered my voice. "But it doesn't have to be. You can keep the baby and not marry him." Evie's head turned to the side, her jaw stiff. "He left you once before, Evie. How can you trust him?"

"Look," she said, turning to meet my gaze. "Not everybody's perfect. Maybe he left, but he came back. And whatever kind of asshole Stephen can be, I can handle it."

"But you shouldn't have to."

"Well, I do." Evie glanced over her shoulder to the man collecting gowns to put in her dressing room. "I do have to, and that's just how it is. And you can either support me on that or go home."

The gnawing hollow in my stomach deepened, and I raised my hand to my face, rubbed the bridge of my nose, and closed my eyes. *Go home.* I couldn't even remember what home felt like. Spring semester midterms would be underway right now, and if I was at home, I'd be in school, my brain focusing on Brit Lit and lab rats and binary equations instead of intuiting my way around living in a world without my father. I needed to be here. I needed Hatteras to be home. "Of course, I support you," I said. The words toppled over each other in a rush. "I always will. You're the most important thing to me. That's not what I meant." My voice dropped out from under me.

"Okay, then." Evie said, her chin raised. "Let's go try on dresses."

I didn't notice the sequin between my fingers until I dropped it on the floor.

———

I messaged Michael. "*Rogue waves are spectacular and dangerous waves. As wave trains travel across the ocean from various storms, they frequently meet each other. When this happens, the waves will either cancel each other out or reinforce each other.*" *Page 14.*

Michael wrote back. "*If the wave crests coincide with other crests, they will have positive interference, which really means that the two intersecting waves will become one wave, with the combined height of the two.*" *Also page 14.*

Then he sent me a GIF of the Spice Girls singing "Two Become One."

———

Staying on Hatteras for more than a few weeks at a time had, for the first time in my life, the effect of the magic becoming routine to me. I lost sight of how much I loved Hatteras until I left and came back. Crossing the Bonner Bridge with that wide expanse of water and shallows and birds hopping and boats skimming, then touching down on the island, I felt the magic of coming home. Crossing to the island brought the only sense of peace I'd been able to find lately, a feeling borne of space, nature, isolation. So different from Ohio-home, with its rolling hills and green trees, its orderly sidewalks and neighborhoods, its clatter and closeness of family, its gaping hole where my dad should be. The sky on Hatteras that evening was cerulean blue, and clouds mirrored the upswept sand dunes. Mrs. Austin had caught a ride up the island, and we met her in Manteo to choose flowers. Evie settled on pansies because they were in bloom. This ride, Evie sat in the back seat with her mother, and I rode up front with Michael. He drove with his right hand at the bottom of the wheel, elbow resting on the console, left arm across the windowsill as if he wanted to press through the glass to the outdoors.

"Talked to your cousin today," Michael said to me.

"Is she coming to the wedding?" I asked. I didn't tell him that Troia and I had spoken yesterday, and I received an earful of their relationship woes. She hadn't decided if she was going to come down yet.

"Yeah, I think she might try it," Michael said. "Take a sick day and fly to Norfolk."

"Good," I said. "I haven't seen her since—" I leaned against the headrest. "It's been a while."

Michael's eyes looked like bits of sky when he turned his head to look at me. Meeting his eyes made my heart race, and I motioned him to watch the road.

Evie's voice rose over the back seat in singsong nonsense. "Y'all y'all y'all," she said. "What are y'all talking about up there?"

"Troia's coming for the wedding," I told her. I turned around in my seat to talk to her.

"Maybe," Michael said.

"She'll come," I said.

Mrs. Austin cleared her throat. "Where will Troia be staying?" She pronounced Troia's name like it caused a bitter taste in her mouth.

"I'm not sure," Michael said. "My trailer's pretty cramped." He'd gotten the job with the National Seashore, and it included government housing—a dirt-colored camper van in the Buxton woods that sucked in its sides whenever there was wind.

We drove on, and the first beach houses of Rodanthe crowned the distance. Tall gray towers perched on the ocean, and shorter houses lined Highway 12.

"It would be nice to have an RSVP if she's planning on staying at the inn," Mrs. Austin said. The inn had been open since Valentine's Day, and I'd moved from the Primrose room to bunk with Evie. When she moved in with Stephen, it would be mine. Guests flowed into the inn slowly but steadily in March, two or three at a time, retirees coming down for long weekends, families with young babies traveling in the cheaper shoulder season. In exchange for my staying with the Austins, I was learning to be a Jill-of-all-trades, doing what needed to be done: answering phones, taking reservations, cleaning, restocking the snacks in the guest quarters, running errands, baking. Baking. Me. I wasn't a baker; I was an experienced microwaver. But somehow I found that the elemental kneading of dough, the rhythmic mixing, whisking, and scraping soothed me. They were tasks of home, of making people feel welcome and safe. Somehow, performing them allowed a little of that safety to seep into me.

"We didn't exactly send out invitations, Mom." Evie shifted in the back seat, tapping her index finger on the door handle.

"I realize that," Mrs. Austin said.

"Troia can stay in our room on an air mattress," I said. "If she needs to. We won't be a bother." I doubted that, despite her complaining, she would leave Michael's side for a second of her weekend down here, but sharing a room with my favorite cousin was a welcome prospect. Troia had always been my idol. Four years older than me, she could French braid her own hair without looking in the mirror, salsa dance, and spit watermelon seeds halfway across the backyard. I still saw her as magic.

"Looks like the weather'll hold," Michael said. Blushes of pink wisped up from the horizon as the sun went down. "Red sky at night, sailor's delight."

"I'll have the prettiest little shotgun wedding ever," Evie said.

"Don't speak like that," Mrs. Austin said.

"It's true." Evie curled a piece of hair around her finger.

"We are going to have a perfectly fine wedding with a perfectly fine bride and groom," Mrs. Austin said. She clicked her tongue on the roof of her mouth. "And of course, Troia is welcome to stay," she said.

The last of the villages trickled off into sand and waving seagrass. "It's going to be a lovely wedding." Mrs. Austin said it as though a reporter lurked in the far corners of the car, tape recorder extended, red light on.

———

Hi Charly,

I finally got to cleaning out the closets today. Did you want to keep any of your dad's clothes for any reason? I can't look at them anymore. If not, I'll take them to Goodwill tomorrow. I think I'll look for a new bedroom suite, too. Wish you were here to shop with me. I miss you so much, and James does, too. We'd hoped to come down for the wedding but just can't swing it. I'm glad Troia's coming. At least you'll have some family nearby for a while.

Love,
Mom

Seven

The day of Evie's wedding rehearsal, I sat at the inn's front desk with Mrs. Austin. Mr. and Mrs. Austin had a small staff but did much of the day-to-day work themselves. It had been an odd sensation to see the first guests of the season pull up, unfamiliar faces checking in and shown to rooms, what had been just our living space opened into something different, a strange amalgamation of public and private. Though I'd stayed in Primrose for two months, I felt like I was trespassing when I walked past my old room, now that it was someone else's, many someone else's. Even stranger was when it stayed unbooked, empty and expectant.

Mrs. Austin pointed to the computer screen. "Then you process the deposit and hit *print*," she said. She clicked through several more screens, showing me how to email confirmations, assign rooms and dates, and apply discounts. It was a surprisingly complicated process, and one I had yet to master on my own without screwing up. I'd always been an overachiever. It felt weird to be so bad at something.

I couldn't focus that morning. All I could think about was Evie binding herself to Stephen, becoming his wife. "Is it usually this humid in March?" I asked.

Mrs. Austin walked over to the printer. "There is no 'usual' when it comes to Hatteras weather," she said.

"Life on a sandbar," I said, echoing a bumper sticker I'd seen recently.

The door opened, and I looked over the desk to see a middle-aged couple walk in. In the weeks since the inn had opened, I'd come to recognize a few broad categories of guests: Awesomely Memorable, Pleasantly Average, and Prickly. The guests in front of me asked about check-in with rolling Scottish accents, and Mrs. Austin chatted with them and processed their payment. Her movements were brisk and sure, and I tagged along as she gave a tour of the inn, showing them the sitting room, explaining that coffee comes out at six in the morning and cookies at four in the afternoon. I peeked in Primrose as we walked past, but the Scottish guests were staying in Jasmine, in the other building.

"It's really quite stunning, isn't it?" the husband asked, as we stepped onto the deck connecting the two buildings. We stood and stared at the sound for a moment, slick calm and flat blue that day, before going over to the other side of the inn.

"There will be a wedding tomorrow down by the pool," Mrs. Austin said, "but that shouldn't bother you. It's too cold to swim, anyhow."

"But that will be lovely," the wife said. She had tousled gray hair and a bright smile. "We shall have to try to sneak a look at the bride."

I doubted the bride would find that prospect enticing, but I didn't say anything.

Mrs. Austin showed the guests into Jasmine, pointing out the whirlpool bathtub and private deck. "You're more than welcome to come down around two-thirty and see the wedding," she said. She never mentioned that it was her daughter getting married, and I thought how, if it was my mom, the Scottish couple would not only have known it was her daughter getting married, but who her fiancé was, the fabric and style of the bridesmaids' dresses, the kind of ribbon she'd used to wrap the bouquets, and the flavor of the cake frosting. Not to mention the emotional temperature of the bride.

We said goodbye to the guests and walked back to the desk.

"Pulling off this wedding could work for the inn," Mrs. Austin said. "We want to get to doing more weddings here, so it's good practice." She nodded as if reassuring herself.

"I hope it's good for Evie." I said it without thinking, my usually intact brain-to-mouth filter evaporating. I looked at Mrs. Austin, afraid I'd broken some rule of hospitality by saying what I thought.

She sat down at the desk and clicked on the computer. Then she stopped and rubbed the bridge of her nose. She seemed smaller, her narrow shoulders drooping. "I hope so, too."

When Troia arrived from Norfolk the first thing she did when she saw me was drop her bags on the floor and cry. Michael stood with a hand on her back. I flung down the invoices I'd been filing and ran over to hug her. Troia's face was wet against my shoulder, and I inhaled the vanilla and cedar scent of her hair. She felt unbearably light in my arms, like her bones were filled with air.

"I'm sorry." Troia pulled back and wiped her eyes. "It's just that you look so much like him."

I nodded and shouldered her backpack, swallowing hard.

"How's Evie?" Troia asked.

I led them down the hall to our room. "Good," I said.

Michael hefted the other bags onto my floor. "Sure you want to stay here?" he asked Troia.

She turned away from him and looked out the window.

Michael shrugged, one blue flannel shoulder rising and falling.

I went back down the hall into the sitting room, and Michael and Troia followed. I sat on the chintz sofa. "So, what are you guys doing today?" I asked.

Troia sat beside me. "I just want to get settled in and hang out with you," she said.

Michael picked up a book from the coffee table: *A Celebration of the World's Barrier Islands*. The cover was a swirling blue batik print. He sat down in a rocking chair and flipped the book open. "We could all have dinner later," he said, looking down.

Troia lay down across the sofa, arms behind her head, stretching her legs over mine. "Are the restaurants even open this time of year?" she asked.

I patted her knee. She wore jeans that were a soft faded blue. "Diamond Shoals keeps regular hours," I said. Diamond Shoals was the restaurant we went to at least once every vacation for their crab cakes. "And didn't you get a coupon last time we were there?" I asked Michael.

Michael nodded. "Did you know that there are barrier islands in Iceland?" he asked.

"I've been reading about that," I said. At the end of the last Ice Age, thousands of years ago, glaciers melted, river valleys flooded, the sea level rose. Headlands eroded by the waves were deposited as sandbars where the river flowed into the sea. The deposits grew and created islands, not just here but in certain places all over the world where the magic was just right. But not magic, of course. Just the way the world worked.

Troia turned her head to look at Michael. "I suppose you'll apply for a research grant there next," she said.

Michael closed the book and put it back on the coffee table. "As opposed to studying ocean currents in Michigan?" He stood up. "I should get back to work," he said. His footsteps sounded heavy as he walked toward the door.

Troia sat up and watched him go. She frowned and crossed her arms, then shook her head and turned to me.

"That was awkward," I said.

"Sorry," Troia said. "Old argument. I keep picking at it." She stood and pulled me up beside her. "I'm here," she said, touching my arm while doing a shimmying little happy dance.

I led her out to the narrow deck overlooking the sound and the garden. We sat in a double hammock swing and pushed it back and forth with our toes. The Pamlico danced where the sun brushed it, bits of light pricking up on wavelets of water. Troia took a deep breath at the same time I did, and her laugh when she exhaled was silver like I'd remembered.

"I can see why you need to be here," Troia said. Her hair blew forward over her face, but she didn't shake it off. The breeze rippled soft and cool.

"It's healing," I said. "And Evie needs me." A trio of mallards swam by in the sound, honking and quacking. I thought about the time James found a picture of me as a baby feeding the ducks, wearing a hooded sweatshirt. He swore up and down that the picture was of him. We fought about it for days.

Troia pulled her legs up and wrapped her arms around her knees. The swing moved off kilter with just me pushing it. "Do I really look like Dad?" I asked. People usually said I resembled my mother.

She nodded. "I always felt like he was my father, too, you know?" Troia's father and mine were brothers. Her dad had left when she was ten, and my dad never really forgave him.

A ruckus erupted from the garden below. From where we sat, Troia and I could see the empty swimming pool covered with a tarp and the garden that stretched out to the sound. A few yellow jessa-mine twined along the water and bleached-gray marsh grass waved in the wind. Nate was balancing stacks of folding chairs on both his arms. "I don't know where to put them," Evie hollered. "I don't even know why we have them. I don't want the whole damn island show-ing up." She circled around the covered swimming pool and walked down toward the sound.

"Line them around either side of the walkway," Mrs. Austin said. Her hair was tied back in a ponytail that fluttered in the wind, and from this distance above them, she and Evie looked alike. "The guests can come in the front of the inn and go down the back steps. Evie will come down that way, too."

Mr. Austin walked out with another load of chairs. He and Nate clattered them to the ground and began unfolding.

"Not like that." Mrs. Austin sliced in front of her husband and snapped a chair open, setting it squarely on the walkway facing the sound.

"What if it rains?" Evie's voice whinged with desperation. She kicked a chair away from her feet.

"That's what the tarps are for," Mrs. Austin said, jerking another chair into place.

"Now, Evie." Mr. Austin put his hands on his daughter's shoulders. "I don't want you worrying over details. Why don't you go find Charlotte?"

Evie wrenched herself away. "Dad, I'm not twelve," she said. "It's my deal. I want to help." But she strode up the walkway toward the inn.

I stood up from the swing. "I should go help."

"I'll be down in a second," Troia said.

I ran down the back steps to meet Evie. "Hey," I said.

"They're driving me crazy," Evie said. She went inside to the inn's basement floor, and I followed. Evie rummaged in the office that held random decorations for guest weddings and events. "Where the hell is the ribbon?"

I reached up to the top shelf and handed it to her. "Yellow," I said. "Nice."

"It's going to look like a bunch of dandelions exploded." Evie exhaled and blew the hair out of her eyes.

"I've always thought there's nothing more festive than pollen," Troia said, poking her head inside the door.

Evie squealed and dropped trails of ribbon to the floor.

Troia hugged Evie. "Why don't you and I go get some tea and catch up?" Troia asked.

I picked up the ribbon and twirled it through my fingers. "You should," I told Evie. "I'll get this."

"You have to update me on Charlotte and Nate," Troia said. "I can't get anything out of that one." Troia nodded her head at me.

Evie raised an eyebrow. "Your cousin, my brother. Who knew you and I could potentially end up relatives."

"Evie thinks Nate and I are getting married just because we've

been on a few dates," I said. "Don't listen to her." I wound and un-
wound the ribbon around my finger.

"I only think it because I know how Nate's mind works around
girls he's in love with."

I stopped playing with the ribbon.

The basement door slammed open and closed, and Mrs. Austin
came by, stopping beside Evie. "If you want to deal with this, then
get out there and do it." She punched up the steps to the second floor.

"I told her we could just do the chairs tomorrow." Evie shouted the
last part toward the staircase. She handed me the rest of the ribbon
and turned to Troia. "Let's go get some tea."

I knelt and tied the last yellow trim to the last brown metal chair,
then stepped back to admire my work.

"Looks good," Nate said. He stretched one arm across his body
then the other. We had been dating, if you can call living in the same
inn in the same town on the same island and occasionally going out
for dinner dating, for two months now. I wasn't sure if he was in love
with me, and I wasn't sure if I was in love with him. I was sure that
I needed his solidity, his anchoring presence, the brush of his skin
against mine, to keep me from falling too far into my own head. I
couldn't think much further beyond that. His presence kept me distracted enough from myself that, paradoxically, I felt like I was coming back around to reinhabit my own body. In the riptide of my grief,
he was a life preserver tossed into the current.

The rows of chairs fanned around the garden and shone softly in
the late afternoon sun. "I hope it stays this nice," I said. Nate reached
for my hand and spun me in a circle.

"Charlotte," Mr. Austin said, coming up behind us and dropping a load of blue tarps to the ground. "Could I see you in the office for a moment?"

Nate squeezed my hand, and I shook it loose. "Sure," I said, following Mr. Austin into the inn. We went upstairs and he settled into a brown leather chair behind a wide desk. I sat across from him and crossed my legs at the ankles, shifted, and put my right leg over my left knee. The room was covered in nautical maps of the area, tiny numbers scattering across intersecting lines. I wondered at what latitude and longitude my father would come to rest. A flash of his broad smile, how his eyes squinched closed when he laughed. I shook the images away. "Is everything all right?" I asked Mr. Austin.

"Fine, fine." He leaned back in the chair and tapped a white pen on the desk, its nib poking in and out. The pen clinked down, and Mr. Austin spread his hands over it. "Evie's mom didn't get to have the kind of wedding she wanted," he said. "And I know she's been a bit—" he paused and raised his bushy eyebrows to the ceiling. "Hard to live with lately."

I made a small protesting noise, but Mr. Austin held up his hand. "But Mallory and I just want you to know that we appreciate all you do around here." He picked up the pen again and walked it from one finger to the other and back. "Now, we've talked it over, and when Evie moves down to Hatteras with Stephen, we'd like to offer you a real position here at the Pamlico." Mr. Austin was the only one who called the inn anything other than the inn.

A door closed and voices cascaded from the sitting room. I heard Mrs. Austin's brisk steps and Evie's chirp of laughter, so rare these days. "Thank you," I said. "I don't know what to say."

I thought about my dad telling me to start college, even though he knew I'd be grieving. He'd been moved to a hospital bed at that point, positioned in front of tall French doors looking out over the woods behind our house. He was bald, emaciated, his feet swollen and cold from lack of circulation because his body had already started to shut down. The icy fact that he was about to die had finally slid down my throat, and my body radiated numbness like a shield. I'd just told him I didn't think I could start school in the fall. Of course, I'd start school in the fall, he'd responded. "What are you going to do instead?" he'd asked. "Sit around the house and do crossword puzzles?"

It was a betrayal that I was even here to begin with.

Mr. Austin leaned forward. "You take your time," he said. "Talk it over with your folks." His mouth hung open for a moment and then he glanced down at the desk. "With your mother," he said, looking up at me and nodding.

"I suppose I should go home sometime," I said. Dust motes caught in a sunbeam, and over the sound a sea gull cawed. "I'll think about it."

Mr. Austin patted me on the back as I walked to the door. "Just know you got a place here, kiddo," he said, then hitched his thumbs in his pockets and started down the stairs.

———

After Stephen and his family filed out from what Evie termed the as-close-as-it-gets-to-a-rehearsal dinner, Troia and I walked down to the pier. The early evening air was cool and damp, and I pulled my sweater tighter around me. "I thought you'd be at Michael's by now," I said.

Troia brushed her fingers over the top of a post, peering down into the water. "It looks like tea," she said.

"It's different every day."

"We're not okay." Troia sat down and crossed her legs, denim brushing against itself.

"You and Michael?" I sat beside her.

"We don't laugh anymore," she said. "I can't breathe around him."

A flicker of annoyance jumped in my chest, bright and startling. "Then why did you come?"

"I thought it might help, or that I was wrong." Troia sighed and leaned back on her palms. "Maybe I am." Troia looked at me, and in the gathering night I couldn't see her expression, just the line of her straight nose and the curve of her chin. The water lapped rhythmically against the dock.

"Let's go inside," I said, standing up. But I saw Evie picking her way down through the tarp-covered chairs, Nate and Michael behind her. I raised my hand in a wave and waited on the pier for them. The inn lights flicked on, illuminating their figures as they walked down the pier.

"No red sky tonight," Evie said. She sat down and dangled her legs over the water. Nate and Michael lowered themselves to the dock, and I sat back down, too. We formed a crooked semicircle.

"That's mostly folklore anyway," Troia said.

Nate shifted. "It's in the Bible. Matthew, I think."

"I never knew that," I said. Sometimes Nate surprised me.

He nudged my thigh with his elbow. "I know some things."

"It's dust particles," Michael said. "When the sun sends light through a high concentration of dust particles, we see the red. It usually means a high-pressure system. Stable air."

The way he said it made me smile. He sounded like a weatherman. I liked the idea of stable air, the atmosphere calm and paused like a dome.

"Such a scientist." Troia said it lightly, but the words pricked along my scalp.

"I don't care if Jesus or Newton said it, I just want rain tomorrow," Evie said.

"You do?" I asked.

"Do what?"

"You said you wanted rain tomorrow," I said.

"I said I didn't want rain tomorrow," Evie said.

Nate shook his head. "Enough with the weather. It'll be fine."

"It's getting cold," Troia said. "Feel my hand."

"We should go in," I said. But we all sat there, silent, listening to the crickets' chirp and the water slip back and forth against the posts of the pier.

———

Hey, kiddo,

Aunt Darcy and I went shopping today. We found some furniture for the bedroom, whitewashed oak. Looks beachy. The car magically swerved into Red Lobster of its own accord, so of course we stopped and ate. Sure isn't as good as the fresh seafood you must be eating every day.

I'm still so worried about your brother. He won't talk to me. Maybe you can get something out of him. At least his grades are better. Give Evie and Troia a hug for me and write soon.

Love,

Mom

———

Michael texted me: *"The most spectacular changes in beach shape, changes that can happen in a matter of hours, occur in storms."* Page 34.

I responded: *"If you've ever visited the beach after a storm, you probably noticed that it is wide and flat at low tide, wider than you've ever seen it before."*

Michael wrote back: *"Beaches do not exist in isolation."* Page 37.

I wrote: *Neither do we.*

Eight

On the morning of the day Evie married Stephen Oden I woke early and walked the lighthouse beach at sunrise. The waves were heavy with seaweed and hovered at the crest before plopping into the sand. Five pelicans belly-skimmed across the horizon, heads tucked back into their bodies, bills thrust forward. I scuffed at the sand and watched as the sky plumed orange and pink.

"Should be okay until this afternoon." Michael's voice came from behind me, and I jumped.

"You're up early," I said.

Michael walked toward the rows of sand dunes with their stalks of dormant seagrass waving over them in slender sticks. He carried a fishing pole over his right shoulder. "Up late," he said.

"Rough night?"

Michael shrugged. "A few of the guys and I went out to Pop's."

I knew Troia hadn't gone with him because she'd spent the night with me. This fact danced brightly in my chest for a moment before I squashed it down. I was dating Nate. Troia was my family. I would not be drawn to Michael. "What are you doing here?" I asked.

He looked at the fishing pole. "Thought I'd go chop some wood," he said.

We sat in the sand. Gray clouds stifled the earlier blue sky, and the wind bit through my jacket.

"I ran into Lester O'Neal in the parking lot out there," Michael said. Lester O'Neal was an old islander who passed his time sitting on the porch of a small store in Frisco. Conversations with Lester were interesting because his brogue was thick, and he had no teeth. It was my goal each vacation to make Lester smile.

"Did you have a good chat?" I asked.

"I think he said to use mullet today. Or he was telling me I had a mullet." Michael scooped a fistful of sand and let it trail through his fingers.

"Your hair is getting long," I said. I twirled a piece of dried seaweed around my finger. "But I wouldn't go so far as to say mullet-esque."

"You should have been there," he said. "Lester could've used a smile."

Michael's face in the fading sunrise was sharp and beautiful, and for a moment I understood my cousin's pain. I couldn't breathe around him.

———

The inn buzzed warmly when I got back, the regular morning bustle taken up a notch. I stepped in the kitchen to check on breakfast and found Aunt Fay standing in front of the refrigerator, demure in a black lace dress. "You taking the job?" she asked. News really did travel fast on an island.

"I don't know yet." I checked the fridge to make sure there was enough juice, then put on another pot of coffee.

Aunt Fay cracked an egg onto the griddle. "Lord helps those who help themselves," she muttered. "I'm helping myself to this egg," she said to me, nodding at the popping mass of white and yellow.

I handed her an apron to put over her dress, then wiped off the counter and looked out the window. Nate crossed over the walkway to the kitchen, his hair dark and tousled in the gray morning, his feet bare.

"Ladies," he said to us, grinning and grabbing an oatmeal bar. "Charlotte, I need to show you something." Nate swept his arm forward like an usher and held open the door.

We walked down to the garden. Pink camellias spotted the sloping ground and Nate picked one for me, tucking the damp stem behind my ear. We wound our way to the water's edge, and I paused. "Should I take off my shoes?" I asked.

"Nah. It's not far." Nate strode along the thin strip of mucky sand that bordered the sound and disappeared among the reeds. I followed him. The land bent into a shallow cove, and Nate splashed over to a small, flat-bottomed boat. Its white hull bobbed happily as Nate patted it. "You think Evie will like it?" he asked. "I figured they might want to make a getaway after the ceremony."

I kicked off my flip-flops, rolled my pants, and waded into the cold water to stand next to him. "When did you do this?"

"A few weeks ago, Billy Scarborough found a skiff washed up on the shoals." Nate ran his hand along the smooth rail of the boat. "He didn't want it, so I fixed it up for Evie."

I touched Nate's hand, brown against the white boat. "She'll love it."

Nate leaned forward, hesitated, then kissed me, his lips dryly brushing mine. I wondered how, surrounded by all this water, his lips were not moist. I wondered why the deepest feeling I could muster for him was tenderness when we could be so good for each other, and I wondered why I kept picturing Michael's face at sunrise. Nate was so kind, so thoughtful, so solid. I laced my fingers around Nate's neck and pulled him closer, but my feet were cold, and a fish flipped out of the water, breaking my focus. I moved away to go find Evie.

I went back to the kitchen and ended up helping out until breakfast was done.

"Have you seen Evie yet?" I asked Mr. Austin as he scrubbed dishes.

"Sure haven't," he said. "Figured she was with you or her mom." He turned off the dish water, crossed to the other side of the kitchen, and started prepping the hors d'oeuvres for the reception. Aunt Fay came in, still in her apron, and Mr. Austin put her to work. I started chopping, but he told me to go find Evie.

She wasn't in the main office or the family quarters, so I checked downstairs in the storage room and office combo by the pool. Evie hunkered on the floor by her wedding dress, scissor blades poised, dark hair falling over her face. "What are you doing?" I asked.

"Do you see this?" Evie pointed with the scissors to a row of fluffy white balls lining the hem. "I don't want to get married standing in a vat of cotton balls."

"It'll be better once it's on," I said. I slid the scissors from her grasp. Evie narrowed her eyes at me and grabbed for them. "I'm just going to take these to my room," I said. When I came back, Mr. Austin was standing in front of Evie, a green velvet box in his hands. I stopped at the doorway, unsure if they'd heard me and I should enter or if this was a private moment.

"They're pearls," he said. "My mother's." Evie hugged him fiercely. The top of her head barely brushed his shoulder.

Evie pulled back, her eyes glinting. "I'm sorry," she said.

Mr. Austin lay his hands on her shoulders. "Evie, honey, I'm proud of you."

I backed away and went back up to Evie's and my room, leaning against the cool yellow wall. It hurt to remember that my father wouldn't see me get married. I'd had months to register that fact, but it hurt. The grief that was just barely beginning to tamp down flared and rose in my chest, up to my face, wild like flame. Troia had left the closet door open, and the box of ashes poked out. I kicked it and closed the door, then picked up the scissors. They were heavy and cool in my hand, and I remembered how that bite of physical pain distracted me, how I still had to help with the food, do Evie's hair, get ready, and be presentable for her wedding and reception. I couldn't be a sobbing mess all day because my father would never see me get married. For the first time in months, I placed a sharp silver blade to my skin.

"Charlotte." Troia's eyebrows drew together as she caught sight of me.

I smacked the scissors on the dresser and dodged around her, but Troia grabbed my arm. "Let go," I said. She wouldn't. I sat down on the bed and hugged a pillow to my chest.

"Are you cutting yourself?" Troia said the words softly.

"Of course not." I threw the pillow down and crossed my arms.

Troia put her arm around me, but I shrugged her away. "Charly—" she started, using my mom's nickname.

"Did you know Michael went out last night?" I asked her.

"Oh." Her face was still and smooth.

I wanted to see her as angry and upset as I felt. "I'd be pissed if Nate did that to me. You know, if we were long distance and it was my first night in town."

Troia stood up and fiddled with a tassel on the drapes. "We had dinner last night. It didn't go well."

I went to the dresser and put the scissors in a drawer. It closed with a satisfying *thunk*. "What's so wrong between you guys, anyway?"

"It's hard to explain. I guess I just feel like something's missing. Or maybe that we want different things, or that we grew apart. Some cliché like that." She sat down on the arm of a chair.

"That's pretty vague," I said. But I was starting to feel bad for bringing it up, guilty for wanting Troia to reveal some fatal flaw in Michael, or a hidden affair on her part that would make him fair game.

"It's like the opposite of where you are. You and Nate are just starting out, and everything's exciting and new." Troia stepped over to me, and I let her.

"I guess."

"Just promise me you'll go talk to someone if you feel like cutting yourself, okay?"

I heard Evie call my name from down the hallway. "I have to go," I said to Troia. This time she let me walk away.

I sent a message to Michael: *You ready for this wedding? Two become one?*

Michael wrote back: *All I wanna do is zig-a-zig ah.*

Evie and I stood in the doorway of the downstairs office, flowers in our hands, waiting for the cue to take our walks down the aisle. Mr. Austin shuffled for something in the office behind us.

"Holy shit, holy shit, holy shit," Evie repeated softly, her eyes squinted shut. The fluffy white balls lining the edge of her dress had disappeared.

"You don't have to do this," I whispered.

"I totally have to do this," she said. "Holy shit."

Pachelbel's Canon in D Major started playing, and I looked at Evie one last time before going down the aisle. Guests filled the folding chairs—I spotted the Scottish couple—and the sky remained a uniform gray. No rain. The Pamlico waved gently under a light breeze, and Stephen stood at the front of the aisle, his blond hair bright against his tuxedo. At Evie's insistence, he had shaved the mustache, and even I had to admit he looked handsome. He seemed calm, his high cheekbones sharp in the planes of his face.

The satin of my lilac dress blew against my legs in the breeze. Nate stood beside Stephen, his face composed. He raised an eyebrow at me, and then the music changed, and Evie was walking down the aisle. She clutched her yellow flowers with one hand and Mr. Austin's arm with the other, a frozen smile across her face. Most of the guests, standing now, smiled, too. Troia and Michael looked uneasy; in my imagination, they had just finished a terrible fight and had decided to break up. Mrs. Austin wiped her eyes, but I couldn't tell what sort of tears, and Aunt Fay nodded, chewing something slowly and methodically.

The minister started the ceremony. "Who gives this woman to this man in marriage?" he asked.

Mr. Austin cleared his throat. "Her mother and I do."

I squeezed my flower stems and stared into the audience, desperate for a distraction. Anything to avoid picturing my dad saying, "Her mother and I do." Michael's hand rested on his knee. If his hand were on my knee, he would glide it across the satin of my dress, the texture of his course palm occasionally catching the fabric, the rough-and-smooth combination causing gooseflesh as his hand moved up my leg.

Evie's flowers tickled my arm; I grabbed them from her. Mr. Austin had sat down, and Evie turned to take Stephen's hands. "Dear friends and family," the minister began. "We are gathered here today to witness and celebrate the union of Evelyn and Stephen in marriage."

He continued, and somehow, unexpectedly, the ancient, oft-repeated words of the ceremony caused something to rise in me, a feeling of hope and calm, like maybe Evie was making the right decision, that maybe everything would be okay. It was something in the diction, the way the language flowed like soothing water—*to love and to cherish, through joy and sorrow, in sickness and in health, for better and for worse, for as long as you both shall live.*

"I do," Evie said.

The minister blessed the rings, *circles of wholeness; perfect in form, the sign of your love and fidelity.* The language stepped me out of time, into a different place, a world where fragile, intangible things like love and faith fluttered in the air, a cascade of brightly colored butterfly wings against the slate-gray sky.

Stephen's face remained calm and serious, and when he placed the ring on Evie's finger *as a symbol of my love*, even I believed him.

Love is a biological need, a necessity born of the magnetic pull between two molecules arcing toward one another. If you could fall
beneath my skin, through my bones and into the spiraling waterslide of my DNA, you'd see the way the cells dance, the swing and
sway of attraction, the push and pull of life as it combines and re-
combines. Alone, standing on the bridge between the two parts of
the inn, I looked down over the white tent where everyone had gathered after the ceremony. I'd gone upstairs to grab a CD for the Scottish lady, who turned out to be a retired opera singer and promised
Evie a serenade. From above, I watched the choreography of pairs,
couples dancing, Mr. Austin reaching over to brush down a strand
of Mrs. Austin's hair, Evie taking Stephen's hand as she pulled him
onto the dance floor. And at the end of a long table, Troia and Michael sat together, talking. They started out symmetrical, bodies facing each other, two straight lines. Then she took his hand.
Their knees turned and touched. His arm went around her shoulder, their legs sliding parallel, pressed together. She curled against
him like a comma. I wondered what it was that pulled them to each
other, whether it was the same force that bonded one molecule to
the next. What was that called in chemistry? Was that the way the
world worked? I couldn't remember. My father would know. If only
I'd thought to ask him.

I moved off the bridge and went downstairs, back to the party.

———

Troia came over and sat beside me with a plate of hors d'oeuvres. She
held out a pig in a blanket. "Want one?"

I shook my head. I was trying to stay upbeat, but as the reception progressed, the reality sunk in. Evie was married to Stephen. Evie was married to Stephen, and they were going to have a baby.

"I think if I had the opportunity, I'd eat a pig in a blanket every day," Troia said. She took a sip of wine. "Come dance with me."

The band played jazzy love songs, and I let Troia take my hand and lead me out to the dance floor.

"Do you know anyone else?" Troia asked.

I looked around. The Scottish lady had sung a truly impressive aria and was now downing wine and hitting on one of Evie's relatives as her husband looked on. I knew Evie's immediate family and a few people who worked at the inn, but nearly everyone else was familiar only in the see-them-often sort of way—the bookstore owner, the cashier at the Food Lion in Avon. Troia was the only one here who shared bits of my DNA, the two of us twined together through our fathers' genes. "Not many," I said. We spun in a circle. I turned her toward a man with a blond, dreadlocked beard. "That's Stephen's cousin," I whispered. "He was once arrested for surfing naked."

Troia nodded. "A valiant cause."

Nate swung over to us, dancing with Mrs. Austin. He was beautiful, his wavy hair curling to his collar, and if my atoms got distracted by Michael again, I'd forcibly redirect them to Nate. I wouldn't hurt Troia. And Nate, on paper, in reality and not the ether of my imagination, was a wonderful person. I would focus on Nate.

Aunt Fay walked up on stage and took the microphone from the singer. She clinked her fork loudly against her glass. "It's time for a toast," she said.

Evie got up from where she'd been sitting with her mom's family and moved to the dance floor, Stephen joining her.

Aunt Fay raised her glass. "I know what you're thinking," she said. "What's Evie's spinster aunt know about marriage? But let me tell you what I do know about—that's Evie." Evie put her hand on Stephen's. He threaded his fingers through hers. "And I know if Evie cares enough to commit herself to this man, then she knows what she's getting into, and she darn well deserves our support and love. To your health." She raised her glass and drank. Mr. Austin grabbed the microphone from her and handed it back to the singer.

After the dancing and the cake, Evie tugged on my arm and motioned back to the inn. Troia was dancing with Michael, Nate entertaining two young cousins. We walked away from the noise and went into the large bathroom downstairs where we had changed before the ceremony. "Get me out of this thing, okay?" she asked. I unzipped Evie's dress for her. She stepped out of it, sat on the cold tile floor in her underwear, and cried.

"Evie." I wrapped my arms around her and stroked her hair. Sobs shook through her body, and her face flushed red. The pearls around Evie's neck grew slippery with tears.

"I can't do it," Evie choked. "I don't want to be married. I don't want to be a mother." She raised a hand to her face and wiped her nose with her palm.

"Shh," I said. I tried to lean forward to grab some toilet paper for her, but Evie wouldn't let go of my arm. The pansies haloing Evie's head crushed against my collarbone, pink and sweet. We rocked back and forth. I let her cry until she stopped.

"I think I need a Kleenex," she said, face mottled and blotchy.

"I think you need a fire hose."

Evie laughed hoarsely, and I passed her a handful of toilet paper and hung up her dress. It floated from the hook in the wall like a wraith, forlorn and deflated. Evie stood up and foraged around the cabinet for the clothes we'd brought down earlier.

"You ready?" Aunt Fay's voice came from the other side of the bathroom door. "Folks are gathering out front to see you off."

"Almost," I answered. Evie buttoned her pants over the small swell of her belly. "You can go out the back," I told her. "Nate has a surprise." Evie nodded and pulled her shirt over her head, petals from the pansies flitting to the floor.

She splashed off her face. "How do I look?"

I tugged the hem of her shirt straight. "You're beautiful."

Evie rolled her eyes. "Okay," she said. "I'm ready to go."

***

The raindrops rolled in with the darkness that night, and I turned on my side in bed, aching with exhaustion. Troia went to Michael's and would leave from there in the morning. I'd managed to avoid any conversations with her before she had to go. My eyes burned, but sleep would not come. I slipped on a robe and padded down the hall. Light glowed from the office and illuminated Mrs. Austin's form, bent over the desk. She looked up at me, the lines on her face deepened in the lamplight. Old pictures of Evie were scattered around the desk. She picked one up by the corner and showed it to me. "She's known Stephen since kindergarten. They'll be a good match."

"I hope so," I said.

Mrs. Austin sighed. "Would you open up that window?" she asked.

I raised the blinds and tugged the window open, bracing myself against the frame as the wind coursed in. Rain drizzled off the eaves and pattered onto the deck. I turned back to the room. Mrs. Austin's hair blew around her face as she gathered up the photos and put them in a drawer. Her shoulder blades rose through the thin cotton of her nightgown, and suddenly I wanted my own mother so badly I almost cried. Instead, I said goodnight, walked back to my bedroom, and cracked my window open. The sheets were cool against my skin, salty and moist. Sheathed in water, I slept.

———

Hi Baby,

Just a note before bed. Hope everything went well with the wedding. I bet Evie was a beautiful bride. Wish I could have been there, but, of course, there is always work. Those kids won't teach themselves, that's for sure!

Any news on the boat? I'll feel better once it's all settled and we know who is taking us out. Wouldn't it be easiest to have Nate do it? Let me know what you find out about the houses, too.

I miss your daddy every day. It's so hard sometimes.

Well, I should get off to bed. Write me when you get the chance.

Love,

Mom

———

PART THREE
May

Nine

I took the job. Mr. Austin wanted a combination receptionist, prep cook, and accountant. I told him I was hopeless with numbers, but he hired me anyway. Spring slipped on to Hatteras in whispered shades of green and a return of birdsong. The sea oats lining the beach turned from brown to tan. Little white flowers popped out along Highway 12, and Mrs. Austin's garden was awash in pink and yellow. It was May, but I couldn't shake my autumn frame of mind. I learned new recipes, walked different beaches, even fished with Nate. But not even collecting the related new vocabulary—*back-cast, crankbait, gaff*—made me feel like myself again.

Evie was only seven miles away, but she might as well have been seven hundred. Her little white house on Elizabeth Lane was chipped and peeling inside and out. She had a new job at a real estate agency in Hatteras, and during her free time, Evie primed and caulked. The paint would wait for Stephen, who was going to return from school soon. I envied Evie's new life, however lilting and tenuous it seemed to me, her relationship with Stephen never seeming to be set on solid ground.

I messaged Michael one morning as I sat in Evie's old room, now mine—though it still didn't quite feel like mine without her in it. It was my day off, and the time stretched in front of me, empty and echoing. *As mentioned in Chapter 1, the gaps in bars are often sites of rip currents, the deadly offshore fast-moving currents that drown swim-mers every year. Page 28.*

Michael messaged back. *Do not let 'er rip.*

If you can see a consistent gap in the white line of breaking waves, keep away from that portion of the beach even if you can't spot an active cur-rent. The gap in the wave pattern indicates a gap in the bar, and swim-ming there is asking for trouble, I wrote.

You all good over there? Michael messaged.

I sighed, irritated. Everything irritated me. *I'm fine.*

I'm gonna swing by the inn, he wrote.

You don't have to.

But a few minutes later, he knocked on my bedroom door. "Kid," he said, sitting at the foot of my bed, "you're worrying me."

I turned around in my desk chair and looked at him. "Don't be ri-diculous," I said. "You don't have to worry about me."

"Have you thought about talking to someone?" Michael asked, solid and masculine against the delicate sprigs of the flowered bedspread.

I didn't answer.

Michael leaned forward, elbows on his knees. "I didn't mention this before because I was keeping an eye out and didn't see any signs, but Troia thought you might be cutting yourself," Michael said.

My cheeks burned. I hadn't cut myself since Evie's wedding, and the thought of Troia talking about it with Michael, of Michael har-boring the idea for months while he watched over me, roiled in my chest. "She's always had a vivid imagination." I chipped at the an-tique wood of Evie's desk, the hard splinters satisfying under my nails. "Remember when she believed Evie that the lighthouse was falling down and raised hell because she imagined how bad it was going to be?"

"Troia's got an imagination, but she's not always wrong."

I stared at the picture of a seagull that hung over the bed. I hated that picture. The gull had beady eyes. "Do you want to pad my walls?" I asked. "Take away my shoelaces?"

"It's not like that," Michael said. He stood up and looked over my head, out the window.

"You're getting sand on my floor," I said, brushing my bare foot along the carpet.

Michael walked over and put his hands on the desk, bent over to look me in the eye. His body radiated warmth. "Charlotte," he said. I couldn't focus. His eyes were too blue. "Are you in a rip current?"

I stood up and brushed past him to walk to the door. "Look, Michael, why don't you think for yourself instead of doing Troia's dirty work?"

"You didn't answer me," he said.

"I'm not going to." I grabbed my sweater and left. Down at the pier a little boy threw crumbs into the air for a gathering flock of cawing gulls. He looked at me when I approached, then squealed and tossed another handful at the birds. I felt a twinge of irritation that he'd taken my thinking spot. I turned and walked back to the inn.

———

The next day, layers of clouds stacked the May sky, flat periwinkle into tufted gray, the sun filtering through in streaks. I came to Hatteras Marina to find a boat. I was in the right place. Lines clanked against masts, and white hulls lined the sound like a row of perching gulls. It smelled of fish. I stood to the side of the marina store listen-ing to the putter of an outboard motor before I went in.

The motor died. I took a deep breath. Talking to strangers was never my forte; let alone talking to strangers about my father's fu-neral arrangements. I walked up the wooden steps to the marina store. A bell jangled when I opened the door, but the store was de-serted. I walked around, thumbed through racks of brightly colored T-shirts with thrashing marlins superimposed over American flags, thinking of the ratty shirts my father would wear. One year he had found a vibrant turquoise T-shirt in an abandoned campsite, *Schwar-kopf Family Reunion* emblazoned across the front in bubbly font. He wore it for years.

"Can I help you?" A man spoke from the back of the store. He was bald with a clipped gray beard and was standing beside a line of fishing rods, wearing a denim shirt, denim jacket, and jeans. Once, when I was a kid, I'd worn jeans and a denim jacket and James had called me a denim-elope.

I nodded. "I need a boat."

He moved toward me, his head shiny under the fluorescent lights. "We got boats," he said. "Anything in particular you're looking for?"

I spun a rotating rack of sunglasses. "It's for ashes." My throat tightened. I swallowed. I should have been able to talk about it, but I wasn't. The room filled with the high-pitched hum of the lights.

The man gestured to the right side of the store where a chest-high desk lined the wall. "Richard can take care of you over there."

I didn't want Richard to take care of me, didn't want to have to say it again. "Do you have a restroom?" I asked.

"Right around the corner, under the grouper," he said.

My shoes squeaked on the shiny linoleum, and I greeted the big orange fish mounted above the bathroom door as I went in. "Sorry about your luck," I said to it. The grouper stared back at me with a glassy eye and jutting lower jaw. I closed the bathroom door and rested my head against it, pulled away. It was cold and damp. I washed my hands and swished them under the air dryer. I sat down on the floor. Grief is a strange animal, placated by the most random things. I counted floor tiles until I thought I could talk, then stood up. *I'm Charlotte McConnell,* I whispered to my reflection in the mirror. *I'm here to rent a boat for my dad's funeral.* When I went out, the Weather Channel was broadcasting from a small television over the cash register, the forecast calling for abundant sunshine.

I walked over to the tall desk and rang the bell. *I'm Charlotte McConnell.* The bell reverberated over the synthesized music accompanying the forecast. *I'm here to rent a boat for my dad's funeral.* Out the window, boats swayed in the sound.

"Yeah?" Richard said, walking out from around a corner. He was chewing gum, and he wore a baseball cap that covered his eyes.

"I need to arrange for a boat in July," I said. Dammit. I was saying it wrong. I took a deep breath. "For an ash scattering."

Richard flipped open a large green notebook. "Any particular day?" he asked.

"July fifteenth," I said.

"Two months from today." He skimmed a finger along the page.

Today was the fifteenth. My dad died on August fifteenth. Every fifteenth of every month since then had been unbearable, an onslaught of unprovoked anguish. But today I'd forgotten.

"It's available. Should I put your name down?"

I nodded. "McConnell," I said.

"You'd be surprised how many people want this to be their final resting place," Richard said. "Once I arranged a boat for the ashes of a dog." He popped his gum.

"Wow," I said. "A dog." I drummed my fingers on the desk.

"Could I get your address and phone number?" he asked.

I gave Richard my information,

"Want to come take a look at the harbor?" Richard asked, shrugging toward the water.

"I think I have to go. But thanks."

I walked to the door, flicking the little gold bell on my way out.

———

Sometimes the trick of pretending to move with strength and grace is that a bit of it actually seeps into your real life. I felt brave after setting up the boat for the scattering. I turned on the radio and drove through Hatteras Village to see Evie. The realtor's office where Evie worked was set up on stilts, like many houses on Hatteras. Graceful white pillars lined the front porch; the ceilings were high, the floors shiny and wooden. The whole building smelled new, like rich people. I couldn't remember the old office, which had been destroyed in Hurricane Isabel. Another thing not remembered today. Glossy brochures sat in stacked carousels inside the door. Windsurfing. Kiteboarding. Hang gliding. I picked one up and tucked it in my pocket. *Bungee jump at Waterfall Park.* I thought my brother might like it.

Evie walked out from the private offices on the left and placed a book on the bookshelf tucked beneath the stairs. She hadn't quite gotten the hang of business casual. She wore khaki pants and an old, red, long-sleeved T-shirt with a frayed neckline, her stomach and breasts swelling against it. Evie had ordered a couple pairs of maternity pants online but was still making do with the loosest clothes she could find in her closet, wearing long shirts and leaving her pants unbuttoned or lacing them shut with a hair band. We hadn't been maternity shopping yet; there weren't any stores that sold maternity clothes on the Outer Banks, even up the beach in Nags Head and Kitty Hawk. Virginia Beach was the closest we could find, and that was a day trip we hadn't yet taken. Evie saw me and walked over.

"Are you free for lunch?" I asked.

"I packed my lunch today," Evie said. She stepped behind the curved receptionist's desk and tapped at the computer keys. "I usually eat outside. I'll share if you want to stay."

"No, I don't want to eat your food," I said. "Besides, I'm getting paid now. I could take us both out."

Evie rattled the computer mouse back and forth. "Stupid thing sticks," she said. Her fingernails were polished a bright blue. "I don't want to waste what I brought."

"Okay," I said. "I'll stay with you while you eat."

Evie reached beneath the desk and pulled out a brown bag. "Come on," she said.

I followed Evie to the back of the building. Offices bracketed the hallway, and somewhere a phone rang. We went outside and down steep wooden stairs. The sky was clearing, the smears of gray flattening into a blue horizon. We walked across the scrubby grass to a grove of live oak trees clustered in the corner of the yard. They grew close together, limbs jutting out horizontally and low to the ground. Evie sat on a branch that bent a few inches from the dirt. Light speckled through the canopy of leaves, and with her lunch bag in her lap, Evie looked young and fragile.

"Don't freak out," Evie said, opening the bag. "But there are gravestones just behind that pampas grass."

I parted the tall tufts of grass and peered forward. Three weathered gray stones slanted out of the ground. "You eat in a graveyard?"

"It's just a little family plot," Evie said. "When you live on an island there's not much space for bodies." She crinkled her nose.

"I guess it's kind of peaceful." I let the grass close back together and sat on the ground. "In a morbid sort of way."

Evie rummaged in her bag and pulled out a banana. She held it up against the sky. "I was thinking of this color for the baby's room."

"I like it," I said.

Evie peeled the banana, broke it in half, and handed me part.

"You could do inner-banana color for the living room," I said.

"My house will look like an ice cream sundae." Evie leaned back against the tree. Her stomach rounded out in front of her. She laid the banana peel on top of it.

"The baby's room could have a border of sprinkles," I said.

"The baby's name is going to be Sprinkles at this point," Evie said. "Do you know how often I have to pee? And it's not even big yet. It's only as big as a papaya."

"Boy or girl, do you think?" I asked. She and Stephen had decided to not find out at the ultrasound.

"Boy," Evie said. She looked up at the green leaves waving in the wind. "Stephen thinks it's a girl. Then he gets mad because he wants a boy." Evie took a sandwich out of the bag.

"Have you thought of names yet?" I asked. I raised my hand to decline Evie's offered half sandwich.

"We decided not to tell people," Evie said, brushing crumbs off her pant leg. "I told Mom one of my names and she made a face. We figure it's our baby, we should be the ones picking the names."

"Oh," I said. I picked a leaf off a tree root that curved into the ground like a talon. "Didn't you always want Katherine for a girl?" Her reticence bothered me; I knew it was childish, but I felt like she was choosing an alliance with Stephen over me. I wanted to shake her back into the way things were.

Evie wiped her mouth with a napkin with little blue teddy bears on it. "Yeah," she said. "But Stephen's got an aunt and a half-cousin named Katherine, so that's out."

"How about Lily?" I asked. I drummed my fingers on the tree trunk.

"We're just really not going to talk about it," Evie said. She pushed the napkin into the bag and crumpled it closed.

"We always used to talk about names for our kids," I said.

Evie stood up. "That was when they were imaginary," she said. "I should get back to work. We got a new listing today."

I stood up, too, knocking leaves off the backs of my legs. "Did you still want help painting this weekend? I can do it, so you don't have to be around the fumes."

"Yeah, that'd be great," Evie said. "Stephen gets home tomorrow, and then he'll be busy looking for a job, so I want to get it done."

Evie and I walked across the lawn. I paused at the steps. "I think I'll go around the side to the car," I said.

"See you later, Meehonkey," Evie said. She walked up the steps, feet splayed sideways, and disappeared inside.

Charlotte—
Seriously. Enough with the not talking. Call me tonight.
                                        Troia

Michael messaged me: *"Although delicate and even fragile in appearance when viewed from the air, barrier islands are actually both durable and flexible. They absorb the ocean waves that otherwise would affect the mainland. But if the waves are particularly large, the beach protects the island by changing shape to better absorb the storm waves. And if the sea level rises, the islands migrate landward, more or less intact."* Page 55.

I wrote back. *More or less.*

More or less.

It was a busy evening at the inn, with the microwave breaking and new guests arriving late. I checked in a retired CIA operative who spoke five languages and her husband, who called me *Liebling*. I found an old microwave in a kitchen cabinet, dusted it off, and rigged an extension cord around the common area to make the plug fit the outlet. Nate wanted to go out. His hair had gotten longer and curled around his face and the back of his neck. He looked so sad when I told him I was busy that I said I'd meet him on the pier when I got a break. After I checked in the last guest and retrieved DVDs for two more, I put the front desk's cordless phone in my pocket and walked down to the water.

The weather on Cape Hatteras never ceased to astonish me. Moments shifted from gray and shrouded to sheer, crystalline blue. That evening, the clouds lifted, and the sun set in swaths of pink and gold. Nate sat on one of the Adirondack chairs at the end of the dock, gazing out at the water. I thought he looked like an old sea captain.

"I should get you a pipe." I said, sitting down in the chair beside him.

"Why?" Nate asked.

"So you look more like a salty old tar," I said.

"That's not all I am, you know." Nate squinted at the sunset.

"I know," I said. A flutter of white edged into my line of view as an egret sailed in and landed on one of the dock posts beside my chair. It tucked its head into a backwards C against the rise of its back.

We sat still and watched the bird and the sunset until I slapped at a mosquito and the egret flew off. I fiddled with the phone in my pocket; the anxiety of it suddenly ringing made me unable to relax. The sky turned purple, and finally I got up to go.

Nate stood up, too. "Can you come with me?" he said. "I want to show you something."

I looked back at the inn's slanting roofline and warm yellow windows. "I still have some work to finish," I said.

"We could meet a little later," Nate said.

I kissed him on the cheek, his five o'clock shadow prickling my lips. "Okay," I said. "I'll see you later."

Nate's car was a square, old Isuzu Trooper with a stick shift and a lingering dampness. A black-and-white oval sticker clung to the bumper. It resembled the ones tourists stuck on their cars and SUVs, proclaiming to have visited the OBX—Outer Banks—but Nate's read BOI for Born On Island. Not many people could claim that. We got in and started south on Highway 12. The road unfurled like ribbon in the moonlight, a luminescent strand between rows of tall pine trees.

"Where are we going?" I asked.

All Nate would say was, "You'll see."

We rode on. "I saw Evie today," I said.

"Me too," Nate said. He cracked the driver's side window, and cool wind streamed over my face. "I've been having breakfast with her before Captain Harlon needs me to load up the charter boat for the day." Nate glanced at me. "We'll have enough money for a new buoyancy compensator soon." Nate had started a small wreck-diving venture with his friend Harlon Jenkins. Between the shoals off Hatteras and the German U-boats of World War II, they never lacked for shipwrecks.

We turned onto the twisting road that led to the National Seashore campground.

"I never thought the beach would get back to normal after that nor'easter this winter," I said.

Nate nodded and flicked his brights on. A rabbit scurried across the road. "Barrier islands are fragile, but they're tough," he said, turning right and steering the car into the tiny parking lot of the Billy Mitchell airport.

"What are we doing here?" I asked. The airport consisted of a small wooden open-air building with a pay phone and a radio tower, a skinny landing strip, and a patch of tarmac behind a chain-link fence.

Nate got out and opened the door for me. He took my hand and led me across the pavement. A small flock of planes nestled on the tarmac, moonlight licking their wings. Nate walked to one, reached up, and touched the hull. "Someday," he said, "she's going to be mine."

"An airplane?" It was a stupid question. "I mean, right, an airplane." I nodded and walked around it like I knew what I was doing.

Nate followed me, kicking at the tires and touching the nose. "I figure I'll get the wreck diving up and running, then use the profit from that to finance a plane."

I had to admit, flying did have a certain romance to it. "You'd have to take lessons," I said.

"Already started." Nate's smile was bright in the moonlight. "The way I see it, you can always count on rich tourists." Nate rocked back on his heels, hooking his thumbs through his belt loops like I'd seen his father do. "This way I can ferry them across air and sea."

"It's a good idea," I said.

Nate put his hand on my cheek, his touch rough and smelling faintly of motor oil. "I'm not just screwing around on boats all day," he said. "I've got a plan. For the future." He kissed me, then pulled back. "It's a whole other world from up there," he said.

He kissed me again. I pulled away. Future talk made me nervous.

"What's wrong?" Nate asked.

"Nothing," I said. "Pilots are sexy." I'd always thought of pilots as fantasy material, in theory. Now I pictured Nate in a hat and uniform, settling into the cockpit, trying to make the image align with my imagination.

Nate moved closer, wrapping his arms around my waist. I stepped back and bumped my head on the belly of the airplane.

"Ouch." I said into Nate's neck.

Nate braced his hands against the plane and looked into my eyes. He was so close, and I could feel the intensity radiating off him in waves. He felt so deeply. I was barely beginning to be able to feel at all, the atrophy of my emotions just starting to release. I ducked under his arm and stepped away. "We should get back," I said. "Your parents will wonder what we're doing."

"I'm not ready to go back," Nate said. He bent his head and breathed out heavily. Then, "Goddammit." He slapped his hands against the airplane. It rocked back and forth, groaning against its chains. "Can't you see I'm doing this for you?"

"You're buying a plane for me? That doesn't make any sense." I squinted out toward the dune line, but it was too dark to see it.

Nate turned to me. "Michael says you need stability in your life right now. I'm trying to show you I can do that." Nate looked up at the sky, rubbed his jaw. "I'm trying to say that—"

"Maybe I don't want stability from you," I said. I immediately regretted saying it. That was shitty. "I mean, maybe I need to find it on my own."

Nate crossed his arms. Uncrossed them. Took my hand. "I'm trying to say that I love you."

My stomach dropped. "You do not," I said. "You don't even know me." I strode across the lot toward the building. Then from the emptiness in my center, anger rose, hot and unexpected. I smacked the silver chain-link fence on my way. Nate followed me.

"Why are you getting so upset?" he asked.

I spun around and faced him. I hit the fence again, satisfied by its clanky rattle. "You know I'm not ready for this." What surprised me was how emphatic I felt, how certain I was that I was uncertain about Nate. The feeling nestled in my chest like a hard kernel.

"Then what have we been doing for the last four months?" Nate said. He gripped his fingers in the diamonds of the fence.

I swung away and ran up the steps of the building, searching my pockets for my cell phone. It wasn't there. I picked up the old pay phone and slammed it back down. It still worked. The crickets paused and then started humming again. "Do you have a quarter?" I asked.

"Who are you calling?" Nate asked. He looked sad and confused under the flickering yellow lights.

"I'm calling Evie to come get me." I held out my hand for a quarter. I knew I was being impetuous and dramatic. Somewhere in the back of my mind, I thought it might push Nate away.

"Charlotte, don't do this," Nate said. "Evie'll be asleep by now anyway."

I sighed, put my hand down, then raised it to my face and rubbed my forehead. My eyes blurred, and I turned away from Nate and the lights and walked to a small wooden bench.

Nate sat beside me. "It's okay," he said. Slowly, he put his arm around my shoulder.

I stiffened. "I like you," I said. "I like getting to know you. Just don't push love on me right now." How could I love someone else when I didn't know who I was anymore? How could I know what was love and what was hormones, lust, biological attraction?

Nate lifted his arm away. "Sorry," he said.

I bent myself in half over my knees. I'd hurt him. Grass waved in the breeze beneath the cracks in the wooden plank floor. I sighed, sat up, and faced him. "Don't apologize," I said.

Nate brushed my hair off my face. "I'm sorry I pushed you."

I put my hand on his leg, squeezed the tight muscle. Nate started to bend toward me, stopped, leaned back on the bench. As much as it frightened me earlier to be close to him, I was scared he'd move away.

Nate rested his arm on my shoulder again. I linked my fingers with his and rested back. I couldn't think of anything to say.

"We can go slow," Nate said.

"I'm not really sure how I feel about anything right now," I said. Nate's arm was pulling on my hair, but I didn't want to say so.

"I'm sorry I swore back there," Nate said.

"Not a big fucking deal," I said.

Nate smiled, sweet and lopsided. "I was raised not to take God's name in vain, that's all," he said.

"You really believe that stuff?" I asked.

Nate jiggled my hand back and forth in his. "Yeah," he said. "I think. Don't you?"

"I don't know," I said. *No. I don't think so. I want to. Maybe.* I watched the shadow of our hands move across the floor. "My dad didn't."

"Really?" Nate stilled our hands.

"He was a scientist," I said. I shifted under Nate's arm, tugging my hair loose.

"Doesn't mean he couldn't have faith," Nate said.

"You think he was wrong?" I asked.

"I wouldn't say wrong," Nate said.

The building's lights flickered and buzzed. I wiggled my hand loose from his. "Let's go home," I said. Nate and I were quiet on the ride back, the moonlight showering the road like melted silver.

———

C-to-the-harlot,

I'm getting a new surfboard for summer. Bribery from Mom for pulling my grades back up. I'm not above it. What else? Learning to play the guitar, fucking loud. The thing is, I was pretty pissed at you for leaving. I still am.

James

———

I texted Michael: *"The amount of water that must flow through an inlet is determined by the amplitude of tides and the volume of nearby rivers. Because the volume of tidal and river water passing through the inlet is more or less constant over time, when one inlet forms, another usually closes." Page 57.*

Michael wrote back: *"In other words, nature maintains just enough openings between islands to handle the local water volumes." Page 55.*

I wrote: *Nature maintains.*

Michael wrote back: *The Dude abides.*

Ten

Early the next morning I stopped by Michael's trailer on my way to Evie's. He answered the door bare-chested wearing green plaid flannel shorts. He rumpled his hair and yawned.

"I did for a while," I told him. If I didn't say it right away and without thinking, I wouldn't say it at all.

"Cut yourself?"

I nodded. I'd felt empty all night after my conversation with Nate, even though distance was what I'd thought I wanted. But that morning, I craved intimacy, wanted to feel laced together with another person.

Michael opened the screen door and motioned inward.

"I can't stay long," I said. His trailer was dark and narrow, and the brown wood-paneled walls seemed to taper it further. I hesitated in the doorway, then turned sideways to brush past him and go inside. Michael stepped aside at the same time, and we bumped into each other, then did an awkward bobbing dance as we each tried to get out of the other's way. He finally flattened himself and I walked past. I moved a pile of papers off an easy chair; the fabric scratched my arms when I sat. "I really don't want to talk about it," I said. "But I didn't want to lie to you."

"I did some research," Michael said.

"I'm doing better now," I said. The depth of aqua Michael's eyes held in the dim room startled me. I looked away. "I couldn't feel anything right after."

"From what I've read, it's not an uncommon reaction to grief." He stood up, went to his bedroom, and came back pulling on a T-shirt.

I wanted him to understand. "I arranged a boat yesterday for the ash scattering. I feel like it'll really be over after that."

"Is that good or bad?" Michael asked.

"I don't know," I said. I looked around the trailer, and my eyes adjusted to the faint light. Michael had posters of waves and water taped up on the walls. "Would you ever want to live here for good?" I asked.

Michael leaned forward and grasped his hands together in front of his knees. "I wonder about it sometimes," he said. "Good spot for research, that's for sure."

"But pretty isolated," I said. "I can't imagine growing up here like Evie and Nate." I looked at a poster of a tiny surfer poised on the tip edge of a surfboard, a wave cresting over his head.

"I wonder if I would've learned to resent all this wind and water the way I can't stand being closed up inland," Michael said.

"It's like our book says, how the beach is a very dynamic system."

Michael nodded. "*The global pulse of the tide*, right?" He jiggled his leg up and down. "I love it here."

"I'm not ready to go home," I said.

"Not even for a shopping mall?" Michael asked.

"Maybe for a mall," I said. "If there was a sale."

"Can't resist a good sale," Michael said.

I stood up, feeling lighter. "Evie's waiting for me," I said. "I'm painting today." I tugged on the ratty bandana covering my head as evidence.

Michael walked me to the door. "Stop by any time, kid," he said, pulling me into a quick tight hug. His skin warmed me.

"I will," I said.

I made sure my hips swayed a little as I walked down the trailer's steps to my car.

——

Evie's little white house nestled back from the road in a grove of loblolly pines. She was one of the few locals living in the neighborhood; most of the other houses were tall pastel rentals or old, gray-shingled squares perched on stilts. Gables peaked up over Evie's screened-in porch, and shallow steps led to the front door.

"It's starting to feel like summer," I called out as I walked into Evie's kitchen and plunked a box of doughnuts on the table. It was a warm day, and everything seemed pulled by the wind. Clouds tugged out in streaks across the sky, and trees bent their branches sideways. Somehow in the last few days the season changed like a switch had been flipped, and I realized that morning that it was because the humidity had returned. The air felt thick and sweet again.

Evie's kitchen sprawled across the right side of her house like a lazy cat. Appliances stuck out at odd angles over the countertop, and cardboard boxes huddled in the corner near the door. Evie walked in and sat at the table. She picked out a jelly-filled doughnut. "Stephen's out, so it's just you and me," she said. She raised the doughnut in a toast. "Here's to paint," she said.

"To fresh coats." I grabbed a glazed and met it to Evie's. "But you're not painting."

"It's not like I'm going to suck on the walls," she said. "We'll open the windows. It'll be fine." She licked red jelly off the side of her hand.

Evie stood up, and we walked through the small living room to a side-by-side set of bedrooms. She gestured to the one on the left with her half-eaten doughnut. "I've been sleeping in here, but I think I'll move my stuff," Evie paused. "Our stuff, out to the other bedroom, since it gets the morning light. That way it won't bug the baby."

I went to the living room and sat on the floor beside a small tower of paint cans. "I just saw Michael," I said. "I could call him. I'm sure he'd come help."

"Nate's working all day?" Evie knelt and passed me a screwdriver to pry off lids.

"He's taking out charters until dinner," I said. "I'll go call Michael."

Michael agreed to come over. I went back downstairs and found Evie standing swaybacked on a dresser, reaching up with the paint-brush where the wall met the ceiling. Her belly poked out between her jogging pants and T-shirt, and a hospital mask covered her mouth and nose. She looked like a pregnant bandit.

"You getting ready to rob banks?" I asked.

Evie looked down at me and dripped paint on her shoe. It pud-dled like drops of buttercream. She tugged her mask down. "I stole it from the doctor yesterday," Evie said. "She said I'd be okay to paint in it."

"You didn't tell me you had a doctor's appointment," I said. I picked up a brush and dabbed it in the paint tray, the fibers separat-ing then glomming together. "I would've gone with you."

Evie turned back to the wall. "It's no big deal," she said. "I have a sonogram in Nags Head on Tuesday if you want to go."

Michael poked his head into the room, swung a paper sack forward like an offering. "Hey kids," he said. "I brought bagels."

Evie put down her brush and hunkered to her knees, then slid off the dresser. She gave Michael a hug and took the bag. "Carb-o-rama," she said.

"Maybe you can convince her to stay away from the paint fumes," I said. I globbed some paint at the wall.

"Nice technique there," Michael said.

I handed him the brush, trying not to feel giddy that I got to see him twice in one day. "Teach me, then, wise one."

He gave it back to me and closed his hand around my hand, stretched our arms up and down, stroking V shapes against the wall. "Like that," Michael said, his face close to mine.

Evie pulled down her mask. She looked at me. "I think I do need to go get some air," she said.

———

Michael and I painted quietly on opposite sides of the room. I stretched my arm up and down in Vs, the ghost of his hand around mine as I grasped the brush. My phone rang in my pocket, and I jumped, blushing, convinced it was Troia. I put down the brush and took out my phone, but it was my mom. I debated with myself about answering for a moment but decided I needed to take a break anyway. To get away from the paint fumes for a minute, I told myself.

"Hi, Mom." I wandered slowly through Evie's house, straightening a blanket here, adjusting a picture frame there.

"Hi sweetie," Mom said. "What are you guys up to today?"

I told her about painting the baby's room, mentioning that Ste-

phen was conspicuously absent. "I had to call Michael for rein-
forcements since Nate's working," I said. Somehow it felt like saying
Michael's name conversationally would help dissipate the feeling
that I'd crossed a line in asking him over.

Mom didn't seem to notice or care. "Any word on the boat?" she
asked.

I stopped walking, stilled for a moment, the fizzing distraction
of Michael evaporating as I remembered everything else. It's funny
how loss and emptiness and absence all carry weight. A hollow light
hot at my core, radiating the compressed mass of *gone*. "It's all set
up," I said, and I told her about the grouper on the bathroom door.

That afternoon the doorbell rang. Aunt Fay walked in, leading Walter on a leash. He held the leash in his mouth, snarling and shaking
his head.

"Hey, beast," Evie said, putting her paintbrush down and walking
over to pet the dog.

"It's British Cemetery Service planning day," Aunt Fay said.

Here's what I knew about the British cemeteries on the Outer
Banks: in Buxton, there were the graves of two servicemen, their
bodies washed up on the coastline during World War II. I didn't
know their stories, their ships, or which particular horror brought
them, their lives smearing into the blur that was the German sub-
marine assault.

Off Ocracoke, though, I knew the ship, the HMT *Bedfordshire*, was
blown up by a U-boat—torpedoes sluicing through the waves, piercing the ship, the explosion killing all the British sailors immediately
in a rising ball of heat and fire. A whole ship of men dead, their fam-

ilies jolted, split, reconfigured. Four of those men's bodies, or parts of them, came ashore on Ocracoke and were buried. The ellipsis of history stretched right up to now, a single generation's twist of DNA grasping those men's wet uniforms in their hands, sodden bodies dragging deep furrows in the sand as they were pulled to the dune line. "Buxton or Ocracoke?" I asked. Walter looked up from Evie to me and smiled, pink tongue poking out of his mouth.

Aunt Fay nodded. "Ocracoke. Plan a service there every year," she said. "Evie's coming with me. Paint smell isn't good for that baby."

"I told you," I said to Evie.

Michael came in from the kitchen with glasses of iced tea. "More lovely ladies," he said, kissing Aunt Fay's concave cheek.

Aunt Fay patted Michael's chest. "I like this one," she said.

"When are you going to Ocracoke?" Evie asked. "I've got to finish these rooms." She sat on the floor to play with Walter, waving her hand in fluttering motions around his head.

"I called up your dad," Aunt Fay said. "He's coming over. Isn't any sense in you doing all this, especially when I saw that husband of yours out on a jet ski when I did my drive down the beach. That boy didn't even wave, just turned back to the water like he knew he was caught doing something he shouldn't have been."

"I thought he was looking for a job," Evie said softly. Walter stood up, licked her on the chin, grabbed her painting mask and tugged at it. Evie pushed him away.

"Let's go outside," I said, an undetonated torpedo of anger rising from the gape at my center, a gathering of rage at my spine. I wanted to get Evie out of the paint smell. I didn't want to be there when Mr. Austin arrived to help. I wanted to rewind time, unspiral DNA, unfracture those British families across the sea. I wanted to go find Stephen and push him off his jet ski. I wanted *my* dad to come help me, and I felt guilty and juvenile for even letting that thought rise. Evie, Michael, and I walked onto the porch, and I sat on the railing. Mr. Austin's truck rolled up, and he stepped out, waving.

"Why don't you go down to Ocracoke with Evie and Fay," Michael said to me. He rested his hand on my back, his touch coalescing with the spark of my fury. "Mr. Austin and I can finish up here."

"Yeah," I said. I leaned against his hand, wanting the friction to ignite, wanting everything inside me to explode into heat and chaos. I thought of Troia, the spirals of her DNA entwined with mine, and sat up straight.

Mr. Austin walked up to the porch and wrapped Evie in a hug.

"I'll take Walter for a walk before we leave," I said, taking the leash from Fay before she could reply.

"We're not in that much of a hurry," she shouted after me, but I was already down the street.

At the end of the block a small pond lined with tall waving pampas grass sat tucked in a curve of the street. Walter sniffed around the edge, clouds coursing in a reflective flow beneath his nose. A warm breeze blew across my skin, and I steeled myself against the cavalcade of memory that had been building since I'd heard my mom's voice. The breeze on the day my father died, the sliding-glass door of my parent's bedroom open all that last night, breeze wafting against the sheet covering his body, blowing over the peaks of his cheekbones, his bald head. A sticky night, but with a cool breeze. I tried to push away his rasped breathing, his open jaw. My mom hunched on a stool beside him, holding his hand. His bones in the moonlight. James curled on the bed, knees to his chin. Was there moonlight? I don't know. Walter and I walked down the street and turned toward the Pamlico. Walter barked, and I turned to see Michael jogging down the street. I walked toward him.

"You look sad," Michael said.

"Sorry," I said.

"It's allowed."

Michael stared out at the sound, crossed his arms. Walter thrashed the leash against my leg. "Do you ever just feel like running?" he asked.

"Running away? All the time."

"No," he said. "Just running. Like when we were kids." He sprinted down the road, flailing his arms like an eight-year-old late for a kick-ball game.

Bonkers. But I ran after him, Walter yapping at my heels. The wind on my face and a burn in my thighs, my flip-flops slapping the pavement, all somehow dampened the conflagration inside me. I turned around backwards so I could see Michael and tripped over something in the road, landing hard on my hands. They stung, bits of gravel imprinting my palms.

Michael ran to grab me, but I was already on the ground. "That didn't feel good," he said, kneeling beside me. He took my hand and helped me up, held on, and looked at me. "You know you can talk to me, right?"

I gave Michael the dog leash and brushed off my hands and my pants. "Did your dad ever put Mercurochrome on your cuts when you were little? That red stuff? Mine did. It stung like hell. I always hated falling down when he was home and mom wasn't." Walter sat down on the pavement. The wind blew and he shivered, looking up at me with round eyes.

"You know that Chihuahuas were bred to resemble babies, right?" Michael said. "So that rich ladies could carry them around."

"That's creepy as hell," I said. "And Walter's a Yorkie."

"I know," Michael said. "Still."

Michael and I took Walter and walked back to Evie's house, together.

———

The ferry boat to Ocracoke ran from 5:00 a.m. until midnight every day, and every day the road through Hatteras Village swelled a little more with traffic as summer approached. I pulled my painting bandana off my head and leaned out the window of Aunt Fay's truck. We crossed the bridge over the canal that marked the center of the village, passed the grocery store and post office and library and giant taxidermied marlin that hung by the community center. I leaned across Evie to talk to Aunt Fay. "Why aren't we taking the *Celtic*?" I asked.

"Getting her painted," Aunt Fay said. "Green to match the beach bus."

Evie shifted the seat belt around her waist. "I'm getting so fat," she said.

"At least you stopped throwing up," I said. "No way you'd be sitting in the middle seat a few months ago." The truck bounced past the marina and a pastel-painted shopping plaza to the ferry terminal. We waited in the line of cars until it began inching forward to the boat, the truck all heft and bounce and jerk as we transitioned from pavement to boat.

Aunt Fay waved out the window at the men directing cars onto the boat. "Going to go say hello to Jerry," she said, sticking her hand out the door to block it from hitting the car beside us, slithering out of the truck and walking over to one of the blue-vested men chucking wooden blocks under car tires. Aunt Fay knew or was related to most people on the island.

"I'm going to the bathroom," Evie said. She wrenched herself out of the truck with a twist.

I got out and stood by the railing, looking over at the ferry terminal and the green water. It was a warm spring afternoon with a soft breeze. Children filed out of cars, tearing up bread to throw at the gathering seagulls as the ferry took off with a slow bump and a blare of its horn. Little rain clouds puckered across the horizon as the ferry lumbered through the Pamlico. I went to the bathroom to find Evie, knocking on the heavy door. "You okay?" I asked.

Evie cracked the door open. "Come on in," she said.

"What's wrong?" I closed the door. The room was tiny and dark and sloshed back and forth against the waves.

Evie looked in the mirror, scrunched up her nose at her reflection, turned to the side, and smoothed a hand over her rounded stomach. "Nothing. I'm just so pregnant." Evie blew her nose. "You and Michael looked cozy when you got back to my house," she said.

I flushed. "We were just talking. And running."

"Charlotte 'I-only-run-if-I'm-being-chased McConnell,' running?" Evie looked at me hard. "You know Nate would do anything for you, right?"

The sudden thud in my chest matched the lurch and thump of the ferry knocking into the trough of a wave. I pressed open the thick door, leaning my shoulder against it to pop it open. I snaked through rows of cars to the front of the boat, my heart pumping with her insinuation. With the fact that she saw what I'd been trying to hide. "Let's look at your track record," I said under my breath.

Evie followed me, her stomach brushing the doors of the cars as she hedged her way forward. The wind blew strong at the front deck, my hair streaming back from my face. Evie shouted to be heard. "Anyone can see the way you look at him."

I turned around to face her, rattling my leg against the heavy chain separating me from the water. "He understands me, that's all."

"Why?" Evie asked. "Because you both went to fancy schools before you dropped out and decided to slum it with a bunch of ignorant islanders?"

I looked away from her, over the chop and slosh of water. "You know I don't think of you that way."

I wound my way back to the truck and shut myself out of the wind, the cab a cocoon of isolation, a sudden absence of noise. But Evie slammed in beside me. We sat, each looking straight ahead, the muted grinding of the boat's motor and the slap of the waves suddenly audible, the anxiety of conflict in my throat.

Evie turned on the radio, fiddled with the knob, turned it off. She sighed. "You're going to make me talk first?"

I shrugged.

Aunt Fay's gray head bobbed along outside my window. She opened the driver's side door and propped her foot on the running board. "Getting close to Ocracoke," she said. "Can't imagine riding this boat twice a day to get to school and back like those O'cocker kids do." She studied me and Evie, her face pinched. "What's wrong with you girls?" she asked.

"Nothing," I said.

"Affaires de la coeur," Evie said, faking a French accent. "If you must know."

Aunt Fay climbed into the truck and settled her arms across the steering wheel. "I never married, but I sure had my share of love affairs in my life. I didn't always look like this, you know." She gestured to her caved-in jawline. "When I was your age, I was real pretty."

"And you got pregnant once," Evie said. "You told me before."

"That was Charlie. The mainlander," Aunt Fay said. "I was going to tell you about his rival." The boat geared down and slowed, turned toward Ocracoke harbor. Gulls perched, squat and frowning, on grayed pilings poking out of the water.

Aunt Fay reached down to the floor. She brought up a pink flowered purse and rummaged through her wallet, then slapped a photograph against the dashboard. I picked it up. A fair-haired man in a uniform looked back at me. I handed him to Evie.

"He looks like Stephen," Evie said.

"He'd be Stephen's great-uncle," Aunt Fay said. "Tom Oden. Went to school together, then he joined the service. He was a good man, Tom Oden." Aunt Fay paused, and for a moment I saw her as a young girl. "He'd take me bottle hunting. Could always count on him. And then Charlie came to town one summer." Her pronunciation of *town* sounded like *tain*.

"What's bottle hunting?" I asked.

Aunt Fay glanced at me. "It's hunting. For bottles."

"Like beach glass?" Evie asked.

"Like bottles," Aunt Fay said. "You go out to abandoned houses and look for bottles. Medicine bottles, drink bottles, it doesn't matter. But that's not the point. Point is, Charlie came along and made my heart beat fast. Couldn't believe such a fancy thing would look twice at someone like me, but he did. More than twice, in fact." The ferry boat docked, and men walked around removing the wooden blocks. One of them waved at Aunt Fay, but she didn't notice. "So, I took up with Charlie but at the same time didn't tell Tom any different." Aunt

Fay started the truck and followed the other cars off the ferry. "Heard there's a chowder cook-off tonight at Blackbeard's Tavern."

We drove onto Ocracoke, clunking off the ferry, and turned right. Ocracoke was known for being the place where the pirate Blackbeard was beheaded. Blackbeard, lighted matches under his hat, smoke billowing, swords swinging, beheaded body swimming around the *Queen Anne's Revenge* three times. It's told that he buried his gold somewhere in Ocracoke's sand, but that's just a legend. He wasn't actually all that successful. The land as we drove was bare except for the dunes lining the beach and the reedy seagrass. The sky turned gray as the clouds thickened and spread out, foreboding like Evie's anger with me. We drove for miles in silence, sticky and viscous.

"Fine, I'll ask," Evie said. "What happened to Stephen's bottle-hunting doppelganger after you hooked up with that philandering mainlander?"

Aunt Fay pulled the truck over in a parking lot and got out. A tall split rail fence stretched in a large square along the side of the road. Behind it, three tan ponies swished their white tails. We got out to watch them.

"Shame they had to fence in the wild ponies," Aunt Fay said. The wild ponies of Ocracoke were descendants of Spanish stallions shipwrecked on the island many years ago. Another telling had the ponies coming onto Ocracoke from Sir Walter Raleigh's settlement on Roanoke, miles and miles to the north. In my imagination, they leapt from the bows of ships plunging through storm-tossed seas, front legs churning the waves, whinnying and tossing their manes, wild-eyed until hoof met shore. *This place is good*, they thought as they sloshed through the breakers to the shore. *Let's stay here.* The Park Service fenced the ponies in during the 1950s because the newly paved highway made it too dangerous for them to roam. One of the ponies neighed and shook its head.

"Did you love him?" I asked.

Aunt Fay stood with her hands in her pockets. "Which one?" she asked.

"Either," I said.

"Yes," Aunt Fay said.

I sighed.

"What happened?" Evie asked. The wind blew her hair back from her face, blew her shirt against the rise of her stomach.

"Same thing that always happens when you love two people at once. Someone got hurt."

Above us, seagulls swooped and cawed through the salty air.

"I remember the Boy Scouts used to catch those ponies, then float saddles onto them in the sound," Aunt Fay said. "Back when the world was wild."

"I have to urinate," Evie said.

"Let's go," I said.

But Evie and Fay didn't move. A fine rain misted down.

"I'm not going to say I'm sorry," Evie said to me. "I don't want you to hurt Nate." She looked out at the ponies, their manes lifting in the breeze.

"Nate can handle himself," Aunt Fay said.

"I'm not trying to hurt anyone," I said.

"Well, of course you're not," Aunt Fay said. She took my face in her hand. She smelled like Vicks VapoRub. "Men aren't something worth fighting about. Now let's get down to that meeting."

I lifted my face to the cool rain for a moment, then followed them to the truck.

———

Charles—

I've been rereading Wuthering Heights *lately. It makes me think that we would have been like the Brontës if we were born in that time. You know, provided that we were actually sisters. And had any literary talent. And looked good in bonnets. But oh, Heathcliff. I mean, problematic, yes, very, but oh.*

Anyway, I'm so ready for the beach. I need to get away. Guess I'll settle for the moors for now. I am going to a wedding this weekend, anyway. Why is it everyone I know is getting married lately? It strains the imagination. Should I wear the blue dress, you think? Or go shopping for a new outfit? Ridiculous question.

Love you,

T.

Eleven

n all my time working at the front desk of the inn, I never got used to the sudden jangle of the ringing telephone. It spiked my heart rate every time. I never got comfortable verifying people's credit card numbers, convinced I'd ruin someone's vacation by transposing the digits. I hated the convoluted computer program for taking reservations and marking which room needed cleaning or had been finished. But the caretaking aspects, those things I loved. I loved doing a walk-through every hour, straightening a pillow here, noting a light bulb out there. I loved walking outside into the soft, salty air to cross from one side of the inn to the other, that infernal phone in my pocket. I loved stepping into empty rooms, pretending that I was a guest admiring the view. And as much as I detested talking to strangers, I loved giving new guests my rehearsed tour of the inn.

The inn worked in rhythms, mornings coffee-smelling and buzzing with guests coming down to breakfast. I figured out who was checking out and who was due to check in and coordinated with Xiomara, who did the housekeeping, on which rooms were ready and which still needed cleaning. Guests tended to come to the desk asking about things to do that day, so when the CIA linguist and her husband walked up to me at my desk, and the husband said, "I am dying, Leibling," it startled me out of my routine as much as the ringing phone did. They were already in my memorable guests category, but this launched them higher on that list. The husband looked a bit like Captain Kirk, and he leaned forward on the ledge of the window that separated my desk from the front room and he said, "We are here because I am dying. What would you see here if this was your last trip to Hatteras Island?"

What would I do? Nate walked by as I gathered an answer in my head. He gave a little sideways half wave. "Dad out back?" I nodded yes, then looked at my guests.

"I mean, the lighthouse is a must-see, right?" I asked them. "Tallest lighthouse in America." The linguist's husband nodded, *Yes, we know this*, his eyes a bright blue. He was dying. Soon, his body would shut down, and he would be gone. This fact did not bring me to my knees.

"But here's what I would do. I'd sit on the beach and listen to the waves," I told them. I'd try to wind myself into that pause between curl and crash, to suspend time in a silver thread before the moment coalesced onto itself, splashing and frothing to the shore. "My favorite access is ramp 49," I told them.

"We will seize the day at ramp 49," the linguist said.

I stood to watch them walk out the door, out to seize every moment, then sat down at my rolling chair and poked the computer awake, thinking I'd work on rewriting the descriptions of the rooms for the website. I got as far as coming up with a word to describe the morning light flowing through the east-facing Magnolia room— *pearlescent*—when the phone rang, startling me like it always did. "Pamlico Inn, this is Charlotte speaking. How can I help you today?" I asked, hoping I was speaking with a smile in my voice like Mr. Austin wanted and not dripping with leftover phone-ringing adrenaline.

"I was wondering if you could recommend someone to drive up to Nags Head with me tomorrow for a sonogram?" Evie said.

I relaxed in my chair and swiveled it around. "I think I know a person, but she's going to want to listen to old Spice Girls albums on the ride and get Diet Cherry Limeades at Sonic."

"I can live with that."

I hung up just as Nate came into the office, stopping behind my chair. I looked up at him, trying to judge the air between us, if it shimmered with tension, attraction, anger, or something else. "Hey," I said.

Nate picked up a pen from my desk and walked it down his fingers. He cleared his throat, and I braced for an announcement, a proclamation, an edict that would determine who we were to one another, how we were supposed to act. "Would you like to have lunch with me later?" he asked.

I thought about it. And I decided I would.

———

Evie and I sat in the waiting room of the Outer Banks Center for Women. We'd made it to the doctor's office in under an hour, just the two of us, while Stephen looked for a job—for real this time. Brightly colored parenting magazines sat in stacks on the coffee tables and black-and-white photos of angelic baby faces lined the walls. Evie started to draw her knee up to her chest, frowned, put it back down. "I can't sit like that anymore," she said.

A nurse called Evie's name. We went into the dim, cool room. Evie undressed and put on a faded blue hospital gown printed with fleur-de-lis. She grinned, put her hand to her mouth like she was trying to stop smiling, then turned to me. "Check out my boobs," Evie said. "They're enormous." She flashed me, then sat on the table.

"Nice," I said. I looked around the room. Fish swam through coral in pictures on the walls, and a big monitor sat on a cart beside the bed.

The sonographer came in and squirted Evie's stomach with jelly. "Cold," Evie said, looking down as the sonographer rolled the wand over her belly button.

The monitor turned gray and swooshed with sound like a paint-brush on dry canvas. The gel on Evie's stomach smelled rubbery, and blobs of color and light swam in a curve along the screen. Evie's heartbeat, or maybe it was the baby's, I couldn't tell, rolled like ocean waves. The picture on the screen stabilized, and I saw a white line of spine, a round head. Here, on the screen, in Evie's body, was the rise of something new, eyes that had not opened yet, had everything to see. This fact settled in my chest, emerald-green and lustrous.

"It looks like a lava lamp," Evie said.

The sonographer pointed to the screen. She had gold rings on every finger. "There are the baby's hands." She tapped at the keyboard, zoomed in. Two hands like tiny blossoms pressed against the top of Evie's belly, curled back in.

"Wow," I whispered.

Evie reached over and touched the screen.

"There are the legs," the sonographer said. "See, they're crossed." The baby kicked up, flipped over, and the image blurred. "Did you want to know the sex?"

Evie looked at me. "I shouldn't," she said. "My husband isn't here." She chewed on her lower lip.

"Can you feel it move?" I asked.

"Not yet," Evie said. She turned to the sonographer. "Is it healthy?" she asked.

"Everything looks normal, as far as I can tell," she said. "We'll get the doctor to review the images in a minute, and then you can go." The sonographer moved the wand around a few more times, shut the monitor off and wiped Evie's stomach with a towel, smiled, and left the room.

"That was incredible," I said. "It was moving around so much."

Evie looked down at her stomach. "I feel like a science experiment," she said. "Maybe I should have found out the sex."

"Does Stephen want to know?"

"I don't know," Evie said. "I don't know if I want him to know." Evie sat up, dark hair falling around her shoulders.

"Do you think Aunt Fay's right?" I asked. "All men are pricks?"

Evie shrugged. "No more than anybody else, I guess. Nate's not. Michael's not either."

"Maybe they're just the good ones."

"Maybe. My husband, on the other hand." Evie raised her hand into the air. "High probability of bad prickdom. You don't know how lucky you are."

"Are you kidding? I'm confused and crazy, and right now I don't want either of them," I said.

"Liar."

"Okay, fine. Maybe I want them both."

"I thought so," Evie said. She leaned back on her elbows. "If you screw over my brother I might have to hate you."

"Are you going to leave Stephen?"

Evie breathed out, lay down the rest of the way. "This ceiling looks like it has coffee splattered all over it."

We sat in silence.

"Hey, Charlotte," Evie said.

"Yeah?"

"You want to see my rack again?"

I messaged Michael: *"Every grain of sand on a barrier island once came across open ocean beach or, to a smaller extent, the lagoon beach on the landward side of the island. Sand is either carried by storm waves or by the wind. Windblown sand may go back and forth between land and sea depending on the direction of the wind." Page 59.*

Michael wrote back. *"Two forces, one catastrophic and one gradual, eventually caused the sand-ridge-covered spits to become islands." Page 60.*

I wrote: *"Once the sand spits became islands, a whole new set of evolutionary processes took over." Page 61.*

Michael responded. *Evolution gonna evolve.*

That night, I dreamt I swam in the ocean, dove through clear, cold breakers, broke across the silver line of paused time, and floated on the waves. My dad bobbed beside me. His hair was dry, brown streaked with red. "Are you my favorite daughter?" he asked.

"I'm your only daughter," I said.

He hugged me tight, and the sun shone bright in my eyes. We floated up over a wave. "Alley-oop," he said as we went up.

We floated back. "Alley-down," I said. My dad chucked me on the chin, winked and clicked his tongue, and swam away.

PART FOUR

July

Twelve

High summer on Hatteras Island as a resident working at an inn was a distinctly different experience from high summer on Hatteras Island as a tourist, the way I first fell in love with the place. As a tourist, I lived in a swimsuit, delighted in walking through the Rod and Gun barefoot to buy postcards and pop, and stayed coated in a film of sand and salt. High summer as a tourist meant thick, salty air, the sides of our canvas tent camper catching in the breeze. Crickets and tree frogs thrumming in hypnotic rhythm, waves of heat rising from the campground's blacktop. The ocean, so clear and cool, the bright blue-green shimmering with diamonds of light. Bright blue-green like Michael's eyes; Michael, who was, I continued to remind myself, my favorite cousin's long-term boyfriend.

High summer on Hatteras as the inn's desk clerk meant cardigan sweaters against the sharp, pinching cold of the air conditioner, sweeping sand out of the front entrance dozens of times a day, rolling out of bed and straight into guests who needed something. The coffee was too cold. The coffee was too hot. The blankets were too thin. The blankets were too thick. The Pamlico didn't have enough waves, and the Atlantic had too many. High summer meant avoiding the Food Lion and Conner's grocery on Saturday afternoons, check-in day for most of the beach houses on the island. Except for today, because today I switched modes, back to tourist, back to who I was before. Today my family arrived to scatter my dad's ashes out to sea.

Michael and I stood in my room overlooking the garden, and then we both reached for the cardboard box that held my father's urn. I couldn't remember how I'd gotten it inside the inn in the first place; Mr. Austin must have carried the box. Michael and I, our heads so close our foreheads bumped, his hand brushing mine as we both reached to find our grip, lifted the box out of my room and into the hallway, then we stepped on each other's feet and got tripped up, dropping the ashes on the floor. "Sorry, Dad," I said. I sat on the floor, the old feeling back, the old all-encompassing grief vibrating through my body in surreal waves.

Michael sat beside me, stretched out his long legs on the blue carpet. "Okay?" he asked. I stared up at a picture of a small sailboat plowing through rough waters. In my imagination, the thrum of the constant air conditioner became the throaty rumble of breakers. Was I okay? Our arms brushed as I shifted the cardboard box and leaned against the wall, the fizz of energy between us silver and bright. When I focused on that, everything else went away. No boat in rough seas. No noisy air conditioner. No dead dad. I was fine. "We're meeting at Bubba's now. Did you know?" I said.

"No, Troia didn't say," Michael said.

The thwack of flip-flops echoed down the hall, and I looked around Michael. Nate stepped over both of us and sat on the other side of me. The big toe on Nate's right foot was wrapped in white gauze. "What happened?" I asked.

"Cut it on the propeller." He spent all day and part of every evening out on the water, then prepared the boat for the same thing the next day. We hadn't seen each other much during high summer. "I thought you might want some extra company," Nate said. "I took time off."

"Yeah," I said. "I do. Thanks." Nate stood and picked up the box, and he and Michael and I walked down the stairs and through the inn, holding the door open to go out to my car. The heat was gauzy in midday, something you could almost touch and run your fingers through. Nate placed the box in my trunk and slammed the lid closed. My dad, his whole life, his whole body, circled in an urn, closed into the trunk of my car. Just like that.

"You driving?" Michael asked me.

I nodded yes. "You two will have to flip for shotgun." But Nate got in the front, and I sat beside him and started the car.

"Excited to see your family?" Nate asked.

"I am," I said, as Michael said at the same time, "It's going to be weird, right?"

What was going to be weird was being in the same room as Troia and Michael, watching them be *together*.

I rolled down my window and let the air, warm and cool at the same time, stream over my face while I turned in at the pink pig on the Bubba's sign. My family had decided to converge at Bubba's Bar-B-Q, a small wooden shack on the side of the road in Frisco, famous for serving some football team ribs after the Super Bowl. Picnic tables spread under airy roofed pavilions to the left of the building, and a man sat at one, his shirt puffed out in the breeze. We got out of the car, and he smiled at us, raising a half-eaten cob of corn in greeting. A tiny white dog with a shiny brown head and great cups of ears stood with its front paws on the man's legs, its thin, pink tongue pulsing in and out. Nate and Michael and I sat at the table behind them and waited.

Out on Highway 12 a horn honked, a flash of platinum hair flying by. My Aunt Darcy, most likely lost and going too far south, though I always maintained that it was impossible to get lost on Hatteras because sooner or later you'd fall off. And then a different car, a car usually parked under the leafy maples in our driveway, a car that had dropped me off at school in Ohio, a car that I drove away from when I went south like a bird, or a girl dodging her grief, a crunch of gravel under that car's tires, a slamming door, and, after six months, there standing in front of me, my mother.

She took up less space than I remembered; everything about her more compact, compressed. But so very much *here*, warm and sticky and rumpled from the hours on the road. She held out her arms. I ran to her, and she smelled the same, like cedar and herbal shampoo, all softness, all swell, the opposite of hollow, the opposite of *gone*, my mom, here. Our bodies stuck together in the heat. My mom. I'd left her to deal with all of this alone, and I felt a twinge of regret shoot through me.

When I stepped back, James was shaking hands with Michael, the action unfamiliar and grown-up, something that wouldn't have occurred to him six months ago. I ran over and grabbed my brother, and I could no longer rest my chin on the top of his head. Mom put her arm around me, and we stood there, the three of us, linked—the trinity I'd been so unable to bear when I'd left Ohio, shadowed by the cold ghost of where my dad should have been, hovering in the thick, humid air. I wiped my face.

"Hey, turd," I said to James. "You're getting tall."

"That's what happens when you disappear for six months," he said. My brother. I'd left him too.

I sighed. "Where are the aunts? I saw Darcy heading south?"

My mom finished hugging Nate and Michael, then walked over to the pavilions and sat at a table, motioning for us to do the same. I sat between Michael and James with Nate and Mom across from me. Over Nate's shoulder the tiny, big-eared dog panted in the heat, and I pointed it out to James.

"It's a pavilion Papillion," he said.

Mom reached across the table and held both my hands. "Aunt Darcy should be here any second. You know she drives like a bat out of hell," she said. "Gwen stopped following her somewhere in Virginia, so God knows when she and Troia will pull in, but they shouldn't be far behind." She reached over and brushed the hair out of my eyes. "You kids ready for some food? Where's Evie?" My mother had a habit of talking all over herself. "What are they feeding you at that inn, Charly? You look like a rail."

I did not look like a rail, and in fact had been feeling distinctly un-railish in my chunky cardigans, but I sat in my tank top in the heat and marinated in my mother's concern. What would my dad have done if he weren't in the trunk of my car? He'd have made some kind of pun, *don't rail on her* or *I rail-y think she looks great*. His ghost still hovering but at least making puns in my head.

"That's because she does the cooking," Michael said.

"Don't listen to him, Mrs. McConnell," Nate said. "Charlotte cooks just fine."

"I don't cook," I said. "I bake. Muffins and stuff. Evie had to work. She'll come over to the house later."

"You know to call me Sarah," Mom said to Nate. And to me, "How far along is Evie now? Does she like the realty office?"

James stood up. "I'm going to get this barbecue order rolling." Again, something he wouldn't have thought of six months ago. He walked inside, the sun making a halo out of his blond hair. When James was little, he used to cry that he hated his hair in the summer because it turned white; he said it made him look like an old man.

Michael got up too. "Pig for everyone?" he asked.

"And all the sides," I said. "Seven months," I said to Mom. "She likes the realty okay, I guess. She found us a good house for the week."

Evie and I had chosen an old, gray-shingled four-story house on the tip end of Hatteras. Evie said it would have to do even though it screamed tourist, and she was right. There was nothing local about the house or the big pastel behemoths surrounding it. Still, it sat right on the ocean and would fit us all. And we weren't locals; we were tourists. Like all the big beach houses, it had a name, *Beachdreams*, but at least it wasn't something like *A Shore Thing* or *Buoys and Gulls* or *LunaSea*. Evie ran across all kinds of cottage names at the realty office and passed the especially heinous ones on to me. My personal favorite remained *WhimSeaGull*.

Michael and James came out with the food, and the rest of the caravan of relatives arrived one by one, unfurling me into who I was *before*. This Charlotte, the one who lived and worked on the Outer Banks, who'd been on her own, receded into Ohio Charlotte, surrounded by family. Aunt Darcy, my mom's sister—round, loud, cheerful, and red-faced—rolled in with her convertible top down and platinum hair blown back from her face. "I thought we'd never get here!" Darcy shouted across the parking lot. She folded me to her, and the glitter from her shirt stuck to my arms. Aunt Darcy—everything about her a little over the top, while her husband, Emmet, was the opposite, long and somber, with legs like a stork. My cousin Sean followed Uncle Emmet out of the car. Sean, fifteen, with his mop of brown hair and T-shirts emblazoned with heavy metal bands, flames, and eagles.

Right beside them in their green Jeep, Aunt Patsy and Uncle Mark parked, not really kin but childhood friends of my parents, so close they'd become family, there for every birthday, popping in for coffee in our kitchen without needing to call. Patsy—short with shiny brown hair cut in a bowl shape; Mark, equally short, with no hair left to speak of. They reminded me of teddy bears. People did hug them an awful lot. Their son, Joshua, nine, artistic, imaginative, hopped out of the car, waving enthusiastically, shaking his curls out of his face. Everyone stretched and gathered and laughed and talked, their voices a cacophony of familiarity.

Finally, in the last car came Aunt Gwen, Troia's mom, and Troia herself. Gwen—permed hair and sensible shoes; she'd married my dad's brother, who left them when Troia was little. My dad never really forgave him for that, and my uncle wasn't coming to the scattering as far as I knew. And Troia, golden, elegant. If I was an artist painting this scene—the people who formed the scaffolding of my whole life all converging on Bubba's Bar-B-Q to scatter my dad's ashes, my worlds colliding, the one I left and the one I'd been building, alone—I'd dab them in with a gauzy impressionist blur, soft and indistinct because of how much they'd always been there. In the kitchen of our house; playing in the yard; me and Sean running outside to spy on the boxers at Don King's training camp, the claim to fame of our little hometown; Joshua falling on our sidewalk and needing stitches in his forehead; James pulling the heads off my Barbie dolls as I screamed; Troia and me spinning in circles in the yard pretending to be butterflies. An impressionist blur of the time when my life had not been broken into *before* and *after*. The me they knew was the me *before*, the me whose dad was part of the pastel blur, who's death left a scraped-out core in the middle of the scene.

Nate and Michael stood out in sharp relief to the smudge of my always-been-there people, the planes of their faces in shadow and sunlight, the curl of their hair in the salty breeze. And Troia, there beside Michael, with her artfully ripped shorts, hair toppling out of a topknot, her hand so casually on his arm as if she didn't feel the shimmer of energy rising from his skin.

Through all the noise and hubbub and barbecued ribs, Troia stood, unfolding herself from the fluent brushwork of the scene in my head and waved me over to the side of the pavilion. I looked around for Michael and found him plugged into Sean's iPod.

"Let's go shopping," Troia said, her face tight.

We stood side by side, a pair like we'd always been. Like we used to be. "Did you forget something?"

"Just all my good sense," Troia said.

"Oh, Troia," I said, squeezing her shoulder. "Neither one of us had any of that to begin with."

Troia thumbed through racks of brightly colored dresses and floral bathing suits at Daydreams in Buxton, topknot undone, hair dangling down her back. I'd tried to convince her to go someplace in Hatteras because the house was south and Buxton was north; driving up and down Highway 12 had gotten old for me, but she was en-

chanted by the views of the Pamlico and Daydreams was her favorite
store, she said, and I was her favorite cousin, so I shut up and we left
the others at Bubba's.

I'd been here with Michael just last week, realizing that I needed
another swimsuit if I was going to be at the beach every day with my
family instead of wrapped up in a cardigan behind a desk. We'd texted that morning to meet up for lunch because he'd been surfing at
the lighthouse beach, and when the little bell jangled as he walked in
the restaurant, I'd tried to squash the thrill that chased up my spine.
Looking at Troia now, I tried to squash something else.

Troia pulled a teal one-piece off the rack, spread it against her
stomach, and put it back, the hanger clinking. "It's just like, I don't
know," she said. "It's like there's this hollowness when we talk to
each other. Where we used to be *us*."

"So, he doesn't listen to you, you mean?" I glanced around the
shop and nodded hello to the girl working at the counter who'd gone
to school with Nate. She also waitressed at Angelo's Pizza in the evenings. If Michael wasn't invested in Troia, it made sense for her to
leave him. "You deserve someone who shows up for you."

Troia and I thumbed through the bikinis. "I do," she said.

"You do." My phone vibrated in my pocket. My mom. *At the realty,
keys are ready.*

Beneath her message, Michael's from last night: *"A swash line is the
last clue left by the edge of a small dying wave, but its erasure provides the
grains that will become part of the next swash." Page 106.*

"I'm telling Michael tonight," Troia said. She stood very still, looking straight at me. She'd always been a pretty crier, something I'd
never been able to accomplish. "What do I say? How do I say it?"

The bell at the door jingled, and a group of sandy-footed teenagers walked in. That floor would have to be swept when they left. I picked up a necklace with a wave charm and held it to Troia's throat. "You should go classic? 'It's not you, it's me'?"

"It's kind of him, though," Troia said. "He's been distant since he moved down here." She handed me a bracelet.

"Tell him you need someone who's there for you," I said. We put the jewelry down and slowly spun a rack of postcards.

"I don't mean to stir anything else up this week," Troia said. "I just feel like I have to do this."

"It's fine," I said. It was fine. Michael was going to be unattached. The shimmer of his energy no longer merging with my cousin's. I needed to change the subject. "Did I tell you I got to see Evie's latest ultrasound?" Troia shook her head no. "She still won't tell me the names she and Stephen are thinking of."

"Stephen-don't-call-me-Steve," she said. "Call me Stevie and I'll hold my breath and turn blue? That Stephen?"

"Stephen-don't-call-me-if-you-need-help," I said.

"Stephen-I-actually-think-mustaches-are-a-thing?" Troia took a small pile of postcards and the necklace with the wave charm to the counter. "Poor Evie."

"He's working in his dad's store now, at least." I smiled at Nate's classmate as she checked out Troia's souvenirs. "They're both coming to dinner tonight."

Outside, a gull sat on a weathered gray post and cawed—four short times and two long. The heat shimmered and the breeze lifted my hair. "I'm sorry about you and Michael." I meant it, mostly.

Troia folded down the edge of the brown paper bag that held her postcards, her movements small and precise. "I need a platitude," she said. "It's for the best?"

"It just wasn't meant to be?" My phone vibrated. Nate: *I placed your dad's ashes in the bottom floor of the rental, right by the door. See you at dinner.* My mom must have had her set of my car keys. Now my car would be waiting for me at the house, and the task I'd most dreaded was done. It was heartbreakingly kind of him. And yet his name wasn't the one I wanted to see at the top of my messages.

———

Dinner that night was a noisy affair. Mark grilled snapper while James and Sean rushed in and out carrying plates to and from the table. I sat in a wicker chair near Nate and watched Evie open a jigsaw puzzle with Joshua, swearing when her stomach bumped the pieces, scattering them. "You said *shit*," Joshua said.

"Sorry. I meant to say *snot*." Evie stood up. She wore a sparkly white sundress that stretched tight across her stomach. From the back she looked exactly the same, tiny and stick-straight from her ponytail to her bare feet. When she turned to the side my mom said it looked like Evie had swallowed a bowling ball. Evie and my mom—here was a dynamic I hadn't dealt with in a minute. They were like a pair of gulls chattering and laughing and circling each other. They were an inlet and a delta, my mom the open inlet and Evie the fan-shaped deposit of sand on one side, two components of the same whole. I was the water. Did I even want to be the sand? Evie and Evie's mom—they were all fresh cuts and disconnect. Mrs. Austin had stayed at the inn tonight, but Mr. Austin stood outside grilling with Mark and Emmet, talking about fishing and the weather.

"Did she tell you Stephen's not coming?" Nate asked. He rocked back in his chair, hands interlocking behind his head.

I shook my head no. "I mean, there's a *River Monsters* marathon on," I said.

"Man's got to have priorities," Nate said.

"You can't just jump into Shark Week untrained," I said.

Nate lowered his arms and took one of my hands in his. "I still don't think I've figured out who everybody is," Nate said.

I focused on the texture of his hand in mine, soft and rough at the same time. I'd stay focused on him, his kindness, his steady presence. I would. "You'll get it," I said.

Aunt Gwen called us to the table. When the shuffling of fourteen people sitting down at once subsided, Mark started telling stories at our end of the table about my dad. "See this scar?" he asked me, waving his hand in front of my face. "That's from the time your dad had me hammering out bent nails so he could use them again."

"I'll never forget riding in that car he was fixing up when the brakes went out and we were headed straight for the Seventh Street Bridge," Emmet said. "'What do we do?' I was hollering, and Cal's shouting, 'Hang on to your nuts, we're pulling the emergency brake!'"

Aunt Gwen, her frown lines relaxed, said, "I remember telling my mother about taking a ride in Cal and Sarah's convertible, and she was just aghast. 'Only chippies ride around in convertibles,'" she said. Everybody at our end of the table laughed, and the other end of the table asked what was so funny. Aunt Gwen told it again, louder, and there we all were, lined up and down the big table—my family and Evie and Nate and Mr. Austin, and fish on the table and glasses clinking, and outside, the setting sun striping pink and orange across the indigo sky, and my dad's ghost, around us, not quite so cold as before, maybe a little bit comfortable inside with the air-conditioning, maybe not quite so much at odds with the world here and now.

———

After dinner, my mom and Evie and I washed the dishes. Mom insisted on running water in the sink and scrubbing the bright yellow fish-shaped plates by hand.

"If only my husband could see me now," Evie said. "Barefoot and pregnant and doing the dishes."

"Where is Stephen?" Mom asked, her voice an arched eyebrow, a question mark crooked, the dot at the bottom firmly pressed.

Evie shifted at the sink and brushed her hair away from her face with a damp hand. "He was tired after work," Evie said. "He's managing the hardware store now. It's busy. Last night he had to go in and open up the store so these people could buy some real tent stakes after their tent flew off a dune." She blew her bangs out of her eyes. "The plastic ones never work."

Patsy walked over and patted Evie's shoulder. "Why don't you go rest? Joshua's been asking for someone to work that puzzle with him. I'll do these," she said, motioning to the pile of dishes.

"Don't we have a dishwasher, anyway?" I asked. The house was packed with amenities—swimming pool, hot tub, game room, whirlpool tubs.

"I just like to do them by hand," my mother said. "It's such a good feeling to take something dirty and make it clean."

"Just like Jesus," Evie said, sticking her hand in the water and blowing the bubbles at my mom.

"For God's sake, Sarah," Aunt Patsy said. "We've got a dishwasher, use it. You don't have to do everything yourself."

"I'm not by myself," Mom said, drying off her hands and putting her arms around me and Evie. "I've got my girls." She nuzzled her nose in my hair. "Oh, I've missed you."

"Well, you know what your girls have?" I asked. "A dishwasher."

"Two, actually," Evie said, pointing at them.

Patsy and I loaded them up while Evie and Mom went to the living room with Joshua. "She'll be okay if she doesn't drive herself crazy this week," Patsy said. "I think she just wants it over with."

"I've got the boat ready to take us out across from the campground beach. That's where he wanted to be," I said. I ran my finger around the rim of a green glass, then loaded it in. Just a girl loading a dishwasher, casually talking about where her father wanted to be buried, or not really buried—dropped in, dissolved, the pulverized bits of his body sifting to the ocean floor. I said it without the awful wrench of grief in my chest, and the absence of it reverberated through my body, a hollow sore space, a purple bruise.

In the center of that bruise sat the Frisco National Seashore campground, across the sand from where my father would be not-really-buried, where yaupon trees grow low to the ground, twisted in the salty breeze. Cicadas and peepers strum rhythmically, and the wind is alive, a wild thing. From campsite P68, high on a ridge of dunes with sea oats waving golden and full, the ocean would lull me to sleep, the roar of that upturned arc of ancient sea zones, ancient depths, crashing on the scar of the shoreline.

In the center of that purple bruise, I imagined the ocean depths, what's under the surface—the warm, vibrant, life-filled coastal shoals blending into the wide-open ocean of the pelagic zone, then down, down, down into the unimaginable pressure of the hadal trenches, so deep it's like another world. So deep, so dark, it doesn't seem like it's part of the same ocean I'd heard from the sandy ridge of campsite P68 on North Carolina's Outer Banks. This same ocean where the ashes of my father's body would dissolve tomorrow. Patsy rubbed my back. "It's hard," she said. "Letting go."

In the rooms behind me, the noise and energy of my family echoed and cocooned. Outside, above this narrow, fragile strand of sand in the middle of the ocean, this impossible island, this in-between place, the horizon deepened, bright stars pinpricking across the sky, the light of long-dead suns glowing like magic in the night.

———

James and I left the house together and walked on the beach, the air thick and sticky and still and those stars above us. Under the moon James's shadow was nearly as long as mine, and the sand squeaked under our feet. The quartz in the sand has to be just the right spherical shape, clear and tiny and smooth, impossibly precise, to make that sound.

"Are you scared," I asked James. "To do the ashes?"

He nodded, kicked at the sand with a loud squeak. "I'm afraid of the sound it'll make." When I looked at my brother, he seemed smaller than he had a few moments ago.

"Maybe we should turn in circles like we're throwing a discus and heave them so far away we don't have to hear it," I said.

"Or skim it across like skipping stones," James said. We walked, the ocean waves lulling in their rhythmic shush.

"We can do the miracle," I said. When James was three and I was eight, we spent one rainy December day coloring pictures. James had asked me to draw a baseball, and I did. He'd drawn squiggly lines all around it. "That's the miracle," he'd said. "The spinning. The round and round and round." The more I thought about it, the spinning did seem to be the miracle. The round and round and round. The waves crashed and the water shimmered silver, and something splashed in the distance, a fish, maybe.

"Why did you have to leave?" James asked flatly, like he didn't really care if he heard the reply or not.

I walked a bit before answering. "Do you know why the sand squeaks?" I asked. "It's the quartz particles rubbing together, and the air has to escape."

"Thanks, Bill Nye."

"It was like, you and me and mom, and not dad, and me scooting off to school like nothing had even happened—I don't know. That didn't seem like the right thing to do, but neither did staying home since Dad wanted me to go to school. I just felt like I had to escape from all of it."

James dodged a ghost crab that scurried in front of him. I always thought that the way they moved was like translucent sand coming to life—a pop and a scuttle and the sand was alive. "Are you coming back?" he asked.

I rubbed my arms, the breeze coursing in from the ocean cool and damp. "My savings account is looking pretty healthy right now," I said. In my mind, a specter on each shoulder, one the jolt of a ringing telephone, the other a pile of books and the squeak of chalk on a board, my hand moving rapidly across the lined pages of a notebook.

James and I walked, turning around to head back at some silently agreed upon point. We passed a young couple holding hands, and I wondered if Troia had told Michael that they were done. But escaping to thoughts of Michael didn't work with my brother beside me. James was here, and my mom was here, and my family was here, and all of them were here to place my father's ashes in the sea.

"I'm so scared it'll be like losing him all over again," I said.

"How can we lose him? He's right up there in the house."

"You're so wise," I said.

James knocked his fist against the side of my head. "Of course, I am, compared to you. Get it? Because you're so dumb?"

I bumped him with my shoulder, and we squeaked our way over the tiny impossible spheres of sand, the crystals smoothed and rounded by the roll and pound of waves, the air compressed until it broke free, all the way back to the house.

Thirteen

woke early the next day, steeped a cup of tea, and stood in front
of the tall picture windows overlooking the beach. The sunrise
blushed in striations of orange and yellow and blue across the sky,
deep and bright. I'd grown used to sound sunsets living at the inn,
with their long stretches of simmering color. Sunrise over the ocean
seemed faster, full of movement, the day starting with a pop. I had
the week off work, but standing at the edge of the ocean with the
orange ball of sun rising into the bluing sky made me miss the cool
gray mornings on the sound, and I decided to go visit Mr. Austin and
see how things were going at the inn. The stairs squeaked under my
flip-flops as I ran down and out of the tall house to drive through
the morning humidity, thick and warm on my skin, to the inn. I
found Mr. Austin in the kitchen, cracking eggs into a bowl. The
warm, bread-and-sugar smell, the bustle of breakfast prep movement draped me in a cloak of familiarity and distraction. Here, I was
after Charlotte again, distanced from who I'd been before, and why. I
picked up a whisk and frothed the eggs in their big silver bowl, falling into our regular rhythm. "I've been thinking," I said. "That the
Dancing Turtle should sell our muffins."

"Can't go wrong with coffee and muffins," he said. Mr. Austin
slipped a pan in the oven, shut the door, and stood looking at me,

one hot pad–encased hand on his hip. He patted my back with the other hand. "Your family all settled in?" he asked.

"They're not really awake yet," I said. "But I think they're all set."

Mr. Austin took carafes down from a cabinet, and I got orange juice out of the fridge. "I got this under control," he said.

"I'll go back to the house for breakfast." I hovered my hand over the skillet, testing the temperature against my palm. It reminded me of the way the heat shimmered over the campground's black-top, and, unbidden, there was my family, me with one foot on my bike pedal, one on the pavement, my dad in his yellow swim trunks, poking hot dogs on the grill, my mom reading in a striped chair with her feet in the sand, James pushing Hot Wheels off the picnic table bench. The *caw-caw-caw-caw, caw caw* of gulls, the thrum of crickets and peepers. The breeze soft on my sun-crisped skin.

Aunt Fay walked into the kitchen, all clatter and energy, Walter in one arm. "Morning," she said, pulling first me then Mr. Austin into fast, hard, one-armed hugs. Walter barked at Mr. Austin, and he narrowed his eyes at the dog. Aunt Fay wore cutoff denim shorts and galoshes, and her hair stood on top of her head like a bubble. She must've come over on the boat.

Aunt Fay reached into the cabinet for a glass and filled it with to-mato juice. She put Walter down, and he scurried around, sniffing under the cabinets. "Where're you hiding the vodka?" she asked. Evie had told me about Aunt Fay's periodic Bloody Mary breakfasts, but I'd yet to witness one.

I pointed to the liquor cabinet as I stirred the eggs. Mr. Austin stacked plates and saucers and mugs on a tray and carried them to the dining room, and I took the eggs off the heat, then opened the fridge and took out some celery.

"Good girl," she said, breaking off a stalk and stirring it into her drink. "You doing the stuff today?" she asked.

"It's today," I said.

"Then what the hell are you doing here?" she asked. "Get back up there with your mama." Walter barked. I didn't need him agreeing with her.

Mr. Austin swung back into the kitchen, and I went over to organize the rest of the things that needed to go to the dining room. Aunt Fay was right; I should be at the house with my mom. But still, I let the clank of silverware rattle with my annoyance.

"Go on up, honey," Mr. Austin said.

I placed the silver down on a tray and nodded. "Let me know if you need any help during checkout," I said. Aunt Fay raised her glass in my direction before taking a drink.

On the porch, I kicked an errant oyster shell off the top step. I wished I had a whole pile of them to kick, wished I could flail at them and scream, nick the skin of my arms and legs with their sharp edges, wished I could beat and stomp and bleed.

––––––

Hurricanes build around an eye of low pressure. Pressure, low and simmering, bands of thunderstorms spiraling out, warm ocean water the fuel. In my chest, gathering pressure. I couldn't go back yet. I backed out of the driveway, gravel churning under my tires, and turned left onto Highway 12. I drove past the clear expanse of the Pamlico, past Pop's Raw Bar, the gabled high school, the small, gray bookstore; past the long, green grocery and the tall surf shop and Angelo's Pizza, my annoyance fading as the landscape rolled by. I pulled in at the National Park entrance, then turned left to park at the original lighthouse site. This drive had been old hat for a while now, my normal commute up to the Food Lion or the post office, but it looked brighter and complexly beautiful again, seeing it as it would look to my family, just arriving.

I texted Evie. *It's today.* The swirl of pressure sat heavy in my chest. I got out of the car and walked through the salty air to the circle of low stones that marked the spot where the lighthouse used to stand.

How's your emotional temp? she wrote back.

Not exactly 98.6, I wrote. *I left the beach house and then your dad kicked me out of the inn so now I have to go back to my family.* I shoved my phone in my shorts pocket and ran my hand across the rough, sandy stone. Thirty-six stones, each inscribed with a lighthouse keeper's name. I spiraled around the stones, saying the names in my head. *Fabius. Ephraim. Jabez. Ethelbert. Zion.* At *Unaka Jeannette* I sat down. *Unaka Jeannette.* I put the name in my pocket, on my list of words that are poems.

What type of medicine do you need? Venting? Tough love? Evie wrote.

Sometimes it felt too much to me, the world. That these men lived and carried oil to the Fresnel lens and stood against the wind, beards flecked with salt and sand, and that they died, that their lights went out, that they left behind their children to navigate the dark world. And those children lived and died and their children after that, and what we have are slabs of granite carved with unwritten poems. Out in that water, two currents clashed. Spumes of sea spray shooting high as they collided, and beneath the surface, skates gliding on their impossible silent wings, grains of sand upswirling in their wake. All of it born from deep space, from nothing, all of it only here for a moment. *Maybe a little tough love,* I wrote. *But gentle.*

You got this, Evie wrote. *I believe in you. You can do it.*

Back at the house on the ocean, I found my mother in the kitchen, scooping ice cream into bowls. The morning sun streamed through the tall windows, turning the kitchen floor gold. Aunt Darcy, Sean, James, and Troia lined the breakfast bar. Everyone was in pajamas— Troia's covered in small pink cowgirls, James in plaid, Sean in a rumpled AC/DC T-shirt and boxers—except Aunt Darcy, who wore a black sequined tank top, jean shorts, and thick eyeliner. My mother pushed the hair out of her eyes, and I handed her a napkin.

"Take a load off," Sean said, patting the barstool beside him before going back to his crossword puzzle, long hair falling around his face.

I got a bowl and spoon and stood beside my mom. She filled my bowl with chocolate ice cream. "Looks like special breakfast day for everyone," I said. "Aunt Fay was doing Bloody Marys."

"Is that the old lady with the face?" Sean asked, skewing his jaw to one side, and pulling in his lower lip.

"Don't be a jerk," James said.

"I figured this was the day for something unexpected," Mom said. "James, give Troia some of that whipped cream."

James shook the can and circled Troia's ice cream with puffy white.

"Me too," I said, shoving my dish toward him. James looked at me, pressed the nozzle for a single beat, put down the can, and ducked away before I could swat at him.

"Should I leave a bowl out for Michael?" Mom asked Troia.

Troia licked her spoon before answering, carefully placing it back in the bowl. "Michael and I are done."

"Would you like a tissue for those tears?" Aunt Darcy asked.

"It's been a long time coming," Troia said.

Aunt Darcy opened a box of Moon Pies. "I've never understood why they call them pies," she said, opening the cellophane and biting into one.

"Charly, did I tell you I ran into Mr. Drew before we left?" Mom said. Mr. Drew, my high school English teacher, all tweed and elbow patches, as if he was channeling the Platonic ideal of an English teacher. "He said you'd better get yourself back in school or he'd flog you with a semicolon."

"I'm not going back this fall," I said, more adamantly than I felt. I'd thought about it, but the vortex of pressure coiled tighter when I imagined myself tacking posters to a dorm room wall, carrying books into a tall-ceilinged classroom, sitting down beside the girls in their Greek letters and pajama pants. Unaka Jeannette had lived and died, and all that was left was a slab of granite. My dad was about to dissolve into the ocean, his body nothing but a swirl of particles beneath the skates.

"You could pack up your things after this week and have all of us take turns driving back home," Mom said. She took my face in her hand. "You have to go back to your life sometime."

"This is my life."

"Think about it," she said. "Anyone want syrup?"

———

As the morning faded, so did the sun. Fat gray clouds stacked across the sky, lines of light falling through them to sparkle on the water, impossibly sharp in their angles. On the beach, a flock of seagulls spread out in formation like football players, black heads hunched into the wind. One bird cawed, and the gulls on either side took off in skittering sideways steps.

I sat in the sand and watched Joshua splash in the shallows with Aunt Gwen. Sea spray refracted into those crisp rays of sun as his small body spun. My phone rang in my pocket, and a jolt of adrenaline shot through my chest as I startled back into the world. It was Nate.

"I have a surprise," he said. "Not exactly a surprise. It's not like a bar of chocolate or something. Anyway."

"What's up?" I ran my fingers through the sand and picked up a small, smooth coquina shell.

A rushing sound coursed through Nate's phone, as if he was driving or in a wind gust. "I ran into the captain who was going to take you all out for your dad's scattering today." *Was.*

"Is everything okay?" Pings of anxiety sparked along my chest and arms, fine-grained and pointy.

"I arranged to captain his boat today so I can take you out." He took a deep breath. "I thought it would help for you to have someone there."

I stood and paced a circle in the sand. I didn't want him there. I didn't want anyone but my mom and my brother and some anonymous person who would fade into fog while we put my dad's ashes in the ocean. But Nate's voice was so kind, a note of hesitation, a note of pride. I couldn't tell him to undo it. "Nate." On the boardwalk from the house, my mom walked down to the beach. "Okay. Same boat I arranged for?"

"Same boat. Same time," Nate said. "I'll be there."

I hung up as my mom came over and draped her arm around my shoulder. "That was Nate," I said. "There's a been a change in plans."

Mom's eyebrows drew together, her white sundress wrapping around her legs in the breeze. "No changes in plans today," she said, hands on her hips. "I have myself prepared for the exact plan we planned and no other plan. Not today."

Out in the ocean, the gray water churned, all frothy whitecaps, all crash and pop and rush of waves, the lines of light fading. I mirrored my mom, hands on my hips. "Nate decided to take us out. Everything else is still the same plan."

Mom's shoulders lowered, and I put my arm around her, her skin warm from salt or sweat or both, I couldn't tell. "That was kind of him," she said.

"I don't want him to do it. But I can't say anything," I said. "He meant well."

"You can say something," she said. "You don't have to run away from everything."

I sat in the sand, petulant. "This from the woman who only has headspace for one plan."

She sat beside me. Put her head on her knees. "He should be here with all of us. Your dad," she said. "That takes up most of my headspace."

"We're all here together because he's not," I said.

Joshua and Aunt Gwen ran out of the water, dripping, shaking sand off towels, and sat with us. "Aunt Sarah, guess what?" Joshua said. "I was born in a Jacuzzi."

Mom tousled Joshua's hair. "Wet boy," she said. "You should go jump in the Jacuzzi now." Joshua nodded and ran off, kicking up sand in his wake.

"Nate is going to take the kids and I out this afternoon now," Mom said to Aunt Gwen.

"Oh, well that'll be—" My Aunt Gwen liked to leave her sentences unfinished, flapping like laundry on a clothesline.

That'll be nice?

That'll be an unexpected invasion of privacy?

That'll be only the hardest thing I've ever done with someone there who I'm pretty sure I do not want to be there.

"That'll be nice," I said.

———

We didn't dress up. I put my hair in braids. James wore a baseball cap, and Mom tied a scarf patterned in red chili peppers over her head. And at four o'clock we put my dad in the trunk and went down to the marina.

Evie was there, one hand underneath her stomach, one on her hip. James and I carried the cardboard box together through the marina parking lot, down to the dock. We set him down, and I kept my foot in front, touching the box, to ward off the image of it slipping into the water. The Pamlico was brown and choppy under the cloudy sky, halyards clanking on boat masts like tone-deaf wind chimes.

"I just thought I'd come see you off," Evie said. "Then I have to get back to work." Her hair blew across her face, and she brushed it back.

"I'm glad you did," I said. Evie. I wanted her there. I hugged her to me, hollowing my stomach around hers.

Evie squeezed my shoulder, dark shadows under her eyes. "It looks choppy out there," she said. "You're probably going to do some bouncing."

Nate climbed out of the boat and onto the dock. Long legs and windblown hair, serious face. Why did I feel guilty, and annoyed, and apprehensive, and sad, all at the same time, by the fact that he was there? It was just Nate, being kind. Mom gave him her hand,

and he helped her in the boat; it bobbed low on the water, a small, twenty-five-foot fishing trawler with a red hull named *Glory*. Mom sat on a makeshift bench in the bow of the boat, her feet bumping into a cooler. James jumped in beside her and tightened his baseball cap down. Nate lifted the ashes in and set them at Mom's feet, and I got in too. I waved to Evie as we left the dock.

The engine was loud and throaty and smelled like tires. Nate steered the boat out of the harbor, into the sound, opened up the throttle, and we skipped and bounced across the water. From the boat, the land of Hatteras arched into the Pamlico, unbearably narrow. How was it still here at all, after all those years, all those storms? How much longer could it possibly withstand? Water splashed over the sides of the boat, salty and warm, soaking me and James. Mom pushed the box of ashes farther under the bow and covered the front with her legs. "I can just see them dissolving," she shouted.

"Going to be a wet ride," Nate called around the wheel enclosure to us. James turned his hat around backwards and kept one hand on top of his head.

We motored past the last of the houses specking the shoreline, past the bare land at the tip end of Hatteras, through the inlet, and out into the ocean, then back north. If I stayed focused on the splashes of water over the side of the boat, the stick of my tank top against my stomach, the rush of wind, and the stacks of gray clouds thick as cottonballs, I could almost forget what we were about to do. Now, on the ocean side, the pattern from the earlier part of the ride reversed, and empty beach gave way to tall houses perched on the edge of a flat ribbon of sand. The water was greener than the sound, clear and deep. Every time the boat hit the trough of a wave, we got wet. I checked under the bow that the box was dry; Mom gave me a thumbs up.

"There's our house," James said, pointing. Aunt Darcy stood on the beach, her hair platinum and startling even from a distance. She waved, and I imagined her waving at every boat she saw, wondering if it were us. The boat bounced on. Mom took off her chili pepper scarf and stuffed it in her pocket, the outline of the peppers visible through the wet fabric of her dress. We passed the pier in Frisco that stretched out into the Atlantic; James and I used to like to try to walk to it from the campground beach, but we always gave up after the first mile.

"Isabel Inlet," Nate yelled over the motor. He pointed at the stretch of beach that had been washed out by Hurricane Isabel. It was built back up now, sand pumped in, dunes restacked, Highway 12 laid back down. The only difference was a brighter shade of tar on the road, but that wasn't visible from the water. Nate slowed the boat after the next row of beach homes. On the shore, the campground beach was empty of houses, empty of people. Nate cut the engine. The silence was sudden, overwhelming. We rocked on the waves, water slapping the sides of the hull.

My stomach tightened; the ride was over. *No.* Mom squeezed my hand, then took her scarf out and retied it at the back of her head. The boat swayed as Nate walked to the stern. He sat down on the side and looked south over the water, away from us. James opened the cardboard box, the sides scraping against each other. He and Mom lifted out the urn. It looked more like a giant white ravioli than the sombrero I'd been imagining; silly and tragic all at the same time. The edges of the biodegradable paper urn were clipped together with staples, one holding a circular I.D. tag. *McConnell*. My dad, my whole entire dad, inside a ravioli. The boat rocked gently as they set him on the bow.

Mom placed her hand on top of the urn.

"What do we do now?" James asked.

My father—geologist, church eschewer, teller of bedtime stories involving quarks and leptons, dark matter, and the expanding universe—hadn't wanted prayers or ceremony. Mom took a piece of paper out of her pocket. It sagged over on itself. "I was going to read a poem," she said. "It's too wet."

I touched the urn, rough and thick and papery under my palm. My dad—his chipped front tooth and his hyena laugh and the way he could do math without a calculator—this was what was left of him, the last fragments of who he'd been, ground down now into ash and bits of bone. His body that had started as that impossible, invisible collision of molecules, soft and alive, now ash and bits of bone—his chipped front tooth, was it still in there, inside that ravioli?—and now I even had to let the ash and bits of bones go. I had to let him go. As impossible as it was that he'd been here at all, that any of us are, that the universe sprang out of a collision of—what—nothingness— from nothing, from nothing; that Hatteras is here at all, a barrier island, its sand composed from fragments of long-dead sea creatures, an island arched into the sea—impossible, all of it. That it won't be here for long, that geologically we're all already less than a blink, nothing, that someday soon Hatteras will be covered in water, nothing but water, nothing, nothing. What comfort is it that my body was made from his, that I might one day have children who carry the spirals of his DNA? What comfort is that? None at all, just more impossibles. As impossible as it had been to watch my dad's light fade and go out, to watch him die, to watch him leave and his body become just a body, an already decomposing body, it was now impossible to let his body, to let these last bits of ground-down ash and bone, go. Impossible to let him go.

"Bye, Dad," James said.

"I love you," Mom said. She searched her pockets and pulled out a tissue, but it was wet, too. She wiped her nose with her left hand.

"How should we put it over?" I asked.

"Together," Mom said.

We circled around the urn, hands crossing over each other. We leaned over the side of the boat, but we couldn't all fit and still hang on, so Mom let loose. James and I bent over with one hand each and the urn touched the water, slipped in. It sank fast and was gone.

Gone.

Mom and James and I, then, just us, swaying together as the boat rocked on the salty waves, Mom and James and I stitched together, if you could see it, the invisible pulsating cords of grief twisting and spiraling from our chests, braiding together into one great keen, our shoulders touching, the energy rising into one solid column of *gone*.

On the ride back, the wind and sea spray cooled my face, and the island ribboned out against the sea, and gulls cawed, and pelicans flapped, and rain misted. Water no longer splashed up over the sides. Our clothes dried, sticky with salt, against our skin.

"Look," Nate yelled, pointing out over the ocean. I looked, expecting dolphins. But it was a rainbow, pale and arcing through the clouds. Nate slowed the boat, stopped.

Mom grabbed my arm, grabbed James's arm.

"It's not raining," James said.

And it wasn't. The mist had stopped. The colors glowed against the gray sky.

"It's double," I said, pointing. A fainter rainbow shadowed the bright arc.

Here's the science of a rainbow—photons, water droplets, reflection, refraction. White light scattering into seven different colors. Crisp geometric angles, sun to droplet. That's about it. And the mythology—a bridge between the gods and humanity, a link between heaven and earth. A link between this world, with its sand and bone, to something made entirely of spirit, invisible, impossible. My dad, the ashes of his body right now merging with the swirling sand of the ocean floor, would have admired the dispersion and reflection and refraction. Me, always looking for the poetry and the metaphor, always searching for the *why*, for the inexplicable and irrational and impossible, was it so hard for me to believe for a moment that the column of our grief had risen to the sky, had met the lingering energy from the leaping synapses in my dad's brain and refracted into magic, that whatever it was that gave him his *himness*, wasn't entirely gone, to admire dispersion and goddesses and geometric angles and miracles—to believe, just for a moment, in both?

———

That night, there was Michael.

And Nate, and Evie, and Evie's parents, and Aunt Fay. Everyone at the big house on the edge of the ocean, a cacophony of conversation and movement, our own little wake for my dad.

Michael arrived while we grilled dinner, an orange-red sunset pouring through the gaps in the thick clouds.

"That boy's got balls the size of buckeyes showing up here to-night," Aunt Darcy muttered to me as we set the table.

"Buckeyes seem pretty proportional, Aunt Darcy," I said.

"Maybe grapefruits," she said. "Something big and ball-shaped." Aunt Darcy stood with a hand on her hip. She'd changed into dinner-wear, a hot pink and teal flowing caftan and rhinestone-covered heels.

She passed me a handful of forks, but I dropped them. They clattered brightly on the glass tabletop. "He's practically family," I said. "Besides, we're friends."

"Troia does seem fine," Aunt Darcy said. She smoothed out a blue-striped place mat.

Troia and Michael stood together on the deck, watching the sky, both of them with arms crossed over their chests, but chatting and smiling. I went out beside them. "Emmett made sangria," I said. We filled up cups and walked through the house, past Evie organizing seashells with Aunt Gwen, past Mrs. Austin and Nate playing foos-ball, down to the pool. Troia sat in a lounge chair. Michael and I hung our legs into the pool and watched Joshua and Sean chase each other in a made-up game of tag on rafts in which Sean pretended to be an attacking taco.

"Dare me?" James stood on the railing of the first-floor deck, lean-ing out over the pool. He jumped before anyone could answer, can-nonballing into the water. Sean and Joshua ducked away, yelling. "Dude, you've got to try that," James said to Sean.

"Can't you act like a normal person?" Sean asked him. "I know you're not a normal person, but you had to have at least met one once, so couldn't you just pretend?"

"There's something in the pool," Joshua said. He pointed to the corner of the shallow end. "Besides us."

Sean dived down to where Joshua had pointed. "It's a crab," he said. "We're swimming with crabs. And it's alive." He splashed over to the steps and climbed out of the pool.

Troia got a cleaning net and scooped up the crab. She brandished it toward us like a pirate with a sword until the crab moved and she screamed at the surprise of it. Troia flung the crab over the fence, its claws flailing in the air.

"My heart can't take that kind of action," Troia said. "I'm going for more sangria."

Michael watched her go. "We're being friends," he said. He put his cup by the pool on the concrete.

"Friends is good," I said.

"Some of my best friends are McConnell women," he said.

———

At dinner, Nate and Evie sat across from me, Michael on my right, our elbows brushing. Troia was sandwiched between Sean and Aunt Fay at the far end. My family jostled and crowded around the table, talking, laughing all over each other, the swirl of four or five conversations all at once.

Michael cut into the ribeye Mr. Austin and Emmett had grilled. "Everyone seafooded out?" he asked.

"Never," I said. "But we had to represent the Midwest somehow."

"Go cows," Michael said.

Evie shifted in her chair and bumped into my mom.

"How are you feeling, Evie," Mom asked.

Evie blew her bangs out of her eyes. "I feel like hell, and I have to pee," she said.

"Those sure are cute shorts," Mom said to Evie. No pee talk at the dinner table.

"Don't look behind me when I sit down," she said. "They're unzipped. On this end of the island all we've got is tube tops and bikinis for people like her," Evie said, gesturing at me with her fork. "Want to make a pregnant-lady-store run up the beach next Tuesday?" she asked me.

"She might not be here next Tuesday," Mom said. "If she comes home with us."

Evie frowned. "Are you?" she asked. She chewed her asparagus a little more slowly.

"No," I said. "I don't think so. I'm not."

"If you need to go, go," Evie said.

"I have a job, you know," I said to my mother. "At the inn. It isn't just Mr. Austin being nice. I actually do stuff."

"Some rainbow tonight, huh?" Nate said. I mouthed *thank you* to him for changing the subject.

"We all saw it from the house," Aunt Darcy said. "'There's Cal giving us a sign,' I said to Emmett. Tell them what you said, Emmett."

"I said, 'If Cal was giving us a sign, it'd be a race car or a dinosaur, not some rainbow,'" Emmett said. He brandied his fork in the air for emphasis.

"A dinosaur?" I asked. "You thought my father would send you a dinosaur?"

Emmett shrugged. "Sure be a miracle, wouldn't it?"

"If God sends burning bushes, why not dinosaurs?" Michael asked.

"I was a dinosaur, once," Joshua said.

"For Halloween?" James asked.

Joshua wrinkled his nose. "No."

———

After dinner and loading the dishwashers, we drifted off in small groups, drinking sangria, reading, playing table tennis, talking, working on a puzzle. Evie fell asleep on the sofa. Nate sat in a chair across from me. Right there, but also far away.

"I'd better get Sleeping Beauty home soon," he said.

"Thanks for taking us out today," I said. "And for, you know, letting us be by ourselves on the boat."

Nate squinted. "Did you think I was going to try to lead a funeral service or something?"

"I don't know."

"I just wanted to take you out to the right spot. He was your dad."

"Yeah," I said. "He was."

I leaned back, a percolating soreness in my veins, an energy like I'd been in a dentist's chair for the past eleven months and the anesthesia was just wearing off. I said good night to Nate and spiraled down the stairs to walk the beach.

On the lower level of the house, Michael put down his table tennis paddle. "Doing all right?" he asked.

I stretched, arms over my head, spine elongating, muscles awake. Percolating, percolating. "I'm taking a walk," I said.

He followed me—just like I hoped he would.

The sand was damp, the moon covered with low rolling clouds. "It's going to be weird to swim," I said. "With him there."

Michael put his arm around my shoulder, squeezed. We were

friends. Friends do things like that. The electrical quickening of my skin beneath his hand meant nothing. "Remember the carbonate fractions in the sand?" he asked.

It was from the book we'd been reading. "The part of the sand that comes from things that once lived." I remembered. A breeze kicked up, licked over my arms and legs and neck. I shivered and leaned into the cottony dampness of Michael's shirt.

"Fact: the beaches around here radiocarbon-date to between seven and nine thousand years old," he said.

"Fact," I said. Facts felt good. Facts felt safe and secure. "Some shells near Buxton are forty thousand years old. Too old to radiocarbon-test."

"Amino acid dating instead," he said.

In forty thousand years, some scientist would amino acid date my dad's bones that were part of the sea floor, thinking they were shells. Above our heads, galaxies wheeled in motion, gasses colliding into starbursts, into new stars. Black holes swallowing old ones, succumbing to the suck of their gravitational pull.

"I believe in you," he said. "If you're not okay right now, that's okay."

He believed in me. "How about you," I asked. "Are you okay?"

"That's too many 'okays' to consider."

We stopped walking and sat down, waves crashing, sediments stirring, life and death and the unbearable briefness of it all, invisible, all around us. How thin this bar of sand must look from the sky, arched into the sea. The breeze flowed over my arms and legs and neck. I wanted to drape my arm over his knee, trace the constellation of freckles that I couldn't see but knew was there. I wrapped my arms around my chest instead.

His knuckles, in the sand, brushed my upper thigh. I shouldn't even be imagining it. I uncrossed my arms, rested my hand beside his. How many light years away were those galaxies meeting, the invisible edges of their energy pulsating, drawing them together? He interlaced his fingers with mine. Mine with his. Whose hand squeezed first? I don't know. Did it matter? What I needed more than anything, in that moment, was the pressure of his hand in mine. The electric, forbidden spark that consumed everything.

My head, full, on his chest, his heartbeat, the ocean waves, the starbursts, reeling. His hand, sandy, on my thigh, kneading the skin beneath the hem of my white shorts. His touch, rougher, my response, deepening, our faces, close. Our bodies taut.

Energy and matter are essentially the same. Light years upon light years of speed the only difference between me, on this damp sand made from creatures that lived forty thousand years ago, and pure, invisible energy; only speed between the friction of my skin on his and the galaxies reeling. Light years of rushing speed; his lips on mine, our tongues, quick and light. Energy and matter, identical.

I should not be kissing him; we should not be doing this.

I pressed closer against him, kneaded the muscles of his back. His hands moved over my breasts, and I grabbed the back of his head, pulled our bodies together again.

"Charlotte," he said into my hair. I kissed his lips, his cheeks, his eyelids, the top of his head. He buried his mouth in my neck. I wrapped my right leg over his left, drawing him into me. My head was in his hands, his mouth along my neck, my collarbone, his hair brushing my clavicle as he kissed my breasts through the cotton of my shirt. I grabbed his head and cried out from the heat of his mouth.

"Charlotte," he said again. He lifted the shirt over my head and sucked in a short breath, then brought his mouth to me. I pulled away then, sat back, and looked at him. I should want him to stop, I should think of Troia, of Nate, of anyone and anything other than Michael and the incandescent energy of his body.

Light years of speed are the only thing between us and the streaming stars. I grabbed a handful of his shirt and pulled it over his head. "Are we doing this?" He wrapped his arms around me, bareness on bareness. His lips and my lips, his tongue and my tongue. We fell back in the sand. I wrapped myself around him, starlight rushing through my hair, and drew him close, close, closer.

———

Back at the house, Michael and I skirted around to the driveway without going inside, still holding hands. His truck was blocked in. We stood and stared. Troia's car.

He squeezed my hand. "I'll do it." He tousled some sand out of his hair and walked in the front door.

I sat on the porch steps, the cicadas and peepers and soft breeze that usually lulled me now mixed in with the anxiety shock and thrum of guilt of seeing Troia's car up against Michael's. I checked my phone. Three missed calls from Nate. Two from Troia. Three from my mom. One from James.

I put down my phone. My whole body still vibrated from Michael's touch. Michael. What I had just done. The whirl and spiral of galaxies coalesced in my body, just me now, just me and what I had done, reverberating. I paced up and down the driveway. What did I feel? Guilt, anxiety. But awake and alive, alive, alive. Percolation rushing through my veins. Guilt for not feeling guilty enough. How could I have done that? How could I have not? What was I supposed to do now that I'd been shaken back into my body, into myself? I checked my phone.

Text messages. Nate. *Hey, something's up with Evie, where are you?*

Another. *I might need a hand. Evie's got a fever, I think.*

More. *Mom wants to take her up the beach to the ER.*

Again. *Trying to find Stephen, you know where he is?*

Troia. *Where are you?*

Troia. *Evie looks unwell.*

Troia. *For real, something is wrong.*

Evie. Something was wrong.

Troia, walking out the front door with Michael, Troia with the porch light reflecting off her hair, Troia, standing beside him, standing where she'd stood for years, her side of their pair. Michael broke away from her and jogged down the steps to me. I went to him, unthinking, magnetized. Stopped myself.

"Where were you?" Troia said. "Evie's sick, and Nate can't find Stephen." She ran down the steps and hugged me, her skin smooth against the grit of sand in my shirt.

Panic burrowed in my stomach. Panic, guilt. "She has a fever? Is she okay? Is the baby okay?" How was Troia touching me right now, touching me when I'd touched him.

"Her parents took her up to Nags Head. We couldn't find you anywhere." She brushed sand off the inside of her arm from where she'd hugged me. Light reflected off the sand in Michael's hair, Michael's arms, in tiny sparkles. "Or Michael."

"Can you all move your cars so I can get up there?"

Troia stood very still. Tuning in to something, as if she sensed the energy around Michael and me, the residual vibrations of the collide. "I'll take you up," she said slowly. "I'd like to see Evie."

"I can drive," Michael said.

I rubbed my gritty forehead. How did those constellations feel after the magnetic crash? Dizzy, sick, unsettled? "I want to go by myself."

Troia still stood unnaturally still. "Your car will be free once I move mine," she said to Michael. "I'm driving her up."

I didn't have anything left in me to protest again. Nothing but a whirlpool of guilt and worry. "Let's go."

———

I sat in Aunt Gwen's Volvo with my feet on the seat, arms around my knees. The road lulled rhythmically under the car, a feeling that usually relaxed me. I felt sticky with guilt, gritty with stardust. Troia flipped on the radio. She pressed the scan button, and stations fizzed past, finally settling on an advertisement for a crab shack in Norfolk.

"Are you cold?" she asked, glancing over at me.

"I'm fine." I eased my grip on my knees and put my feet on the floor. "Actually, I'm kind of warm."

"Traditional windows or AC?" Troia asked. It was our custom to keep the windows down for as long as possible on trips up the island so we could smell the salt air. Ohio air smelled like grass and leafy green trees, sometimes cows. Beach air was different—salty, and soft, and to be savored.

"Windows," I said. I thought the wind would inhibit talking.

Troia pushed the window button and cranked the radio louder. The cool air rushed over my face, and I leaned my head back against the seat, thinking of Michael, of Michael's face near mine. Then thinking of Evie, of her tight face at dinner, the way her voice had an edge of coldness.

Troia touched my arm, and 1 jumped. She brushed sand off me, rubbed her fingers together. "You're so sandy."

1 crossed my arms over my chest. "1 guess 1 am chilly," 1 said.

Troia rolled the window up, the radio suddenly too loud. Johnny Cash singing about being lost in a sea of heartbreak.

Troia snapped off the radio. "Songs about breakups, right?"

"1 never thought the man in black would make you sad," 1 said.

"Go figure," Troia said.

We rolled to a stop at the red light in Waves. Waterfall Park flanked the sides of the road, the corkscrew waterslide on the right and bumper cars on the left. "See this scar?" 1 showed her a line on my left elbow.

It was too dark in the car and Troia squinted and shook her head.

"It's from Dad plowing over me on that waterslide. He had James on his back, and 1 was too skinny to create any velocity and got stuck in the middle. 1 thought 1 was going to drown when they ran over me."

"1 wish 1 could've come down here more with you guys when 1 was growing up," Troia said. She drove on past the gas stations and T-shirt shops as Waves blended into the village of Rodanthe.

"We'll have to have family vacations when we have kids," 1 said. 1 bit my lip. Crap.

"1 always thought they'd be with Michael," she said. "So, you and Michael were walking on the beach tonight?"

"Yeah," 1 said. My face burned. 1 wanted to tell her. She'd given me an opening and everything.

Don't be mad, but Michael and I have this connection.
It's really rare for me to feel this way about someone.
I mean, technically you're not with him. You guys aren't together.
I did something. We did something.
It's like, constellations, you know?

I couldn't. We drove past the last tall houses, erosion forcing their stilted legs into the undulating sea, and out of Rodanthe, sliding back into darkness.

———

A spotlight illuminated the yellow logo of outstretched sun rays over the Outer Banks Hospital's front door. Yellow hurricane shutters angled over tall windows and pampas grass lined the driveway. The building was cream and blue and looked more like a beach cottage than a hospital. Troia and I found Mr. and Mrs. Austin sitting in plastic chairs in a waiting room on the second floor.

"How is she?" I asked. I sat down beside them.

Mrs. Austin answered. "It had a long name, but what she has is a urinary tract infection. They put her on IV antibiotics, and now they wait and see that it doesn't spread. If it spreads to the womb, they'll have to induce labor."

Mr. Austin stood up and put his arm around my shoulder. "We figure we'll stay here for the night just in case. Have you heard from Stephen?"

I shook my head no and sat down.

"Can we see her?" Troia asked.

"We're allowed in to visit, but she was asleep, so we came out here," Mr. Austin said. "Her room's nice, though. Got a sofa and everything."

Fluorescent lights hummed above us.

"They said the next twelve hours would be critical," Mrs. Austin said. Her face was drawn and tired, but it struck me how much she and Evie resembled one another. She kept talking, more sentences than I'd ever heard her speak at one time before. "They said that Evie probably didn't notice the signs of it because it was just having to pee a lot. Well, she always has to pee a lot. How could she tell? They said it could sneak up on you real quick."

Troia sat down beside me. "She's here where they can watch her, and she's stable, so that's good," she said. She turned to me. "We'll stay with you all. We'll stay here."

———

I wandered the hospital, finding the vending machine, the third-floor atrium, the small chapel with its illuminated cross and terra-cotta pots of brightly colored fake flowers.

I didn't do anything that wrong, right?

I sat down in a pew, the polished wood sleek under my thighs. I'd abandoned my friend when she was sick, and I'd betrayed my cousin. And still, all I wanted to do was go back down the island and find Michael, wind my fingers into his hair. Ride wave after wave of incandescence.

Where do I go from here, Dad? Like I'd have talked to my dad about this sort of thing. This was firmly in friend territory. I'd abandoned my friend.

Okay, Dad. Or God. Or glimmering constellations and really old sea-shells. Someone please tell me what to do.

Nothing but the quiet hum of electric lights, my dad gone, the starlight faded, and I was suddenly so tired. I wound my way back to the hallway outside Evie's room, pushed two chairs together, and dozed. When I woke up Nate was in a chair beside me. I smiled at him, then I remembered. I sat up stiffly and stretched my neck, trying to place myself in this new reality. Troia slept in the chair beside me, curled over on herself. Evie's parents weren't there. I'd been on the beach, been with Michael; my body flushed with the memory. "I went for a walk and didn't see your messages," I said. *Liar. Why are you such a liar?* "Did you find Stephen?" Stephen, the real villain, who was probably out drinking with his buddies while Evie got sick.

"He's in with Evie," Nate said. He ran a hand through his hair. No sand. God, I'd used him as a prop to dodge my grief. He was kind, and I used him. Another layer streamed through my guilt flood, thick with sediment. "She's awake."

"I should go see her." Because I couldn't sit there with him anymore. Because I'd abandoned Evie.

Evie was in one of the two labor and delivery rooms. It had a shiny cherry wood floor and a wallpaper border of dancing teddy bears. Stephen sat on the couch, and Evie was in bed, monitors around her stomach, TV remote in her hand.

"Did you ever really look at walruses?" she asked me. Her cheeks were flushed, but she still looked pale.

I sat on the edge of the bed beside her and stared up at the animals on the television. "Pretty serious buck teeth going on," I said.

Stephen stood up. "I can leave you alone to talk," he said.

"You just got here," I said. It felt good to narrow my eyes at him. Evie rested her head back on the pillow.

"I'm just going to go get some coffee," Stephen said. He walked out of the room.

Evie kicked her feet out from under the covers, chipped purple nail polish on her toes. "He's going through a lot," she said.

"So are you, right?" I said.

Evie jiggled the remote. "I'll be okay. Where were you tonight?"

"I was out on the beach with Michael," I said. "I had my phone off." I patted Evie's hand and said she should rest.

From behind me, in the doorframe, Nate cleared his throat. "You were with Michael tonight?"

Anxiety shock, guilt whirlpool. "Yeah," I said.

Nate crossed his arms. Nodded once.

I looked down at my feet, at the pale streaks from my flip-flop tan, the small line of bare nail that had grown out in the two weeks since I had painted my toes, the same day I'd done Evie's nails purple. Evie turned off the walruses and closed her eyes. I looked back up at Nate. He turned away without saying a word.

Fourteen

The next morning, Evie looked like herself. Still pale, but the brightness had faded from her cheeks. She'd changed from Animal Planet to the History Channel and was watching a documentary about Mata Hari. Stephen sat in a chair in the corner, his eyes focused on the television set. I'd left Nate and Evie's parents and Troia in the cafeteria after breakfast.

"Did you know that my feet will never be the same size again?" Evie asked.

"Really?" I said.

Evie shifted in bed, pulling the clear cord that ran fluid into her arm out of the way. She draped it across the bed railing. "Whatever makes your pelvic bones pliable also changes your feet."

"Good thing you basically wear flip-flops," I said.

"These are the things no one tells you," Evie said. "I wonder what else they're keeping secret about this whole baby deal."

Stephen cleared his throat. "Now that's someone I'd divulge my secrets for."

I rolled my eyes at Evie, but she didn't smile.

Nate poked his head in the room and paused with his hand on the doorjamb.

"Hey," Evie said to him.

"I'll come back," Nate said. He didn't look at me.

"Wait," Evie said. "Are you going back down the island today? I need a few things."

"Yeah," Nate said. "Listen, I'll come back in a few minutes." And he left.

"What was that all about?" Evie asked. She frowned and turned the volume on the TV down.

"I was watching that," Stephen said. He didn't take his eyes from the screen.

"Maybe she wants to talk," I said to him.

Evie turned the volume back up. "What's up with Nate?" she asked me.

I studied the wallpaper border of dancing bears. "He's upset with me," I said.

"Why?"

"I don't want to talk about it right now," I said. I glanced at Stephen and raised my eyebrows.

"Relax," Stephen said. "I'm not even listening."

Evie closed her eyes and sighed. "What happened?" she asked me. I didn't answer.

"Stephen, could you go grab me some water?" Evie asked.

Stephen turned his head to Evie. "I want to see how Mata Hari turns out," he said.

"She was tried for espionage and executed," I said.

Stephen shrugged, then walked over and kissed Evie on the cheek. "I'll get that water," he said, and left.

I rubbed my forehead, a headache forming behind my eyes. "Nate's upset about the *Michael* part of 'I was out walking with Michael last night.'"

"Why?" Evie asked. "You were just walking," Evie said. She pushed herself up in bed, flinching as her hand bent the IV.

The toppling feeling in my stomach was becoming second nature. "Walking," I said. The headache throbbed harder. "Maybe a little more."

"What? Why? How much more?"

I needed it. Him.

It was magic.

All of it.

"I didn't mean for it to happen. I didn't plan it."

"How much more?" Evie asked, her face tight.

If I turned my head just right looking out her window, I could see the shore. "All of it."

"You know Nate's in love with you, right?" Evie asked. "You know you were supposed to fall in love with him and get married and move down here and we'd be a big family?"

Did I know that? Of course, I did know he was in love with me, just like I knew I was in love with Michael.

"You never bothered to find out how he feels," Evie said. She crossed her arms over her stomach. "You ruined everything. Why don't you just go home?"

"Troia and I are going back to the beach house soon," I said.

"No, I mean *home*, Charlotte," Evie said. "Go back to your nice little college and your Midwest and your family," Evie said.

Stephen walked back in the room with a pitcher of water. He set it on Evie's table and poured some in her pink plastic cup.

"Thanks," Evie said.

"Could we have a couple more minutes?" I asked.

"This is my husband," Evie said. "I know you don't support my marriage, and I don't need that right now."

My whole body was a tight knot. "I just want to finish talking," I said.

"We're finished," Evie said. "But have you talked to Troia?"

Stephen put his hand on the top of Evie's head.

"Go talk to your cousin, or I will," Evie said. "Then go home."

"You know what, Evie?" I said. I wanted to tell her that I'd only just begun to feel my own feet again, here on these shifting sands, and I had no idea how to do that back home, back at school, back where the old me used to exist. How did I fall from all that starlight and magic into this hollow pit where I'd hurt everyone? And I still wanted him anyway. How could I just go back? How could I stay here? "Maybe you're right."

———

I went outside into the bright, hot day. A seagull cawed, wheeling above my head against the sun, the morning already sticking to my skin. My cell phone rang in my pocket, and I jumped.

"Hi sweetie." My mom. "How's Evie?"

"She hates me," I said. "But she's okay."

"She hates you? Why?"

"I did something, Mom," I said. "Evie and Nate, they're mad. Troia's going to be hurt."

"Do you need me to come get you?"

I moved under an awning, sat in the shade. I did; I needed my mom to come get me, to drive me down to Hatteras and help me pack and take me home. *Talk to your cousin or I will.* "Troia and I will be home soon." Home. "Back to the beach house."

———

Troia and I drove with the windows down, our hair blowing. The radio stayed silent. We rolled past South Nags Head and the Bodie Island lighthouse, went over the three miles of the Bonner Bridge.

"I hate this bridge," Troia said.

I nodded.

I think I might love him.

If this bridge collapses and we die right now, I will not regret last night. But I lied to you.

By the time we hit Bodie Island, I couldn't take it anymore, the whirl of guilt in my stomach spinning into a hurricane. "I was on the beach with Michael last night," I said.

"I noticed," Troia said. She raised an eyebrow.

"I kissed him," I said. I just said it. "I kissed Michael." My face burned.

Troia didn't stop driving. She didn't jerk the steering wheel or run the car off the side of the road. "You kissed Michael," she said, looking straight ahead.

"I kissed Michael. Or Michael kissed me. We kissed."

"Last night?" she asked. "Before Evie?"

"Yes."

"What else?"

Out the window, sea oats undulated in golden waves over the gently rolling dunes. What else? Only wild magic, only the centrifugal spin of me coming back to myself, coming into him. What else? "More."

Troia drove silently, into Rodanthe, coasting on down the island through Waves and Salvo. The light was green at Waterfall Park, lines of children and parents winding up the waterslide. It seemed stupid to apologize, to say anything, so I was quiet too.

Troia stared ahead at the road. I focused on the other cars, pretended I was driving. At the first light in Avon, Troia spoke. "More," she said. "More, and you intend to do it again?"

I scrabbled along the edges of the abyss, stomach turning, head pounding. Troia. What I'd done. "You can't hate me," I said. "Please."

You can't hate me.

I can't lose another person.

But I deserve it.

Do I?

"Do you plan to do it again?" The light turned green. Troia's foot on the gas was quick and pressured, or maybe that was my imagination.

"I don't know," I said. "I shouldn't have done it. I'm sorry."

"You have feelings for him?"

"Maybe," I said. "Yeah."

"And Nate?"

I rubbed my forehead. I could still feel sand from last night. "Nate's like solid ground. I needed solid ground to find my feet again," I said. "Michael is currents and motion and life."

"Does Nate know this?" she asked.

I sighed. "He does now." Out the window, kiteboarders whirled and leapt across the sound at Canadian Hole, the water a bright stretch of blue. I closed my eyes, exhausted, empty, alone.

We rode the rest of the way to Hatteras in silence.

———

I found my mom sitting with Aunt Fay and Walter on the third floor back deck in a wooden swing, snapping the ends off fresh green beans and tossing them in a colander. The ocean stretched out blue and çalm, and the sky canopied the day.

Aunt Fay swore. "I keep throwing the crap ends in with the good." Walter lifted his head, his left ear flopping over while his right perked straight up. He settled back down, nuzzling his chin on the deck boards and licking his lips.

I sat down on the deck beside him. "What's for dinner tonight?" I picked up a bean and cracked the end off, thick and waxy in my hands. "Beside crap beans."

"Crap beans and cheeseburgers," Mom said. Her hair blew back from her face in the breeze.

"What's the Evie update?" Aunt Fay asked.

I threw my bean in the colander, picked up another. "She looked better," I said. My rib cage hurt when I thought of Evie, of Evie telling me to go home. "She kicked me out before I learned anything else." Mom and Aunt Fay must have thought I was joking. They didn't respond, just kept snapping their beans. The sounds of splashing rose from the pool three stories below, and Walter barked furiously. It would have been menacing if he weighed more than five pounds. I stood up and leaned over the railing.

"I'm not happy when my butt's cold," Sean said to James. He climbed out of the pool, hair streaming down his back. James followed, and they went inside the basement door.

I sat back down on the warm deck boards and looked up at my mom. I wanted to lay my head in her lap, have her pet my hair and tell me that everything would be all right. I leaned against the porch railing instead, coaxed Walter onto my lap, and twirled his silky hair around my finger. "I've messed everything up," I said.

Mom looked at me. "Messed what up?"

Walter jumped off my lap and pounced at a fly.

"Thinks he's a cat," Aunt Fay said. She stood up. "Better take him to do his business," she said. Walter followed her down the stairs, and I looked down to watch them emerge on the ground floor, Aunt Fay's gray head bobbing as she walked her sideways walk, Walter weaving around her feet.

"I hurt Troia," I said. "And Evie. And probably Nate." I brushed my hand back and forth across the ringed wooden planks of the deck. "Definitely Nate."

"Is it something that can be undone?" Mom asked.

"No." I got up and sat beside her on the swing, pulled my knees up, and wrapped my arms around my legs.

"What was it your dad always said? Best way to suck out poison is to—" she paused, looked at me, bit her lower lip. "Something about sucking, anyway. Facing up and sucking."

I leaned against my mother, her skin cool and sticky, smelling like sunscreen and salt. She put her arm around me. "So, what you're saying is, there'll always be suckage," I said.

"I believe in you," she said. "Whatever you did to hurt them, you can suck it out."

———

I texted Nate. *I'm sorry. You're such a good person.*

He replied. *You're sorry I'm a good person?*

You know what I mean, I wrote. Then: *I'm sorry for what I did.* Only I wasn't all that sorry. I deleted it. *I'm sorry that I hurt you. Can we stay friends?* Send.

We were more than friends, Nate wrote.

You're right, I wrote. *I'm sorry.* Again. Sucking the poison out.

It's fine, he wrote. Then a long pause. *You don't owe me anything.*

James and Sean orchestrated a campfire on the beach that night. I held Joshua's hand and watched as they dug a pit below the tide line.

"Charlotte," Joshua said. I was looking back at the house, the tall windows illuminated against the night. Troia was in there, not speaking to me, going in another room when I walked in. Joshua tugged on my hand, dropped it. "There's a 30 percent chance for scattered showers and thunderstorms this evening."

James looked up from his digging. "It always says that," he said.

Sean crouched down and tore up some newspaper to put under the logs. A tiny piece fluttered away into the night. My hair blew across my face, and I tied it back in a quick braid. One of the things I loved best about Hatteras was the wind. Everything was in motion. It made me feel so alive.

"Can you guys create a wind shield for me?" Sean asked.

Joshua put his hand back in mine, small and soft and malleable. We crouched around the fire pit, James on the other side. Above us, the stars pinpricked the night, dim against the round, low-hung orange fullness of the moon. The ocean rushed softly on the beach, and Sean's fire danced in tiny, licking flames.

"Is Troia coming?" James asked.

"I don't think so." I released Joshua's hand and stretched out in the sand, hands behind my head, squinting up at the sky. "There's Orion's belt," I said.

"Mom and Dad aren't coming to eat s'mores," Joshua said. "Aunt Darcy is. Uncle Emmett is. Michael is. Aunt Sarah said, 'You're going to get sticky.' But she's coming, too."

I sat up and looked back toward the house. "How do you know Michael's coming?" I asked Joshua.

"Troia said so."

Dark forms moved toward us. Aunt Darcy with her bright hair, my mom, her arm looped through Aunt Darcy's, Emmett's head towering behind them. No Michael.

"Get out the chocolate," Mom said.

Emmett spread out a blanket, and everyone sat down around the fire.

"Ghost crab," Sean said. A small, almost luminescent white crab skittered around the fire pit.

Aunt Darcy jumped up, edged away from the crab. "No, thank you," she said.

The crab fell down the slope and into the fire, claws grasping.

Joshua reached his hand toward the fire, drew it back at the heat. The crab stopped moving. "His goose got cooked," Joshua said.

"Snack, anyone?" Emmett asked.

Aunt Darcy sat back down, peered into the fire. "Poor little sucker," she said.

"At least we rescued the one from the pool yesterday." The voice came from behind me. Michael. He sat down beside me, rested his arms on his knees. "Nice fire," he said.

My heart pounded against my ribs. My heart a sudden meteor, bright tail flaming. "Our crab karma is breaking even," I said.

Michael's T-shirt flattened against his chest in the breeze. "We could go looking for a rescue mission if it'd make you feel better," he said. He stood up and held out his hand. I took it, could almost see the spark as our fingers met. We walked away from the fire, away from my family, down toward the silver moon-brushed waves. I heard James laugh and, for a moment, wanted to turn back.

"Evie still in Nags Head?" Michael asked. He was right beside me, and he felt so tall and solid, so bright and alive. He put his hands in his pockets.

I nodded. But I wanted his hand in mine. "She's pissed, but fine. The baby is fine."

"Pissed at you?" He was right beside me, so close, just Michael and me and the shimmer of the moonlight on the summer water, soft moonlight and the rush and stream of waves.

"She knows about us." It was the first time I linked Michael and me to an *us*. I looked over to gauge his reaction; he nodded out to the water. "Troia and Nate do, too."

"That was a lot of confessing," he said. "I was going to talk to Troia."

I wrapped my arms around myself. We walked down the beach. I knew the words I was supposed to say next. I tried to get them to form in my mouth, come unlodged from the back of my throat. *This is hurting people. We have to stop.* The moon rose higher in the sky, and the ocean stretched out silver to the horizon. I wanted to be brave and cool, tell him it was just a romp in the sand, that I had no feelings for him. That it was a stupid mistake. "Last night was a mistake," I said.

Michael raised his hand to the back of my head, stroked my hair. "When I talked to Troia, I'd planned on telling her that I wasn't sure what last night was, but that it was not a mistake."

I leaned into him. Together, we moved closer to the water, and a wave crashed, rushed up and over our bare feet, splashing the backs of our legs with water and little bits of wet sand.

I made myself say the next lines from the script in my head. "I'm not in any place to be with you," I said. "I'm barely myself again, and you're barely single."

Michael rubbed his foot over mine in the water, then bent down and sifted out some shells. "Forty thousand years, in my hand," he said. "If you need space, I'll back off."

The thought of space from him, of that solidness and magic and life evaporating into ether—no.

I turned to him, pressed my entire body into his as the waves crashed over our feet. "I don't want space. It wasn't a mistake."

And then I was back in the rush of incandescence, his mouth and mine, the thrum of waves, thick, salty air cascading over our bodies, starlight and the grit of sand. Science and magic, both. We moved up to dry sand, no more words, just me and Michael, together, alive.

Later, back at the campfire, we approached to the sound of Emmett leading a crooked verse of "Kumbaya" as Aunt Darcy rubbed his head and said he never was a very good hippie. Aunt Patsy had joined them, and Joshua curled against her side. James caught a marshmallow on fire, brandished it flaming into the air before blowing it out. He peeled off the blackened outside and offered it to me. Michael and I sat down, hands linked, energy thrumming around our bodies. My mom caught my eye and raised an eyebrow. I shrugged at her and squeezed Michael's hand. The blackened marshmallow dissolved in my mouth, woodsmoke lingering on my tongue.

Fifteen

T he next day was so blue and bright it hurt my eyes. The ocean lay flat and smooth as polished aquamarine. I'd seen bigger waves on Lake Erie. James griped that there was no surfing, so I surprised him with a mask and snorkel, and we splashed into the clear, cool water together. I floated on my stomach, dead man's float, letting the current drift me for as long as I could hold my breath. It was another world, rhythmic and weightless. My hair washed into my mouth, and I brushed it out and stood up. James's feet stuck up out of the water a few feet away, then he surfaced, too. He inspected a handful of sand and shells, shook them back into the water. He took off the mask and pulled the snorkel out of his mouth.

"Fish down there," he said. He extended the mask and snorkel toward me.

I took them, wiping his spit off the mouthpiece with my water-puckered thumb. The sun felt pointed and hot, like it was boring into my head. "You're not sick, are you?"

James splashed me. "Syphilis," he said, "and a bad case of the crabs."

"Probably from the campfire," I said. I rinsed off the mask and put it on, sticking the snorkel in my mouth. I put my head under, keeping one foot on the sand. The water settled around me and a small, nearly transparent fish flickered by. My hair stuck against the rubber strap of the mask, pulling; I stood up and took the mask off. "Did you notice Emmett's hair last night?" I asked.

James shook his head. "Einstein in a Hawaiian shirt," he said.

I leaned back and let a wave wash over my shoulders. Bright white clouds puffed across the sky. "It's so nice to have everyone here," I said. "I thought about making matching Outer Banks T-shirts for us, but I decided it was tacky."

"They make Ohio T-shirts," James said. He floated on his back, his hands figure-eighting at his sides. "Remember that place? Trees? Cows?"

I let my feet drift down into the sand, winnowing my toes around, and pulled up a shell. It was a thick gray clamshell, mottled and ugly. Definitely not forty thousand years old. I tossed it out into the water. "Landlocked?" I asked. "Kind of hilly?" I handed James the mask and snorkel.

James didn't say anything, just wriggled the mask on and dove under. When he surfaced, he was several feet away. I slogged through the water to get to him. "I'm going to tell school I'll be back for the January semester. I can come home for Christmas."

"Great," James said. "I'll start the chestnuts roasting now."

"I can't be there yet," I said. I looked at my brother, his eyes blood-shot from the salt, the green of his irises deep and bright. "There's this quote, right? By John F. Kennedy. 'We have the same percentage of salt in our blood that exists in the ocean. We're tied to it. Being by the sea is like going back from whence we came.'"

James looked at me. "Never say 'whence' again," he said. He body-surfed into the shore and walked away.

I sank back into the water, letting my head go under. Underwater, the throb and rush of small waves flopped on the sand, and a small fish slithered and darted against my leg. I tried to swat it away like I would a fly, but my arm moved slowly. *We are tied to the ocean.* I opened my eyes; the sunlight undulated through the waving surface of water. I raised my face back into the air.

———

My imaginary friends, when I was a kid playing alone on the beach before I met Evie, were named Laura and Maylene Scarborough, and they were characters from *Taffy of Torpedo Junction*. Laura, Maylene, and I, three sandy, brave, little girls, hunted for buried treasure and sculpted mermaids together in the sand. We foiled Nazis and rode our horses down the beach, manes flowing as they galloped. Laura and Maylene dissolved back into my imagination the day Evie found me on the sand dune at the top of campsite P68, but today they returned.

My family played and laughed and lounged and ate and swam all around me that afternoon, but I was alone. My dad was dead, his body gone, really gone, all the way gone. Did his ghost hover in the air anymore, even? Evie was angry and Troia was hurt, and Nate was stoic, and Michael was up the beach, and I was alone. I laid back on my beach towel, the heat of the sun penetrating through my skin. Laura and Maylene had long legs and full figures now, wore eyeliner and lazily paged through fashion magazines. Their fingers, slick with tanning oil, left marks on the pages as they turned them. They weren't as much fun as they used to be, but probably neither was I. Across the sand, Troia spiked a volleyball across a net to James, and he leaped into the air to return it. Troia, who had stiffly asked me to pass her the sunscreen before going back in the water.

That evening, with my family all around me, was full of noise and light and food; Laura and Maylene sat on the sidelines, texting their friends, snapping gum, their hair sleek and flat-ironed and deeply side-parted.

That night—all of us together, my dad gone, it was becoming normal that he was still gone, that he was all the way gone, that my family rippled and swelled around me. My family all around me, an impressionistic blur and swirl, and me, there in the middle, in the eye, alone without even my old grief or imaginary friends to keep me company.

———

At the end of the week, my family dropped me off at the inn before they left. Everyone piled out of their cars to say goodbye. Troia stayed close to Aunt Gwen's Volvo, bending down to check the pressure in the tires. Her hair fell over her shoulders, her arms and legs sunbrowned. I hugged James and then my mom, torn. Part of me wanted to climb into the passenger seat beside her, to read the map and fiddle with the radio knobs and listen to her talk about how to best rearrange the furniture in the family room as we drove home, to feel the road pull out behind me as the terrain changed from waving golden sea oats to flat swaths of green. And part of me still needed the open expanse of air and water, needed to be on Hatteras.

"I remember how you used to cry when we crossed the last bridge onto the mainland," Mom said. She tucked her hair behind her ears and pressed her lips together.

"Get a big turkey," I said. "And I'll make Mr. Austin's sweet potato pie, and we'll have a reunion for Christmas."

"Later," James said. He fist-bumped me.

I grabbed his head and planted a big kiss in his messy hair, then play-shoved him into the car.

Then I walked over to the Volvo, said goodbye to Aunt Gwen, and stood in front of Troia. "I'm sorry," I said. "I'm so sorry."

"I know this was a really hard week," she said. "But you broke girl code."

And so, I stood there, my guilt as thick as the island humidity, as Troia got in the car and closed the door.

Troia led the caravan of cars out onto Highway 12, her profile straight and calm as she drove away. I felt like I'd swallowed something sharp. I ran down the gravel driveway toward the road and watched the cars until I couldn't see them anymore. A rusted red truck rushed past me down the highway, leaving exhaust and dust in its wake.

I walked back up the hill and went inside the inn. My body felt separate from the compressed air-conditioned cold, isolated and empty. The quiet felt odd and overwhelming, my veins still vibrating with the reverberations of having family all around. No one was in the office, so I sat down in Mr. Austin's brown leather chair and picked up the phone. Evie didn't answer her cell. I looked up the number for the hospital in Nags Head and dialed. The nurses' desk patched me through to Evie's room.

"City morgue. You stab 'em, we slab 'em," Evie said.

"Hi," I said.

Evie was silent. When she answered, her voice was thin and tight. "Hello."

I traced my finger along the edge of the desk. "How are you? How's the baby?"

"Fine."

The phone crackled, a scratchy rustle like crumpling paper. "The family left today," I said. I spun around in the chair and studied the blue nautical maps on the walls.

"Tell them I hope they have a safe trip," Evie said. A high-pitched beeping sounded in the background, voices. "Was that all?" Evie asked.

The sharpness came back into my throat. I stood up, took the phone over to the window. Mrs. Austin knelt in the garden below, pulling weeds. Fat bees buzzed, and the peepers thrummed in the calm afternoon. "I guess so," I said. "That's all."

PART FIVE

September

Sixteen

I n September, on the first anniversary of my father's death, all the humidity dropped out of the air. The Outer Banks stretched and undulated, golden and cool and blue, crisp as fresh water. I swept sand out the inn's front door and stood outside, a pinprick against that vast blue sky. My grief, which had nestled deeper inside my chest these months, again expanded into all-encompassing on that first anniversary, once again a wild thing in my throat. I sat on the front step, head on my knees, then got out my phone to message Michael.

Michael, my Michael now, who I'd spent so many evenings pouring myself into. Michael, whose electrically charged body still met mine with a sizzle. I'd tried to talk myself into giving him up—out of guilt, out of girl code, out of the completely rational reason that we were both planning to leave the island soon and go back to our respective schools. I hadn't succeeded. The pull between us was too strong.

I closed the little message box and texted Troia instead. I'd texted or emailed her every day since she'd left the island to go back home, and every day she would respond cooly, but it was better than nothing. *First anniversary. You holding up?*

No answer.

I sent the same message in a group text to James and my mom, then I opened Michael's messages back up. *I'm not okay today.*

I can be there in ten.

I stood up, stretched, and walked through the inn and out the back door to the deck overlooking the sound. Mrs. Austin had hung wind chimes from the corner of the building, and they toned in the breeze, the afternoon sun sprinkling bits of light across the water as a guest in a straw hat strolled around in the garden below. The sliding screen door opened behind me, and I turned. Nate walked out onto the deck, holding a wriggling Walter in his arms.

"Damn dog," he said.

"I'll take him." I held out my arms, and Walter pushed free of Nate, landing with his paws on my chest and licking my nose. "Where's Aunt Fay?"

"Inside with Dad," he said. "She wants him to hang up some painting she did in the dining room."

I put Walter down, and he pranced around my legs. Nate went over to a chair and sat. I pulled another chair over and sat beside him. I still felt gritty around Nate. "I bought Walter a sweater the other day," I said. "When I went up to Nags Head."

Nate nodded. His hair had grown longer, curly. "I hope you got a color to complement his eyes," he said. He leaned back against the chair and stretched out his legs.

Walter sniffed along the edge of the deck, stopped, perked his head up. He barked once, loud and shrill, one paw poised. The door slid open again, and Aunt Fay came out in all her Aunt Fay-ness: corduroy jacket, fishing boots, windblown hair. "'It is a wild and miserable world, thorny and full of care,'" Aunt Fay said. She looked from me to Nate, resting her elbows on the deck railing. "Shelley." Walter pawed up at her boot. Aunt Fay reached down to pat his head, but he darted away and ran across the deck to the steps.

"Why all the thorniness?" Nate asked. "Dad not hanging your painting?"

"Get back here," Aunt Fay said to the dog, leaning forward. "The little shit will run right into the water and swim out too far." Walter barked and dashed down the steps, tearing around the garden and the hatted guest, fast and low to the ground, pink tongue out in a smile, hair blowing back. Aunt Fay followed Walter's path to the garden, standing in one spot, lunging as she tried to catch him while he ran by, missing every time. "Get me a crab net," she called to Nate.

Nate looked at me. I shrugged. We walked downstairs to the storage closet. It was damp and musty inside, and there wasn't enough air between Nate and me.

"Nate, are we okay?" I said before the anxiety at the thought of saying it overwhelmed me into keeping quiet.

Nate pulled down rafts and beach chairs. "Why wouldn't we be?"

I rummaged around the shed. "I very much had feelings for you," I said. Who was I, able to just *say* something like that? But I said it. I stacked kids' sand buckets and pushed aside a pile of skimboards. "I just wanted you to know."

Nate stood still, ran a hand through his hair. He started to speak, then stopped. "I'm glad you told me." He moved some paddles aside and looked behind them. "I'm here for you, if you need me," he said. "I mean, if you need a friend."

I sorted through a pile of sand rakes and found a crab net and handed it to Nate. We walked to the garden and gave it to Aunt Fay.

"This ought to be good," Nate said. He moved up toward Aunt Fay. It looked like he was ready to leap in if the situation warranted, but for now Nate crossed his arms and watched. Walter flashed by in a streak of black and tan.

Aunt Fay hoisted the net over her shoulder, ran out into the patchy grass, and took a swipe at Walter. She missed. Walter stopped running, looked at her, and took off again, this time toward the sound, his tiny legs pumping.

Footsteps clattered on the stairs, flip-flops thwacking the wood, and then Michael was standing beside me. "I heard a ruckus," Michael whispered in my ear. The thrill of his closeness chased up my spine.

Aunt Fay ran after Walter, swung the net down, and missed again. "It is a wild and miserable world out there, dog," she said. Walter ran, gave a leap, and landed in some marsh grass. He looked surprised at the texture of the ground and picked up his feet like he wanted all four of them up immediately, then trotted back to the edge of the garden and sat down. Aunt Fay walked over and picked him up, and Walter lolled, soggy, under her left arm.

"Good show," I shouted at them.

Nate turned to me and grinned, his face still summer-tan, teeth white and straight, then he saw Michael.

My guilt hit me in the chest again, morphing through my grief, wedging into my throat. In the months since my family had left the island to go home, Nate and Michael had yet to be in the same space.

"Hey, man," Michael said. He put his hand on my shoulder.

Nate raised his chin at Michael in greeting and walked over to us. Guy code. When would they ever go back to normal? When would girl code allow hanging out with Evie to feel right again? She hadn't frozen me out, but she hadn't exactly forgiven me, either.

Aunt Fay gave a half salute to us with her right hand and hoisted

Walter higher in her left. She walked around to the steps up to the back deck. "Wild and miserable," she said. "And thorny."

Michael squeezed my shoulder. Did he mean it as supportive and kind, or did he mean it to lay claim in front of Nate?

As the universe expands, it cools. The wild, miserable, thorny universe, stretching out into infinity, cooling as it grows. For the first time, I didn't want Michael touching me, didn't want anything intensifying me or the awkward grittiness in the air. I stepped away from them both and walked toward Aunt Fay and Walter.

Shelley wasn't wrong. It was a wild and miserable world, and Walter had the right idea to run.

———

There's a labyrinth tucked in the reeds and live oaks beside Our Lady of the Seas, the Catholic church that sits on the Pamlico Sound in Buxton. The labyrinth is a symbol of the cosmos, a liminal space to physically contemplate the path of life, going inward and out again, and I'd been wanting to show it to Michael for ages. We drove there together that day, the first anniversary of my father's death.

"Do you know the mythology of the labyrinth?" I asked him. We'd parked in front of the church, and I led him to the labyrinth, stepping onto the curving path.

Michael scuffed his flip-flop along the gravel. "Minotaurs and shit, right," he said. He squinted out at the sound. "Giant balls of yarn? David Bowie?"

"Kind of," I said. He was funny, but I wanted him to listen to me. "That's part of it, but it's also got spiritual significance." We walked along the path, single file, turning in slow, meandering circles.

"It's the circle of life," Michael said.

"I took a class in theology and mythology before . . ." Before what? Before I let the tidal wave of my grief overwhelm me? Before I ran away? "Before I left."

"What classes are you taking when you go back?" Michael asked.

I stood still for a moment. The wind rushed, and I turned in a slow circle in the labyrinth. "Poetry, maybe. Psychology. World religions."

"Cool." We walked, circling each other, each on our own path. "I'll just have my diss left, and then I'll apply for post-docs."

"Where?" I asked. *Where do I fit in to that?*

He reached across the labyrinth and touched my face, gently, electric. "I don't know. It could be anywhere. But the world is a lot more connected now. It doesn't have to mean we're apart. You know?"

I nodded, resumed walking my path. "We'll figure it out." And in the back of my mind, I felt an opening, a quark-small space, a thought about how a long-distance relationship had worked out between Michael and Troia.

I focused on the labyrinth. Labyrinths aren't like mazes. They're not meant to confuse you and make you feel lost, but rather to focus you on your path, on your own way.

"Want to have dinner tonight?" Michael asked.

But I didn't. I circled the labyrinth, one foot then the other, a rocking motion, just me and the gravel path, inward and then out again. "Evie and Stephen are going to come over," I said. Something crystallized. My own plan, my own path. "I'm going to make Evie love me again."

When I looked up from the path, Michael was on the other side.

———

That afternoon, the weather changed. Outside the tall sliding-glass doors of the dining room, the sky was a flat gray tinged with yellow around the edges. Still and eerie, the world an indrawn breath. Evie and I set silverware around the long table. The ghosts of us from months ago floated in the corners of the room, watching, remembering when they had done the same thing, remembering the spiky winter reeds and the heat from the fireplace, the rumples of windblown water and the swoop of pelicans on outstretched wings, the movement and currents wild compared to the silent yellow stillness of today.

"What's up with the sky?" I asked, channeling Charlotte from months ago, when Evie and I interacted without an invisible barrier between us. Setting my plan in motion.

Evie took her phone out of her pocket, poked it, and turned it to show me a red banner scrolling at the top of the Weather Channel. "Tropical depression upgraded to a tropical storm," she said, the annoyance and edge in her voice, Evie from months ago cast to the past. "It'll hit tomorrow," she said.

I clinked down the last of the place settings. "Let's go sit in the garden."

Evie shook her head. "My bones hurt. I don't want to go down the stairs." She opened the sliding-glass door and wedged her stomach sideways through the opening; I followed her out to the deck and sat beside her on a swing. We pushed back and forth with our toes in the silent late afternoon, the only breeze the unsettling one we created.

"Something happened to me today," I said. I wanted to tell her about my dad's anniversary, about sobbing as I dusted the Periwinkle room, but the words didn't come. "I wanted space from Michael for the first time," I said instead, then tensed. That was the wrong subject to raise around her.

"So, take your space back," she said. "It's not like anything's binding you to him."

"It's not that easy," I said.

"It is, though," Evie said. "You can keep screwing around with him or you can stop. You can stay here, or you can go home. You can do whatever you want. You could leave before this storm hits if you wanted to. You're completely free."

On the sound, the water stretched flat and motionless. In the sky, the yellow deepened. The pressure thickened, invisible, tangible.

"Are you ever going to be normal around me again?" I asked. Who was I, that I could just *say it*?

Evie watched the sound. "What do you mean?" she asked.

I stood up. "Jesus. You know exactly what I mean. Stop being fake. Stop being not you." I walked over to the deck and leaned out, then turned around to face her.

Evie looked at me. Her eyes were dull. "I have responsibilities now," she said. "You can't expect me to talk about boys and be like I was before."

"That's not what I mean," I said. I sat down beside her again. Was that what I wanted? Was that what I meant?

Evie pushed herself up to sit straight, grimacing around her stomach.

"I'm not willing to lose you," I said. I took Evie's hand, squeezed it. I wanted to squeeze the life back into her, to squeeze her back to the people we used to be. She didn't pull away. She didn't squeeze back. I dropped her hand and stood up again, crossed my arms and paced the deck.

"I don't know what to tell you," Evie said.

"Tell me you'll come back," I said. "Maybe you're still pissed at me. Maybe you need time to adjust to Stephen and the baby. I get that. But come back."

"You don't get that." Evie turned to me, her eyes bright and sharp. "You're here trying to relive your old vacations while I'm dealing with this. Then you're going to leave."

"That's not fair," I said. "You know what I'm dealing with."

Evie pushed the swing with her foot. Back and forth. For a moment, she looked like herself again. "I guess."

I sighed. "Maybe I don't get it," I said. "But I want to."

"Stop trying," Evie said, her expression closing down again. She stood up slowly, belly first, and walked inside.

———

The most interesting thing about quarks is that they like connection. They *need* it. The farther they're pulled away from their paired partner, the stronger their connection vibrates. If they're stretched far enough apart, if they're stretched too far, the connection snaps, and the energy eruption forges a brand-new quark spawned directly from the lonely one, a twin, a new pair, a soul reborn, doubled, solely reliant on its newly twinned self. Quarks, when they're stretched apart from their partner, create a new one from themselves. It must hurt, though, when the connection ruptures. It must be awful, that energy peaking to the point where the quark can only rely on itself, exploding into something brand new. I think that the rupture must burn.

———

Stephen sat beside me at dinner with Evie on his other side, leaning back in her chair because her stomach swelled forward, the outline of her belly button protruding through the fabric of her shirt. She talked with Nate and Mr. Austin about the real estate market.

Stephen saw me looking out the window. "Earl," Stephen said. "Big enough that they named him. He'll be a hurricane by tonight." He pointed out the window with his fork.

The closest I'd come to experiencing a Hatteras hurricane was getting evacuated from the campground during Hurricane Bonnie, but that was a full day before she hit. Maybe it was because I'd never been out in a hurricane, maybe it was because Ohio didn't have them, maybe it was because I wanted all the tumult and chaos I felt inside out in the open, but I wanted to stand out by the ocean and watch the waves turn into giant, clashing thrashers and lean into the force of the wind, fat wet drops spattering my face. I wanted the wind to tear at my hair. "Is he making landfall?" I asked.

"Looks like," Stephen said. His eyes lit up with storm excitement, and I felt an odd thrill of kinship with him, tinged with the familiar mild disdain.

"It's nothing but an overblown thunderstorm," Mrs. Austin said. She shrugged her shoulders. "The Weather Channel blows everything out of proportion. Jeff Morrow's parents live in Frisco, so he's down here every time there's a raindrop."

Stephen speared a piece of fish and popped it in his mouth. "Still," he said, "we're all moving our cars tonight, so they don't flood out."

Evie looked up. "Nothing is flooding," she said. "If this baby comes in the next two days, it's coming in Nags Head. Nothing is flooding." But she twisted her shoulders and looked out the window, eyes narrowed.

Outside, a pelican skimmed by, breaking the monotony of the still, yellow sky, and thunder rumbled, low and throaty.

———

At Michael's that night, the wind began—subtle at first, brushing my arms as I walked from my car to his door, then sidling against his trailer as I pressed my body into his. Wind, rising and wailing and rocking us side to side through the night. What would happen if I didn't have him to cling to, if it was just me, alone in the night in the wind?

———

Troia—
Here's what happened today. I was up in Periwinkle doing my
walk-through, running my dusting cloth across the windowsill,
and a fly crumpled to dust under my hand. It just . . . it had been
a fly, and it crumpled to dust. To nothing. Just flecks on my yel-
low dusting cloth. And it's been a whole year, but I cried and cried.
Snotty, red-faced sobbing, not pretty like you cry. I've never been
as pretty as you. I've never thought that I could get the things that
come so effortlessly to you. And I'm sorry that I'm doing things
that are hurtful, that I keep doing them, that I never thought he
would want me, and that he did, and that you didn't want him,
and that, despite everything, I need him. I need him to stand be-
tween me and the dust.

                                             C.

———

There are things no one told me about living by the ocean, things that never show up in real estate brochures. The way houses sway with the wind, walls almost fluid. How sand grits its way into the seams of a hardwood floor. How those floors tremor when waves pound at the shore.

There are certain things no one told me about grief. How there are conversations I'll never get out of my head, like when my dad said, "After I'm gone, say a prayer, send one up, and it's over. It's okay. It's important to focus on your studies."

He was lying in the hospital bed, the one against the window where he could look out over the trees, at the green and gold leaves of late summer. He was bald and shrunken, and his feet were cold, and I'll always recall that, no matter how many times I put heating pads on them, I could never get them warm. I'll never forget that he died with his feet swollen and alien and cold.

I'd replied to him, "That's all well and good, but I'm the one that's going to be left here without my dad."

"That would have happened anyway," he'd said. It felt like he was dismissing me.

"It would not," I said. "Not before you walked me down the aisle, not before I had my babies. Not before you taught them about patellas and proboscises and decibels and atoms."

"You'll have to tell them for me," he said. "Stand by the ocean and tell them everything. You'll feel me."

No one told me that sometimes I'd even begin to believe this.

Evie and I once had a conversation about whether it was better to die by drowning in the ocean or floating away from a rocket ship into outer space. Both involve suffocation, sucking in a breath that isn't there. Like all deaths. Evie chose the spaceship. She wanted to be high and weightless and above it all. I chose to drown. To be at home when I die. To be part of the earth.

No one told me that I might travel through my grief and come back to myself, but that I wouldn't be the same. That there would always be a dividing line from who l am now and who l used to be. Who l was before.

No one told me that time would move differently, that I'd recognize how every moment will never, ever happen again, as if l was the one who was dying. That l would begin to realize that l am.

No one told me that I'd feel guilty for still loving the way the sun warms my face, my arms, the back of my neck.

No one told me that I'd always hold on.

That, no matter how hard l tried, l could never draw a tight enough circle around someone else's life.

Seventeen

The wind gusted my car sideways as I drove down Highway 12 from Michael's back to the inn in the dim morning light. The Pamlico tumbled and waved, coffee-brown with small pricks of whitecaps, now all movement and motion after yesterday's odd stillness. An evacuation order had come in the night, and I went straight to the front desk to help check out the inn's guests and send them up the road and off the island. When everyone was out the door and on their way to the mainland, I made some tea and took it out on the deck to watch the sound. Moisture clung to my skin, clammy and sticky; the breeze coursed over and blew my hair back in gusts, sending the wind chimes clanging. I put down my tea and went over to where the chimes hung. They jangled in my hands as I carried them inside.

In the kitchen, Mr. Austin had the tiny TV tuned to the Weather Channel. He opened the oven door and pulled out the pan of zucchini bread. "Looks like tonight for landfall," he said, clanging the pan down on the stovetop.

"Category?" I asked. I fell into a rhythm beside Mr. Austin, scraping plates, rinsing muffin tins, loading the dishwasher. The TV blared synthesized music, and a red bar scrolled across the screen forecasting severe weather.

"Just a cat one," Mr. Austin said. "Like Mallory said, overblown thunderstorm. We won't need to evacuate." He opened a cabinet door and took out a silver filigreed platter, then leaned back against the edge of the counter. "Nate and I'll probably board up the windows a little later just to be on the safe side."

I stuck a spatula under the zucchini bread, lifted it out of the pan, and slid it onto the platter. "I can help if you want," I said. "I'm good at holding ladders. I used to hold the ladder for Dad when he cleaned out the gutters." I wanted to see what boarding up windows for a hurricane was like. I opened a cabinet and took out the powdered sugar, sprinkling some across the zucchini bread.

Mrs. Austin walked into the kitchen carrying a tray of coffee mugs. "Your mom called," she said. "Said she couldn't get hold of you. I told her we weren't going to drown and that you'd call her back as soon as I could find you." She clanked the mugs into the dishwasher.

"Best go put her mind at ease," Mr. Austin said, patting my shoulder.

I nodded and walked out of the kitchen, across the deck walkway to the old part of the inn. Whitecaps dashed furiously across the sound, and the wind blew harder, making its way through the crannies of the inn's shingles. I went inside and called my mother, but James answered the phone.

"Why aren't you in school?" I asked him. I sat down in Mr. Austin's chair and breathed in the smell of the worn leather.

"Teacher workday," James said. I thought his voice sounded deeper than it had the last time we'd spoken. "Why aren't you in school?"

"Regular workday," I said. "At my job." I stood up and looked out the window, straightening the blue plaid curtain swag Mrs. Austin had recently put up.

The wind blew and the phone crackled. "What are you eating for breakfast?" I asked.

"Pop-Tarts," James said. "Mom wants to talk to you. Don't die or anything."

I heard a rustle as James passed the phone to Mom. "Honey, the Weather Channel says there's a chance for flooding down there," she said.

"I know, Mom," I said. I looked up at the thick gray sky. "We've got the Weather Channel here, too."

"I just want you to be safe," she said. "Will you and the Austins leave the island if it gets too bad?"

"We would if it was going to be bad," I said. "Don't worry. We've got the biggest generator on the island, and we're up on a dune. It's just an overblown thunderstorm. I love you, Mom. I've got to go finish up breakfast stuff."

I hung up the phone, and Mr. Austin came into the office. He handed me a list. "Could you run to the store and get a few things?" he asked. "We shouldn't get stuck, but it can't hurt to have a little extra milk in the fridge." Mr. Austin's hair stood on end from being out in the wind.

I headed out to the store in Buxton, listening to the radio on the drive up, the air through my windows laced with pine and rain. The supermarket was fuller than usual, and I recognized almost every face I saw. It struck me that I'd never feel anonymous here again. One of the things I loved best about vacationing on Hatteras was the feeling that no one knew me, that I didn't have to be the same person I was at home, that I could be anyone, that I could be brave and bright and free. Now all of me was here, befores and afters, a familiar face in the blend. I bought what I could find from what was left of the milk and eggs and bread, then swung up to the lighthouse beach to check on Unaka Jeannette and the other dead lighthouse keepers in their circle of stones.

The parking lot was crowded with cars and SUVs with license plates from all over the country. Wave seekers and storm chasers. I walked through the damp, cool sand to the beach, the tide high and fast, closer to Unaka and his ilk than I liked. Closer to us all getting washed away. The ocean churned a deep gray green, and sand blew in sideways swirls, salt spray lacing across the air like a curtain. Surfers' heads bobbed across the water as they jockeyed for waves. I watched the surfers until the sand whipped to the point of stinging my legs and arms and face, tiny cutting specks of ancient life, the world wild and roiling.

I dropped off the groceries at the inn, tucking them into place in the kitchen. Mr. Austin and Nate were up on ladders, nailing boards in place, and I went down to the garden to watch. Mr. Austin swung a board up and nailed it in, the sound of hammer on metal ricocheting across the whitecapped Pamlico.

Nate started singing Michael Jackson's "Thriller," hammering out a beat to go with the music.

If Evie had been with me, before I was with Michael, we would have launched into choreography, swinging our arms into the air in monster poses. If Troia had been there, and I hadn't chosen Michael, we would have laughed and catcalled Nate, and she would have put her fingers in her mouth and whistled in the way I never could learn.

"Did Stephen pick up the plywood he wanted yet?" Mr. Austin asked Nate.

Nate stopped singing long enough to answer. "Not that I know of."

Mr. Austin shook his head. He hammered in a nail.

I cleared my throat; I didn't want to startle them. "Do you need me to take something down to Evie's?" I asked.

Mr. Austin looked down at me. "You want any excuse to get out in this weather, don't you, kid?"

Nate took a nail out of his teeth, pounded it in, and slid down the ladder to the ground. "Of course, she does," he said. He did a little moonwalk move and a spin. His hair blew back in the wind. How could I have resisted his steadiness, his kindness, all those months ago, when I needed it so much? What was I doing, throwing myself to the wild currents now? The wind and water around my ankles, whipping to my thighs, how hard could I dig my toes in and find my own sandbar? Wouldn't I just get swept away?

I looked up at Mr. Austin. "I could take the plywood down to Evie's," I said.

"That's probably a real good idea," Mr. Austin said. He hooked the hammer in his belt buckle and slowly walked his way down the ladder. "She could use a friend right about now," he said.

I nodded, but inside I thought that if Evie needed a friend so much, then she should try holding up her part of the bargain. The wind whipped around my face, and heat lightning streaked across the sky, a rush of energy, the sizzle of electricity rending the air.

———

The windows of Evie's house stared out at me clean and open with nothing covering them. I parked the car and unloaded the plywood onto Evie's porch. Tiny nettles of thin rain spattered sideways against my face, sharp and cold; I rubbed my arms and knocked on Evie's door. She didn't answer. I knocked again, then opened the door a crack. "Evie," I called, "I'm coming in. It's raining." I stepped inside and shut the door, shook out my hair and called again. "Evie?"

"In here." Evie's voice came from the living room. I walked in. Evie sat on the sofa with her feet on the coffee table. She had the remote in one hand and the other hand on her stomach. The room was dark. Evie muted the Weather Channel as I came in.

"I brought plywood from your dad," I said. I wanted to flop on the sofa beside her, put my feet up, compare pedicures, tell her about Nate's Michael Jackson rendition. I perched on the couch's arm instead.

Evie turned her head to the TV and unmuted it. "Thanks," she said. "But I don't think we'll need it."

I watched the radar map splash splotches of green and orange across the Outer Banks before it switched to a commercial for heartburn medication. "If you need it, it's here," I said.

"Thank you for the plywood." Evie walked toward the door. She put her hand to her stomach and grimaced.

"Are you okay? Are you going into labor?"

Evie scowled. "It's just an effing twinge." She took her hand off her stomach, turned slightly sideways, and stared off toward the kitchen. Her eyebrows knit together, puzzled. "I don't say 'effing.'"

"Fuck that," I said.

Evie crossed her arms over her stomach. "I can stop being polite if that's what you want," she said.

"By all means," I said.

"You screwed over Nate, and now you're on to the next guy."

"I'm sorry that I hurt Nate," I said. "I really am. But I love Michael."

"You love him, or he's giving you attention?" Evie asked.

A current of energy gathered in my chest. "You really think I'm that shallow?"

"His trailer, by the way—Lover Boy's—is in a flood plain, so there's that." Evie raised an eyebrow.

Anger streaked through me. All the times I'd put up with Stephen to support Evie's choices, and she couldn't even try to understand. "Thanks for letting me know. I'd do the same for your douchey spouse if his house was about to flood."

The Weather Channel blared a loud alert in a robotic voice from the other room. *High winds, potential for heavy flooding.* "You're coming to the inn tonight, right?" I asked.

"I'll have to see what my husband wants to do," she said.

I squinted at the spattering rain then walked out into the storm.

Charlotte,
One of my kids asked me today, "If I haven't seen my cousin in
a long time, will she look different?" When he said "cousin," I
thought of you. I haven't stopped thinking of you. Once I found
out that my kid's said cousin was twenty-seven, I quite reasonably
assured him that his cousin would remain unchanged. But isn't
it funny how we stop growing on the outside, stop changing, stop
needing new jeans every six months, when we can be so very, very
different on the inside? Or maybe it's strange that we ever did have
those physical markers to go by in the first place. I don't know. I
guess that's all.

Troia

The storm deepened. I drove to Michael's trailer in the floodplain after helping at the inn all afternoon. Dark clouds thickened across the sky, and rain pelleted in fat, sideways-blown drops. Michael stepped outside, golden against the darkening storm, his hair blown back in the wind.

He held out his hand. I took it, but for the first time I only felt the sizzle in the air around me, the charge emanating from the atmosphere and the storm.

"It's getting wild out there," I said. And then I verbalized what had been brewing in me all afternoon, ever since Evie had grimaced and touched her stomach. "I'm worried Evie will go into labor and the road will flood out."

Michael and I walked into his trailer and sat down. He shook rainwater off his hair and looked up at a surfing poster on the wall, showing the blue curl of a tall, hollow wave. "Nothing we can do but wait and see, I guess," he said. "Flooding will depend a lot on the direction Earl takes right before landfall. And how long he lingers."

"But what if we get trapped here?" What if Evie went into labor and she couldn't get to the hospital? If we had to boil water and collect rags and she had the baby by candlelight. What if something went wrong? Wouldn't it hurt? How would she bear all that pain? Should I try to make her leave and go up the beach now, today?

Should I go, too? Should I just go? What if I didn't leave in time to get back to what my life once was? What if I let myself stay for too long?

Michael came over and wrapped his arms around me. "It'll be okay," he said.

I stepped back. Things didn't always turn out *okay*. Sometimes the opposite. "We're in a floodplain right now," I said. "Your trailer is in a floodplain."

Michael nodded. "Would the Austins be cool if I go stay up at the inn?"

All of us in one spot. The anxiety of that thrummed in my throat. But what were my other choices? Stay here with him in a trailer in a hurricane and risk getting washed away?

I grabbed his hand and looked up at the wave on his wall. So tall and blue, so much hidden power. The velocity of water. What it could do. "They're going to have to be."

Velocity's opposite, its paired, quark-like twin, is inertia. Inertia with its dragging feet and Eeyore glumness, inertia holding you back from where your life is pulling to go.

Highway 12 is a narrow little road, prone to overwash from the ocean and the sound. Barrier islands are meant to move, to accrete and erode; roads are not. Barrier islands don't stay in one place, like people sometimes want to do. Somewhere on the drive from Michael's trailer in Buxton to the inn, with the wind buffeting his 4Runner and the rain pelting down, the hurricane stopped feeling like a thrill ride, like some kind of exciting anomaly.

Michael and I drove up the sloped driveway to the inn. With the wind and rain and the thick gray sky, the inn sat darkly on its slope in a Gothic gloom. We parked, I noticed with relief, between Stephen's and Aunt Fay's cars, and ran inside.

My desk at the front entrance was dark, and so was the back room where we put out cookies for the guests. Dark and quiet, rain and wind lashing at the windows. Outside, the Pamlico had already flooded the inn's pier and walkway and was approaching the swimming pool.

Michael and I walked through the inn's rooms, our wet feet squelching on the carpet. I peered around the back doors and spotted a light in the kitchen, across the walkway, and a light in the dining room in the new part of the inn. The power was still on. "Looks like everyone is over there," I said.

Michael nodded. "Hoods up," he said, tugging my raincoat hood up over my head before doing his own.

I opened the door and the wind immediately slammed it flat against the outside wall. Michael and I both pushed and pushed to get it to close. We ran, struggling into the wind, over to the kitchen and banged inside, shaking off our coats and shoes.

"There's my storm chaser," Mr. Austin said. He had sandwich makings spread across the counter and was slathering bread with Duke's mayonnaise. "Michael, you're welcome to stay. As long as you share my view that Duke's is the only mayo allowed in this inn."

My phone buzzed in my pocket. My mom. *The Weather Channel upped it to a Category 3.*

I'm safe, Mom. We're on a ridge. The pool and the pier were not on a ridge, but I left that part out.

Michael and I went to the counter and joined Mr. Austin in a sandwich assembly line. "Everyone's here?" I asked. "Any extra guests?" Mr. Austin usually opened the inn to locals during storms if anyone needed to find high ground.

"Just us," he said. "Aunt Fay and Evie and Stephen. They're all in the dining room right now. We'll eat then huddle over in the family quarters for the night."

I stacked sandwiches on a platter and walked into the dining room. I set the platter down and the lights flickered, then snapped off.

"Holy gloom, Batman," Evie said.

I blinked, adjusting to the darkness, hearing Michael enter the room, feeling him beside me, still solid but no longer quite as electric as before. All the charge from our bodies had absorbed into the storm. He clanked down a plate. "Hey, Austins," he said.

"'Full fathom five the poet lies,'" Aunt Fay said in greeting. My eyes adjusted to the dimness. She sat on the floor with her legs stretched out in front of her, Walter trembling on her lap. Nate and Evie were at a small table by the window; they turned from watching the sound to look at Michael. Stephen and Mrs. Austin sat across the room looking at their phones.

"Looking pretty fathom-y out there," I said. "We brought sandwiches."

Mr. Austin entered behind me and placed pitchers of water on the side table. "That's it for power, folks. We got ice in the cooler and water in the bathtubs. I'll kick the generator on if we need it." He lit some candles.

Michael chose a chair in the middle of the big dining room table and sat down with a sandwich. The others followed, Walter barking and lunging when Mr. Austin got close to him.

I watched for the chair Evie walked toward with her sandwich then sat beside her. "How you feeling?" I asked.

Evie took a bite and shrugged as she chewed. "I feel like everyone needs to stop looking at me like I'm a ticking time bomb."

"You kind of are, though," Nate said. He drummed his fingers on the table.

"She has another two weeks," Stephen said.

Wind whistled through the shingles, pinnacled over the rooftop. At home, when it rained, the tall trees turned their leaves inside out, silver and veined. The smell of damp earth and rain rose across soft swells of grassy hills. At home, in a storm, the water was absorbed; it didn't overtake you.

"It shouldn't be a direct hit, at least," Michael said.

"Can be worse for flooding if it just sits out there off the coast," Nate said.

Aunt Fay placed Walter on the floor with his own sandwich. "In my reading lately, I have learned some things," she said. "The poet Shelley went out on a boat despite storm warnings, and he refused help, and he drowned. He may have wanted to die."

Mr. Austin raised an eyebrow. "Point taken," he said. "We will not go for a sail right about now."

Aunt Fay cleared her throat. *"Nothing of him that doth fade. But doth suffer a sea change. Into something rich and strange."*

"Let's stop talking about drownings," Mrs. Austin said, her mouth a thin line. "You all know not to talk that around me." Mr. Austin put his arm around her shoulder.

"Should we try to leave so you're closer to the hospital?" I said to Evie, low and under my breath. "I'll go with you. If it's not too late."

Evie brushed her bangs back from her face. "We're past time for leaving," she said. "We'd be full fathom five blown off the road."

Michael squeezed my thigh under the table. *A sea change.* A gathering of pressure rose through my body. We were past time for leaving. We were on the tiny, thin sliver of a barrier island in the middle of a Category 3 hurricane, eating sandwiches and talking about drowned poets, the slope of a ridge the only thing between us and the water. Michael would finish his dissertation and move to a different barrier

island. A barrier island where? Australia? Denmark? And here I was
on this narrow strip of land, storm surge on the ocean side, the Pamlico rising on the other. Barrier islands are meant to move. I wanted
to go home to the soft hills and the green, and at the same time I
wanted to go outside into the fury of the storm. I understood why
Shelley set his foot on that boat as it rocked in the wild sea—why he
left land and leaned into the velocity of the storm.

"I'll go light some candles on the other side," I said. Channeling
works-at-the-inn Charlotte, helpful Charlotte. "So we don't have to
turn on the generator just yet."

And I moved out from under Michael's hand and went into the
kitchen, put on my shoes and coat, and shoved the door hard into
the wind. The gusts pushed at my back and sent my feet skittering
across the boards of the deck, plastered the hood of my jacket over
my head and blew my hair into my eyes. I tried to stand still, but the
wind kept pushing. I had to lean backwards to stop moving. Velocity
and inertia. The pull and stretch of a quark when it moves so far away
from its pair, so far away that it only has itself to rely on. My dad was
gone, the burnt bones of his body churning in the sway of the waves,
surging through the storm. My family was at home, Michael would
leave soon, and Evie would have her baby, her own family, and here
I was, a speck in the middle of the bright spiraling galaxy, a speck in
the rocking sea. Just me. *Something deep and strange.*

I was right about the rupture, as it turns out. About the sting and
the burn.

———

Late that night I woke to the rain falling in swaths, escalating and
abating in alternating waves. The wind howled. We'd all chosen

rooms and bunked down for the night, and while I wanted to stay with Evie, she and Stephen had gone to the Sea Oats room to sleep. I rolled over and pressed closer into Michael's back. Michael, who wanted me. Michael, who had brought me back to myself. Michael, who would leave soon.

The heart is mostly hollow. The epicenter of the body, the heart is the size of a clenched fist. Hormones released because of strong emotion affect the heart rate, which is why the heart is associated with feelings, with heartbreak, with death by broken heart.

I had to take control of mine. I had to be the one who left first. I had to go home.

Eighteen

I pressed my forehead against the window overlooking the sound in the room we'd slept in. The worst of Earl had blown north, but the sound still roiled in its wake. The pier, my thinking spot, was gone. Brown water flooded the lower decks and the swimming pool. Michael stirred in the bed behind me. He stretched and walked over to the window.

"Whoa," he said.

I turned my head in slow circles, stretching my neck from side to side. Michael rubbed my back.

"No swims today," I said.

"No swims for the rest of the season," he said.

The rest of the season, which we'd planned to ride out together until Christmas. "Michael," I said. My heart, my hollow, healing heart, pounded in my chest at what I was about to say. "I've been thinking."

"Risky pastime," he said.

"I think I need to go."

Michael stopped tracing circles up my spine. "What do you mean?"

I turned to him, both of us there in our pajamas and with morning breath. "I need to get back on track with school. Move forward. Harness my velocity, you know?"

Michael frowned, scratched his head. Outside, a board from the pier thwacked against what was left of the railing. "What happened to waiting for Christmas and leaving together?"

"It's the waiting part," I said. "If I wait until Evie's baby is born, I'm never going to leave."

Michael ran his hand through his hair. "That's a change in the game plan," he said.

"I don't know where this puts us," I said, before he could bring it up.

"You don't know?"

But I did. I did know. My heart pounded harder, a fist unclenching and tightening again. "I need to go. Alone."

Michael stood still, looking out the window where the water rose and fell. "How alone are we talking?" he asked. "Long-distance alone, or *alone* alone?"

And then, I didn't know. He was standing there, right there, so beautiful, mine, and my sturdy knowing faltered. I just knew that I had to leave. "In the last chapter of our beach book it's all about equilibrium, you know? How trying to fight the erosion makes it worse in the end?"

"You're ready to let nature take its course? On us?"

I sat down on the bed. "That's just it, though. It's the only way to save things."

Michael was still. Eventually, he nodded. "In the long run," he said.

I stood back up beside him, and we looked outside again. Where the water rose and fell and the broken boards banged against each other, where the currents pulled north, pulled south, pulled and swirled as the storm moved out and out and out and into the sea.

———

Michael and I crossed the wet deck to the dining room. Leaves and sand were scattered everywhere, and the wind tugged at my hair. The air was thick and smelled like the sea. Inside, Michael and I poured bowls of cereal and sat down in the dining room. I couldn't quite pinpoint the currents between us. Sitting beside him felt like where I was supposed to be, but the specter of leaving floated between us, an invisible, vibrating space.

Nate and Evie walked in with their breakfast and sat with us. "Hey, gang," Nate said.

"Where's Stephen?" I asked Evie.

She took a bite and talked around a mouthful of food. "I'm starving," she said. "Stephen went to see if he could get down to Hatteras to check on his parents."

"Any word on what the roads are like?" Michael asked.

Nate took a drink of his coffee. "S-turns is flooded."

"Probably bad at motels, then," Michael said. The motels on the north end of Buxton were miles from S-turns, but when one got ocean flooding, that usually meant the other did, too.

"So, what you're saying is we should drive south and see how it is in Hatteras?" I asked.

"If you want to," Evie said. "I mean, Stephen will text me in a minute here."

"Let's do it," Nate said. "I'll drive."

We took our dishes to the kitchen, then walked down to Nate's car. Evie got in the front seat, me and Michael in the back. The ghosts of us a few months ago didn't feel so far away; they hovered close around our heads as Nate pulled onto Highway 12, turned on the radio, and drove south.

———

Just south of the Frisco bathhouse, where Hatteras Island narrows to just a few hundred feet across, where you can turn your head one way and see the Pamlico and turn the other and see the Atlantic, Highway 12 vanished under water. The dunes hadn't breached, but the sound flooded the road, brown water rushing in the wind.

Evie looked up from her phone. "Stephen made it through," she said. "He's at his parents', but Hatteras is a mess."

I leaned forward to look at the water as it lapped against Nate's tires.

Nate pointed. "It's not all that deep," he said. "See the yellow lines on the road?"

If I squinted, I could. "Stephen drove all the way through?"

Nate pulled the car forward, and the water fanned out behind us. He drove slowly for a bit. It looked for all the world like we were driving into a river. Nate stopped and backed up. "We'd make it, but I don't really want to rust out my undercarriage."

Evie nodded. "Tourists fly through the flooding," she said. "Just wait. They'll be coming down for their vacations as soon as S-turns opens and start rusting out their cars right and left."

Nate backed out of the water and turned the car back north.

"Beach stop?" Michael asked.

Nate pulled into a parking lot at the Frisco pier just past the bathhouse. We all got out and walked to the dunes.

Gulls cawed and the sea oats waved in the wind. I held out my arm to Evie as we started up the dune, and she took it, leaning on me as she struggled in the sand. The ocean thrashed and roared against the broken pier, a thin line of sand between the dune line and water.

"If I sit, you all are going to have to get me back up," Evie said. She lowered herself onto the dune, and we all sat with her in the damp sand.

Michael sifted sand through his fingers, and I sat solidly in myself, for the first time. It wasn't that I didn't want to take his hand. I did. But the thought didn't overwhelm me. The thought of touching him didn't overtake me. The ocean crashed and rolled. "I'm going to miss this," I said. The ocean, I meant, and the four of us together.

Nate fluffed some fallen sea oats upright and let them fall again. "It's a special place."

"I'm thinking about leaving soon," I said. "Sooner than I'd planned."

Evie frowned and froze up, a chilly sheen between us. "That will be nice for you." She stared off into the ocean.

"I thought we were done being polite." I dug my toes in the sand.

"I thought you were going to help me with the beginning baby business," Evie said.

I scooted closer to her. "You know how you wake up sometimes in the middle of the night and you don't have your glasses on, and nothing looks like where it's supposed to be?"

"No," Evie said. "I have perfect vision."

The ocean roared with an especially loud wave, and the water rushed up near our feet. "It's like you don't know where you are," I said. "Like you think the door to the bathroom is the door to the hall, or that you're asleep in your childhood bedroom and can't figure out why the window is in the wrong place." I had to make her understand. "I feel like I've been living in that state for the past months now, not knowing where I am. Disoriented. But at some point, I blinked and woke up."

"Really, though, what's your town in Ohio got that we don't?" Evie asked. "Besides grass and cows and that fucker Mike Tyson."

"Her school," Nate said. He bumped his shoulder into Evie's.

Michael took my hand, and I laced my fingers through his, the sand gritty between us. "So she can learn about why Shelley got on that boat," he said. "Or labyrinths. Or something like that."

"Mike Tyson hasn't lived there in like ten years," I said to Evie.

"The cows are still there, though," Evie said. "Why do you want to go live with a bunch of cows and Mike Tyson's dumb house when we've got all these dolphins and pelicans and a fresh baby?"

I couldn't explain it, my need to leave on my own, now, my fear of never going if I stayed too long. "Cows are majestic creatures," I said. "You could bring the baby up to meet them."

Evie chewed on her lip. "I guess you were going to go soon, one way or another."

I didn't have anything else to say. "I love you," I said to Evie.

"I know."

We all sat in the sand, looking out to the stormy sea.

Nineteen

The next morning, Evie went into labor. I'd spent the night at Michael's, wrapped up in him, the air between us distanced but intensified, colliding into *ours* but separating back into *mine* and *his*.

When I drove to the inn the next morning, Mrs. Austin met me in the garden. "Charlotte," she said, "can you handle things here?"

I nodded, a burrow of anxiety in my throat. "Is it Evie?" I asked.

"Her water broke last night," Mrs. Austin said. "Stephen's taking her up to Nags Head now, and we're headed out as soon as Jacob gets down here." She threw a bag in Mr. Austin's truck and got in the front seat, buckling her seat belt impatiently.

"Is S-turns open?" I asked.

Mrs. Austin nodded. "Flood water on the road but it's passable."

Up at the inn a door slammed, and Nate came out. He leaned over the railing. "Dad's ready," he said. "It's uncle time." He clattered down the stairs and got in the truck.

Mr. Austin came out next, down the stairs and over to me. "You got things here by yourself? With the road opening we'll get check-ins."

Mrs. Austin rolled down her window. "I already asked her." She motioned him to the truck. "Call if you need anything," she said to me. Mr. Austin got in, and they all drove away.

Could I handle things here by myself? While Evie was in labor, an hour away, about to have everything change? With Evie, my touchstone, about to become someone's mother?

I stood in the garden, watching them drive away. The blue sky puckered with gray clouds, sunlight lancing through in streaks to the mist-covered garden. A butterfly landed on the bush in front of me, folding its brown-edged yellow wings up and down. Birds twittered and called, and the sound lapped softly along the shore, the air fresh and cool on my bare arms. I stood in the garden in the sweet, sad autumn morning, alone.

———

Inside, I did a walk-through of the inn. Up the stairs and into each room, tidying and straightening, checking that the shampoo was filled and the curtains hung sleek. I crossed the walkway and did the same in the other part of the inn, settling each room. Then I went to my little room, Evie's old room, a room that would soon be cleared out, blank and impersonal. I opened my *How to Read a North Carolina Beach* book and paged through it, then texted Michael. *Evie's in labor.*

Whoa, he wrote back immediately.

"The beach is a benchmark—a scar cut by the edge of the sea into the land." Page 1. I wrote. *A scar. Isn't that something?*

Michael wrote back: *"The key to solving some of the riddles of a sandy beach lies in understanding its equilibrium. The shape of a beach (its width, slope, and general profile) is the end product of sea-level change, the quality and quantity of sand, and the height of the waves and strength of the currents."*

"When one changes, the others adjust accordingly." I wrote. *Page 2.*

Equilibrium, he wrote.

I nodded to myself and set my book down. *Equilibrium*. I had to figure out how to stand alone on the shifting sand.

———

When you lose someone you love deeply, it leaves a hollow space at the bottom of your heart, the vibrant, clenching fist of your heart. All other feeling skims over top of this emptiness so that nothing resonates strong or pure. For months I'd been trying to pierce the hollow, fill it with something new, banish it forever. Nothing worked until I saw Evie's baby. Evie was asleep, and I was allowed to go into the nursery by myself to meet him. I put my pinky finger in his tiny hand. He curled his fingers around it, grabbed on, opened his mouth in a cry that turned into a yawn, flailed his arms. He never let go of me. He never let go.

Newborn babies have the fastest heartbeats of all humans. Evie's baby's heart fluttered like a hummingbird, this brand-new person who never existed before, suddenly *here*, suddenly alive. A constellation of quarks and currents and the speed of light, the suck of a black hole exploding into life. The track and pull of electrons, a rush of blood and the beat of his stunning, thrumming hummingbird heart.

———

I went into Evie's hospital room when she woke, the same one she was in two months back. Evie lay in bed.

"Did you see him?" she asked. Her eyes had purple smudges beneath them.

"He's beautiful," I said. Outside Evie's window the sky pinked in streaks of sunset. "Did you name him yet?"

Evie pressed the button to raise her bed. She brushed her hair out of her face. "Austin," she said. "Austin Charles Oden."

"That's perfect," I said.

"They'll bring him back in here soon," Evie said. "I want to look at his toes again."

"They're like corn niblets," I said,

Evie smiled. She looked over my shoulder. "Mom said you brought me presents," she said.

"Of course, I brought presents," I said. "What kind of an Aunt Charlotte doesn't bring presents?" I reached down for the gift bags I'd set on the floor.

"Perfect," Evie said, opening them and spreading the tiny onesies across her stomach, shaking the stuffed elephant at me, lining up the nail polishes I'd bought for her in a brightly colored row. "Stephen's painting a parade of animals around the baby's room right now. He got the stencils at Home Depot." Evie leaned back and put the presents on her side table. She took a sip of water.

"What was it like?" I asked.

Evie made a face. "I'm still waiting for the amnesia to set in."

I took her hand. Evie. Evie who knew me *before*, who knew me *after*, Evie who would be there as I found my equilibrium. As I'd be there while she found hers. "You've been my anchor," I said.

"I know," Evie said. "You've been mine, too."

Nate came through the door, pushing Austin in a clear, wheeled bassinet. Austin, swaddled in a pink-and-blue blanket, round-faced and impossibly small, screwed up his face and screamed. Nate picked him up, cradling him like a tiny football. Austin quieted for a while, then cried again, and Nate handed him down to Evie.

Evie took the baby out of his swaddle and jiggled him up and down. He kept screaming, his face red and angry, hands in tight fists. "I don't know what I'm doing," she said.

I ran my finger across Austin's taut little stomach. "Are you hungry, baby?" I asked.

Evie switched from jiggling to rocking back and forth. "Boob buffet, you think?" Evie asked.

"That's my cue," Nate said, saluting and walking out the door.

Evie moved the baby to her left arm and tugged at her hospital gown. "Untie me," she said.

I brushed Evie's hair off the back of her neck, where her fuzzy split ends were sticking out, and untied the gown. "Do you want me to leave?"

Evie shrugged her shoulder out of the gown. Austin howled. "You can stay," she said. She pressed Austin's head to her breast. He cried while Evie poked her nipple into his mouth in various configurations until he latched and was quiet.

"I'll stay until you're settled in," I said.

Evie nodded. We sat together as Austin nursed, his tiny fingers clasped tight around mine, not letting go until he fell asleep.

I kissed them both and left the hospital to drive into the night, back down the island to the inn. At the stoplight to turn south down Highway 12, I sat in my car, while time expanded and coalesced like the northern lights, seeing myself packing my clothes into my suitcase, the cardigan I'd worn in the air-conditioning all summer thick against my fingers, the tank top I had on when we put my father's ashes over the side of the boat soft, folding up so thin it took no space, so thin it almost wasn't there. I saw myself standing in the blank space on the floor of my closet where the box of my father's ashes had sat that winter and spring; I saw Evie and Stephen tucking Austin into his crib, romping elephants circling the walls; I saw myself soak in the energy from Michael's arms one last time, my ear pressed against the solid beat of his heart. I saw the golden sea oats waving on the dunes, the bright sweep of kiteboarders skimming across the waters of the sound, my car traveling up the thin line of Hatteras Island, this impossible island, this narrow, resilient strip of sand, full of impossible life, holding against the fathoms of the deep, blue sea. In the night, after meeting Evie's baby, sitting at the stoplight to turn south on Highway 12, I saw myself in the bright morning sun, poised to cross that bridge, ready to turn north, ready to go home.

Acknowledgments

Thank you to Robin Miura for believing in this project, for her smart and insightful editing, and for her friendship. To the Blair team—Lynn York, Arielle Hebert, and everyone else—thank you for giving me a literary home.

To my agent, Andrea Somberg, thank you for your dedication and enthusiasm. I'm so glad we're a team.

Thank you to Kaye Publicity—Dana Kaye, Ellie Imbody, and Amanda La Conte. You crystallized my blurry goals so gracefully. It's been amazing to work with you all.

This book began years ago, as I was writing my way out of a haze of grief. To my mentors at Ohio University who read my messy first drafts, thank you, especially Joan Connor and Darrell Spencer. And to my cohort, my friends, especially Leigh Wisneiwski and Kristen Lillvis (Girls' Club!), Megan Lobsinger, Dave Wanczyk, Carrie Oeding, Jason Kapcala, Jana Tigechalaar, Jackson Conner, Lydia McDermott, Iver Arnegard, Tony Dallacheisa, Amanda Hayes, and Sara McKinnon, thank you. At West Virginia University, I handed over the sunken soufflé of the second half of this book to my new classmates. Thank you to my mentor, Mark Brazaitis, and to Kori Frazier Morgan, Rebecca Schwab Cuthbert, Rebecca Bailey, Patrick Faller, Alex Berge, Jason Freeman, and the rest of my cohort for your guidance on this project.

For Jen Colatosti, my writing soulmate who has read this manuscript from it's very first incarnation to its final polishing more than a decade later, thank you. I genuinely don't know what I'd do without you.

Thank you to Orrin H. Pilkey, Tracy Monegan Rice, and William J. Neal for their scientifically poetic book, *How to Read a North Carolina Beach: Bubble Holes, Barking Sands, and Rippled Runnels*, and to the University of North Carolina Press for allowing me to use excerpts. Thank you to my friend, Dr. Jillian De Gezelle, who loaned me her copy of *How to Read a North Carolina Beach*, which changed the trajectory of this book for the better.

For my Raleigh crew, thank you for your friendship and support as I rewrote this book, especially Barbara Meechan, Crystal Whittenton, and my pod squad: Dr. Shannon Davidson, Marie Wallden, and Jill and J. T. Crook. You all kept me sane during Covid and book promotion. Shannon, I'm so thankful for our continued little pack. Thank you to Megan McClung, who graciously babysat when I couldn't quite pull off rewriting the last twenty pages before the end of the school year. Thank you to all the lovely staff and parents at St. Raphael Preschool and Hunter Elementary, and a shout-out to the Starbucks on Falls of the Neuse and to Deja Brew for being such excellent revision hangouts.

For José, thank you for your support, and for Jonah, Hannah, and Jordi, my little family, thank you for being such lovely humans.

Thank you to my brother, Ben, who moved with me to Athens that first horrible year when I started writing this book. I'm forever grateful. And thank you to my mom, for your constant encouragement and unending love. I'm glad we pulled together during that terrible time.

And finally, for my dad. I owe you so much, and I miss you every day.